3 4028 07530 5897
HARRIS COUNTY PUBLIC LIBRARY

P9-APW-701

WITHDRAWN

Recipe for Disaster

For Sophie, Sam and Hanna— May your reach always exceed your grasp, and may you always travel paths that make you happy.

KCP Fiction is an imprint of Kids Can Press

Kids Can Press acknowledges the financial support of the Government of Ontario, through the Ontario Media Development Corporation's Ontario Book Initiative; the Ontario Arts Council; the Canada Council for the Arts; and the Government of Canada, through the BPIDP, for our publishing activity.

Published in Canada by	Published in the U.S. by
Kids Can Press Ltd.	Kids Can Press Ltd.
29 Birch Avenue	2250 Military Road
Toronto, ON M4V 1E2	Tonawanda, NY 14150

www.kidscanpress.com

Edited by Sheila Barry
Designed by Marie Bartholomew
Cover image © Veer Incorporated

Printed and bound in Canada

This book is printed on acid-free paper that is 100% ancient-forest friendly (100% post-consumer recycled).

CM 09 0 9 8 7 6 5 4 3 2 1
CM PA 09 0 9 8 7 6 5 4 3 2 1

Library and Archives Canada Cataloguing in Publication

Fergus, Maureen
      Recipe for disaster / written by Maureen Fergus.

ISBN 978-1-55453-319-0 (bound) —ISBN 978-1-55453-320-6 (pbk.)

   I. Title.

PS8611.E735R42 2009   jC813'.6   C2009-900008-3

Kids Can Press is a *C©ⲣᵁS*™ Entertainment company

Recipe for Disaster

Maureen Fergus

KCP FICTION

1. Life Isn't Fair — Spread the News!

"Oh, Randall! I always knew beneath that hard, crusty exterior you were filled with a passion as rich and forbidden as my momma's finest cream custard!"

Excerpt from The Cad Who Loved Me by Ima Dormatt

"Honey, can I talk to you for a moment?" asked my mother.

"Uh-huh," I said without looking up from the pages of my True Romance novel.

"It's important," she said.

"Okay," I murmured as I imagined my majestic white stallion galloping through the pounding surf alongside the powerful steed of the swarthy, dark-haired lover who would rather *die* than be parted from me. My perfect hair fluttered behind me in the wind; my perfect breasts jiggled enticingly beneath the bodice of my long, flowing gown.

My mother leaned across the table and waved her hand in front of my face. Slowly, crashing waves gave way to the muted clink of coffee mugs and cutlery; sea salt smells faded into the fragrant aromas that hung in the air of our little neighborhood café.

"Are you back?" asked my mother.

"I guess," I said, shoving my book into my overnight bag. "What's up?"

"I'm afraid I've got some bad news. You know my friend Vivian?"

"Of course," I nodded, rolling my eyes as I leaned over to take a bite of my giant fried cinnamon bun. "She runs an organic catering business and owns twelve cats. Also, she says she's a vegetarian but she always smells like pork chops."

"She does *not* smell like pork chops," chuckled my mother, handing me a paper napkin.

"She does to me," I said through my mouthful of food. "Is she in some kind of trouble?"

"No, but I promised her I'd help cater a party this Friday evening."

I shrugged and wiped a dollop of cinnamon goop off my chin. "So you're going to smell like fried pig until next October. It could be worse."

"It is worse," said my mother uncomfortably. "Somehow, Dad and I got our wires crossed and he took an extra shift at the garage Friday evening by mistake. With both of us gone, the café is going to be short-staffed, so ... I'm afraid we're going to need you to stick around here and lend a hand clearing tables and doing dishes."

For a moment, her words hung between us, like a stink in the air. Then I smiled pleasantly.

"No can do, Mom," I said. "I've got the ninth-grade pool party Friday night. I told you about it weeks ago, remember? I was sitting right here in this very seat and I was so excited I kept forgetting not to talk with my mouth full but you were so awesome and supportive that you only mentioned it to me four times." I reached for her hand. "I'll never forget the way we communicated that day, Mom," I said, my voice quivering with emotion. "It really meant a lot to me."

My mother grimaced and pulled her hand away. "I'm sorry, Francie, but it's too late for Dad to get out of his shift."

"No problem!" I said quickly. "Just tell Vivian you can't help her cater the party after all. Tell her you're allergic to cats. And pork."

My mother shook her head. "She only took the job because I told her I'd help. I can't back out now. She'd have to cancel, and that would make her look unprofessional."

"I DON'T CARE HOW IT WOULD MAKE HER LOOK," I said loudly. Three tables over, a businessman in horn-rimmed glasses glanced up. I bugged my eyes out at him until he ducked back behind his newspaper. Then I took a deep breath and turned to my mother. "What about how it will make *me* look if I don't show up at my pool party, Mom?" I asked urgently. "I'm one of only two ninth-grade representatives on the Student Social Committee. The Dive into Winter event was my idea. Are you trying to tell me that commitments made by your friend are more important than commitments made by your daughter?"

"No ..."

"Well, then, are you trying to teach me that I don't need to honor my commitments?" I asked, widening my eyes as though in shock.

"Of course not!" spluttered my mother.

I flung my arms in the air. "Well, what are you trying to teach me, then? Huh, Mom? Can you answer me that?"

Even before she opened her mouth to reply, I could tell my approach wasn't working. Quickly, I changed tacks.

"Mom, please, PLEASE don't do this to me!" I groveled. "We're going to have access to the hot tub and the sauna — they're going to let us use the high diving board and *everything*. I've never looked forward to anything so much in my entire life, Mom. I'm not kidding! I even bought myself a new bathing suit especially for the occasion."

"I know ..."

"Do you know, Mom? Do you?" I asked. "Do you have any idea how many muffins and cookies and cakes and pies I had to make and sell in order to earn enough money to pay for that bathing suit?"

"A lot?" she guessed in a sympathetic voice.

"That's right!" I cried.

"Those coconut drop cookies you made last weekend were delicious, by the way," she murmured. "In fact, I overheard Bernice Watson from down at the beauty parlor say she's never tasted their equal."

"Really?" I blinked, pressing the palm of my hand against my chest. "She said that?"

"She certainly did," nodded my mother.

I took another bite of my cinnamon bun and momentarily lost myself in a vision of old Mrs. Watson staggering through the streets in a coconut-drop-cookie-induced rapture, raving to complete strangers about her life-altering dainty experience.

Then my mother's voice interrupted my reverie.

"Oh, no, Table Seven just knocked over his papaya juice," she said. Jumping to her feet, she hurriedly ripped three pages off her waitress pad and handed them to me. "Would you be a sweetie and run these dinner orders back to Dad for me, Francie?"

Frustrated by how neatly I'd been outmaneuvered, I was about to deliver a heartfelt speech on the subject of adding insult to injury when I got an idea so brilliant I nearly laughed aloud. Snatching the orders out of my mother's hand, I bolted for the kitchen like a house on fire.

"DAD!" I hollered, shouldering open the swinging door with such vigor that Marguerite, our short-order cook, accidentally flipped a Salisbury steak onto the floor. "Dad, oh, Dad, did you know about this horrible plan to leave me stuck here like some pathetic loser while everyone else on the planet goes off to the pool party next Friday night?" I cried, trying to look as pitiful as I possibly could. "Did you *approve* it?"

My startled father looked up from the half-constructed bacon-and-tomato sandwich on the counter in front of him. He was a man of great moral conviction and strength of character, and sometimes, if I worked him just right, I could get him to fold like a cheap garage sale card table.

Unfortunately, this wasn't one of those times.

"I know it's disappointing, Peanut," he said, his voice as soft as chalk. "But there's nothing we can do about it."

I dropped to my knees.

"Dad," I moaned, raising my clasped hands high in the air. "It's not fair! I promised my Social Committee executive team and our staff adviser that I'd be there. Everyone is counting on me!"

"I don't know what to tell you, Peanut," my father sighed as he turned back to his sandwich. "I wish Mom and I didn't have to take on extra work, but we do. Making ends meet on what we earn from the café has always been a struggle. You know that."

Since I had no good answer for this, I breathed loudly through my nostrils and scowled up at him with all my might. In response, he asked me to go into the back and fetch him a jar of dill pickles. I grudgingly did as he asked, then stalked back out to the dining room, flopped down in my chair and stared moodily at the remains of my cinnamon bun until my mother walked over.

"Holly is here," she said, using her papaya-juice-soaked rag to point to a car idling at the curb outside the café.

Wordlessly, I threw my bag over my shoulder and tried to sweep past my mother in order to show her how deeply the injustice of the situation had hurt me. She completely ruined the effect by telling me I had every right to be angry.

"You had your heart set on something and got the rug pulled out from under you," she said as she reached forward to push my bangs out of my eyes. "I know it's hard, but if you can, try to remember that part of growing up is learning to accept the fact that things don't always work out the way we want them to."

"That's just another way of saying I have to learn to give up," I said loftily. "Tell me, is that what you want, Mom — a daughter who is a *quitter?*"

After assuring me it wasn't, my mother gave me a kiss and a gentle shove out the front door into the bracing January cold. Covering my bare ears with my bare hands, I ran for the backseat of Holly's car, where she sat blowing fog on the cold windows and writing rude phrases in letters just small enough that her mother couldn't read them in the rear-view mirror. When she grinned up at me, the ache of knowing all the fun I was going to miss at the pool party brought a lump the size of a cantaloupe to my throat.

If growing up is about giving up, I thought suddenly as I yanked open the car door and motioned for Holly to shove over, *then it just might have to wait until after next Friday night.*

⁊⁊⁊

Holly and I had been best friends since the third grade. It was eerie how much we had in common — our birthdays were exactly three months apart, our left big toes were the exact same shape, we could both wiggle one ear but not the other, and we both agreed that boys who ignored us didn't know what they were missing, although Holly would often add that she couldn't give a fiddler's fart about any guy who was too cool to give her the time of day, whereas for some strange reason I'd always found that sort of behavior the icing on the cake.

That night, I waited until we were in pajamas and tucked cozily into her frilly pink bedroom to tell her that my parents were making me work the night of the pool party.

"What?" she cried as she put a final dab of sludge green polish on her baby toenail. "Did you point out to them that this isn't Communist China? Did you remind them that child labor has been illegal in this country for quite some time now?"

"No, but I wish I had!" I said fiercely, holding out my hand for the polish.

Holly gave it to me, then leaned over and blew carefully on her perfectly painted toenails. "Well, did you at least explain to them that if you don't go to the party I'll have no one to go with, so they'll be ruining my life, too?"

"If I had, my mother would just have given me her little speech about how nice it can be to have several good friends instead of just one best friend," I snorted.

We looked at each other and then — at the exact same moment! — pretended to barf with such enthusiasm that

Holly's mother anxiously called up to see what was wrong. After a few more noisy fake retches, we sweetly reassured her that everything was fine. Then I reached down to continue painting my toenails and Holly belted me so hard across the back of the head with her pillow that I smeared polish halfway across my foot. With a snarl, I lunged for her right leg and missed. She shrieked with fake terror and leaped onto her bed, where she bounced around, laughing hysterically and pounding on my head with her pillow until I managed to catch the hem of her flannel pajamas and give a sharp tug. At that point, she lost her balance and came down so hard on the bed that we heard a sharp *crack* from below.

In the silence that followed, we held our breath and listened for the sound of Mrs. Carleson's feet pounding up the stairs to see what we'd destroyed this time. When we heard nothing, we had a good, long giggle. Then I began to scrape the sticky, clumpy, utterly ruined polish from my toenails so I could redo them.

I was only half finished when Holly's little sister, Tabitha, burst into the room unannounced, spied Holly's toes and the gummy green ball between my fingers and started hollering down to her mother that we'd stolen her favorite nail polish. Holly immediately leaped up and started hollering that Tabitha hadn't knocked before entering her room. When Mrs. Carleson hollered up for them both to stop hollering, they hollered for a while longer about how she didn't care about their problems and about how she always favored the other daughter. Then Tabitha whispered that she'd found a stack of love letters her dad had written to her mom when they were engaged, so while Mrs. Carleson continued to holler herself hoarse about the fact that she couldn't bear the household hollering a moment longer, we tiptoed down the hall to her bedroom and laughed ourselves sick reading mushy poems that didn't even rhyme.

Later that evening, after we'd finished watching a

ridiculous old horror movie in which a giant blob of jelly terrorized a major American city, Holly and I made crank phone calls using the neon pink cell phone she'd gotten for her last birthday. We telephoned Pizza Palace, gave them my address and asked them to deliver thirteen extra-large anchovy pizzas to a fellow named Rory. Then we called our science teacher to see if his bedside phone really would be answered by the algebra teacher with the lopsided breasts, and made several dozen giggling hang-up calls to the homes of cute boys we knew.

I don't know what time it was when I finally crawled into my sleeping bag on the floor beside Holly's bed, but I know I felt content. For a while, we drowsily talked about what I could do to convince my parents to let me go to the pool party, and how to get the boy I had deep feelings for to stop treating me like a turd. Then I quietly asked Holly if she thought it was weird that in *exactly* fourteen days I'd be turning *exactly* fourteen years old and she said she did. After that, we lay still in the blue darkness without saying anything for a long while. Eventually, Holly began to snore like a lumberjack, so I rolled over onto my side, pulled my pillow over my head and fell asleep dreaming of a time and a place where my baking business had become so wildly successful that I got to make all my own personal decisions, and where handsome boys without attitude problems rode handsome stallions as they galloped along beside me through the pounding surf.

❧❧❧

Monday morning it was so cold that by the time I got to the bus stop I could barely feel my toes pressing up against the ends of my favorite old purple high-top runners.

"Well?" said Holly as soon as I walked up. "Did you talk your parents into letting you go to the pool party?"

"No," I replied. "And this morning my mom said if I didn't get off her case about it she'd make me scrub out the café toilets with my bare fingers the night of the next school dance."

"No *way,*" said Holly, stuffing three pieces of Juicy Fruit gum into her mouth.

"Way," I assured her as the bus pulled up to the curb and we climbed aboard.

Flashing our passes at the driver, we tromped to the back, grabbed for handholds and kept talking. The bus slowed to pick up more passengers; I swayed on my feet. Then I happened to glance outside and notice my mother's friend Vivian standing at the bus stop. When she saw me looking at her, she smiled broadly and began to wave.

"Ignore her," I told Holly. "She's the reason I can't go to the pool party. She also smells like fried meat and has an unnatural attraction to things with fur. Waving to a person like that can only lead to trouble."

"Uh, Francie?" came a deep voice from directly behind me.

Holly let out a little shriek. I jumped like a startled cat. Both of us spun around.

To my horror, it was Vivian's son, Ricky Skametka.

"I think she was probably waving to *me,*" he whispered, looking acutely embarrassed.

Holly smiled. I nodded awkwardly.

Ricky, who was a grade ahead of me in school, had been a good friend of mine until three years ago when he'd moved to Vancouver to live with his father. It hadn't worked out, I guess, and when Ricky moved back earlier this year, he'd turned into a tall, skinny stranger with an embarrassingly deep voice and a tendency to bump into things. I'd been uncomfortable around him ever since.

"Listen, Ricky —" I began.

"Remember what I told you before?" he interrupted in that horribly manly voice of his. "My friends call me Rick now."

I opened my mouth to say something, but nothing came out.

"So call me Rick, okay?" he added softly, reaching over to untwist the strap of my knapsack.

"Uh ... okay," I stammered. "Well, anyway, uh, I'm sorry I said that your mother ... you know ..."

"Smells like fried meat?"

"Yes, and also — "

"Has an unnatural attraction to things with fur?"

"That's right," I said.

Then I didn't know what to say, so I didn't say anything, and after a while it dawned on me that I was just standing there gawking at him with my mouth hanging open. I thought I felt as completely mortified as it was possible for a person to feel until the very next second, when the bus driver suddenly slammed on the brakes and I went flying into Ricky. Not only did we make *full frontal body contact,* but my left cheek got planted so firmly against his chest that I swear I felt the crinkle of crispy chest hair through the thin cotton T-shirt he was wearing under his open black leather jacket. Leaping backward in shock and revulsion, I knocked into a dude wearing wraparound shades, who banged into a blond girl about my age, who tripped over someone's portable kennel and set loose a pair of high-strung Chihuahuas who were so excited to be free that they started peeing all over everybody's shoes.

My only conscious thought at that terrible moment was to flee the scene as quickly as possible. Frantically yanking up and down on the bell cord, I hissed at Holly that we were getting off at the next stop. She started to complain that we were still six blocks from school, but I cut her off with an elbow jab to the ribs, seized her by one arm, galloped us to the back exit and leaped for freedom the instant the doors opened. Unfortunately, neither Holly nor I realized that she was standing on my untied left shoelace, so I only got partially airborne before my body snapped to a sudden halt and I fell to the curb in a heap. As I lay face-first in the dirty snow gasping for breath, it occurred to me that I hadn't even bothered to say good-bye to Ricky, and that in addition to possibly hurting his feelings, this had almost certainly made me look like an immature freak. Scrambling to my feet, I pushed my overgrown bangs out of my face and peered desperately through the grimy windows of the bus, straining to make eye contact with Ricky in order to confirm that he saw me giving him a nonchalant wave good-bye.

But the only person who acknowledged me was the blond girl who'd tripped over the portable kennel, and she was smirking and making circles at her temple with her index finger. Outraged, I gave her what I hoped was a withering stare, tried not to cough as the bus pulled away belching toxic blue diesel fumes all over me, then turned and joined Holly for the long, cold walk to school.

Frozen nearly solid, we arrived eight minutes after the first bell and were promptly handed late slips by Mr. Simmons, who was prowling the hallway by our locker. I found this pretty rich considering the fact that Mr. Simmons, who was the staff adviser on the Student Social Committee, had shown up late for every single meeting we'd had since the beginning of the year. The other kids on the committee insisted that it didn't bother them, but Holly and I agreed this was because they were afraid of Mr. Simmons and the way the veins in his red, sweaty forehead stood out whenever he lost it on us, which was all the time. We also agreed that his tardiness was a slap in the face to young people everywhere, and that until he started treating us with a little more respect, we were only going to give him the minimum amount of respect required to avoid getting pulverized by him.

"Mr. Simmons, couldn't you let it go just this one time?" I asked now as I tried not to gag on the stale cigarette smell that enveloped him like a reeking force field. "I mean, can you honestly say *you've* never been late for something on account of extenuating circumstances?"

He stared so hard at me that for one breathless moment I thought he might actually be about to take back our late slips. Then he bellowed that if we were still in the hall when he finished counting to ten he was going to give us both a week of detentions. Holly let out a little shriek and flew to our locker. Thoroughly affronted by the hypocrisy of the situation, I followed her just quickly enough to ensure that Mr. Simmons couldn't accuse me of deliberately trying to provoke him. I think he felt provoked anyway, however, because just when it looked like we were going to make it before the count of ten, he skipped directly from "seven" to "nine," sending Holly into such a panic that she nearly wrenched our homeroom door off the hinges in her effort to beat the countdown.

"Wait up!" I whispered, but she had already darted through the maze of music stands and beat-up trombone cases and was sliding into her seat.

Our homeroom teacher, Mrs. Cavanaugh — who'd stopped talking when we burst into the room — now said, "Hello, girls. Nice of you to join us."

Holly blushed and sank lower in her seat. I blushed, too, but I also waved and said, "Don't mention it, Mrs. C."

Mrs. C arched her eyebrow at me but didn't say anything as I tromped to my seat and dumped my knapsack at my feet. In addition to being our homeroom teacher, Mrs. C was the school band instructor and, more important, the coolest teacher I'd ever known. She didn't sweat the small stuff, and she always went out of her way to treat me the way a ninth-grade student deserved to be treated. Plus, her hair looked *exactly* the way I was hoping mine would look when I finished growing it out, so whenever a bad hair day was making me tempted to chop it all off, one look at Mrs. C's long, lustrous mane gave me the inspiration I needed to persevere. You couldn't ask for more than that in a homeroom teacher.

"As I was saying," said Mrs. C, picking up from where she'd evidently left off, "I have two more announcements to make before you head to your first class. One is that Performance Band auditions will be held in the next couple of weeks, so if you're hoping to make it, I suggest you practice hard between now and then. Not only is being a member of the Performance Band a great way to get involved in school life, but the band will be performing in an out-of-town festival in early spring and, believe me, you don't want to miss that."

Holly and I looked at each other and grinned as Mrs. C handed out an information sheet about the festival.

"The final announcement is that we have a new student in our midst," said Mrs. C, looking over at someone I hadn't noticed on my way in. Leaning forward in my seat, I couldn't help but give a loud grunt of dismay when I saw that it was the blond girl from the bus who'd set the Chihuahuas free and then had the nerve to make the cuckoo sign at *me*.

"Hello, everybody!" She grinned, bouncing to her feet and giving us all a peppy little wave. "My name is Darlene Donovan!"

Holly looked over at me and raised her eyebrows. I tucked my clasped hands under my chin and batted my eyelashes like a demonically possessed kewpie doll.

"Francie?" called Mrs. C.

Without warning, everyone in the classroom turned to stare at me.

Flustered, I dropped my hands to my sides and bugged my eyeballs out at one person after another in order to get them all to turn back around and mind their own beeswax. Then I cleared my throat and said, "Is there a problem, Mrs. C?"

"Of course not," she smiled, tucking a thick lock of glossy hair behind one ear. "I was just wondering if you'd mind giving Darlene a helping hand until she gets settled."

The truth was that I'd rather have had my eyelids ripped off with a pair of rusty pliers than give a helping hand to someone who'd given me the cuckoo sign for no good reason, but since I didn't want to look spiteful and uncooperative in front of my favorite teacher, I nodded and threw a vaguely welcoming smile at the new girl. She grinned back at me, then immediately turned and whispered something to the girl behind her. Whatever she said sent them both into such fits of giggles that my smile froze on my face and my stomach did a funny sort of flip-flop. Then the bell rang and the moment was lost in the noisy bustle of people getting ready to head to first class.

"This isn't fair," I whispered to Holly as we leaned down to grab our knapsacks off the floor.

"Life isn't fair," she grinned, pretending not to notice that the sight of her bending over in a scoop-necked T-shirt had just caused Randy Newton to walk into a wall.

I glanced across the room to where two more girls were giggling with the new girl, and then over at Randy, who was being sent to the office to get an icepack for his nose.

No, I thought, slinging my knapsack over my shoulder. *I guess it isn't.*

2. Hope and Other Forms of Torture (Part I)

The more desperately a charged particle attempts to attract a similarly charged particle, the harder it will be repulsed, until eventually it will find itself floating through the vast, sub-atomic universe, alone and miserable.

Excerpt from The Wonderful World of Physical Chemistry by Professor Donovan Storm

As luck would have it, the new girl — Darlene — and I were in almost all the same classes.

"I guess that's why Mrs. C asked you to show me around," she said, bouncing alongside me as we made our way to science class. "Of course, if she'd asked me what *I* wanted, I would have told her not to bother asking anyone to show me anything. I've gone to four different schools in the last six years, and frankly, I've always ended up settling in just fine on my own."

"Oh," I said, wondering if there was a polite way to tell her that I was the only person who ever called Mrs. Cavanaugh "Mrs. C." "Why have you gone to so many different schools?"

Darlene detoured into the girls' bathroom without asking if I minded or even pausing to make sure I was following her. "My father is a management consultant whose firm specializes in taking over failing businesses and either returning them to fiscal health or breaking them up and selling off the assets for profit."

"Oh, yeah?" I said, trying not to sound impressed. "What kind of businesses does his firm take over?"

"Failing ones. Weren't you listening?" laughed Darlene as she skipped into a toilet cubicle and locked the door behind her.

"I was ... I just meant — "

"Anyway," she continued, "whenever he's sent to a new city to get involved in a new project, I always come with him."

"What about your mother?"

"That's none of your business," she snapped. Then she laughed. "So what about you, Nancy? What does your dad do for a living?"

"The name is Francie, and uh ... my parents own and operate a café," I said, feeling a little unbalanced by her shifting tones. "It's not very big, but the food is good and—"

"Hey, there's no toilet paper in here. Hand me some, will you?" interrupted Darlene, thrusting her tiny hand under the cubicle door and snapping her little fingers at me. "Then, if it's all the same to you, I'd really like to get going. I know being late for class doesn't bother some people, but where I come from, that kind of behavior is just pure ignorant."

After Darlene finished scrubbing her hands for as long as it took her to hum her ABCs, she followed me down the rapidly emptying hallway to the science lab. It was by far the most awesome learning environment I'd ever had. In addition to the anatomically correct biology posters stapled to the walls, there was a locked supply cabinet full of chemicals that could blind, burn or poison us if handled incorrectly, and a collection of pickle jars containing horrible things floating in formaldehyde. There were twelve long desks in two long rows, two students to each desk. Every desk had its own stainless steel sink, electrical outlet and gas hook-up. The gas hook-ups were for the Bunsen burners that our teacher, Mr. Flatburn, said we'd be able to fire up just as soon as we proved we were responsible enough to use them without incinerating ourselves.

Of all the many fantastic features that made the science lab such an attractive place to acquire knowledge, the most fantastic by far was the fact that by some incredible stroke of luck I'd had the good fortune of being assigned to the same desk as Tate Jarvis, the boy who'd stolen my heart at the beginning of eighth grade and never given it back. Prior to sharing a desk in science, the most attention Tate had ever paid me was one time last year in the school cafeteria when he'd stuffed the crust of his bologna sandwich into my milk as he walked by with his gang of jock friends. Although I'd pretended to be outraged by his juvenile behavior, it had been weeks before I'd stopped blushing at the memory of what a thrill it had been to have that precious moment of Tate's undivided attention. So you can imagine how I felt at the beginning of this year when Mr. Flatburn called our names — one after another! — and then told us we were going to be desk partners. My god! I almost *died!*

So far, it had worked out even better than I could have hoped. True, I had yet to catch Tate staring at me with anything resembling a love-struck expression, but he always chuckled when I pretended to light my hair on fire with the Bunsen burner, and once, when I threw my pencil up in the air, he caught it and handed it back to me. He'd also asked me to supply him with the answers to science assignments a couple of times, but I'd always told him I couldn't do it unless he was prepared to sit down with me and actually try to understand the answers I was giving him. Partly this was because I had principles, and partly this was because I was living for the day when Tate's marks would plunge so low he'd have no choice but to invite me over to his house to help him study.

As Darlene and I approached the science lab, I licked my lips and fluffed my bangs in anticipation of all eyes — including those of a certain academically challenged dreamboat — being on me as I introduced her to Mr. Flatburn. The minute I opened the door, however, she scooted ahead of me and introduced herself with another perky little wave. Quickly, I tried to draw everyone's attention back to me and my freshly moistened lips by declaring myself her assigned caretaker. Unfortunately, this backfired in the worst way when Mr. Flatburn said if that was the case, Darlene could sit with me.

"What?" I blurted, aghast. "No, she can't! I already have a ... a desk partner."

"Well, now you have two," shrugged Mr. Flatburn as though he couldn't care less about the fact that he'd just destroyed my tender hopes of blossoming love.

"But ... but ..." I searched wildly for an argument that would appeal to Mr. Flatburn's intellectual side, since he obviously had the emotional sensitivity of a gnat. "Don't you think that might be a little dangerous?" I asked finally.

With a puzzled expression, Mr. Flatburn looked up from the notes he'd been reviewing.

"I mean, I'm not one to tell you your business, sir," I said, lowering my voice. "But you know what they say — 'two's company, three's a crowd.' Do you really want to be responsible for having created a crowd when it comes time to use those Bunsen burners?" I shrugged as if to say that it was his neck, not mine.

Mr. Flatburn stared at me. I held my breath and crossed my fingers.

"I can move over," called Tate suddenly.

"I can be careful," piped Darlene at the very same instant.

The two of them locked eyes and smiled. It was such an adorable moment that I almost vomited. Then Mr. Flatburn made it about a billion times worse by ordering *me* to go to the classroom next door and get a chair for Darlene. Like I was her slave or something! When I got back, I tried to arrange the desk so that I would be the one in the middle, but Tate wouldn't hear of it. He insisted that he would sit in the middle, with Darlene on one side of him and me on the other. My heart soared briefly when he expressed this desire to have me at his side, but it was all downhill from there.

Tate shared his textbook with Darlene and lent her a pencil when she whispered that she didn't have one (a likely story!), but ignored me completely until Mr. Flatburn caught me pretending to light my hair on fire and told me to grow up or get out, at which point Tate started snickering along with everyone else in the class. Face burning, I ignored my childish classmates, waited until Mr. Flatburn turned his back to give him a dirty look, then put my head down and got to work.

👁️👁️👁️

Later that morning, in the dim, damp-smelling basement cafeteria, I poured out the whole sad story to Holly. Out of a sense of duty, I'd invited Darlene to join us for lunch, but she'd briskly advised me that she had other plans and ditched me without a backward glance.

"You don't think Tate likes her, do you?" I asked anxiously as I picked bits of wilted alfalfa out of my egg salad sandwich.

"Who cares if he likes her? He's an ass," said Holly, ripping open a big bag of salt 'n' vinegar chips.

"How can you say that?" I cried. "You know how I feel about him and you're my best friend. It's your *duty* to agree with me on matters of the heart!"

"Oh, I'm sorry," said Holly through a mouthful of chips. "Obviously, what I meant to say was that he's an ass if he chooses her over you."

"Do you sincerely think so?" I asked, reaching for a chip.

"I sincerely do," she said

"You're a good friend, Holly," I sighed.

"Yes, I am," she agreed, rolling her eyes. "What's she like, anyway?"

"I just told you what she's like. She's like a conniving wolf that dresses up in sheep's clothing just so she can lure the majestic ram from the actual sheep that truly cares for him."

"Other than that."

"She's rich and possibly motherless," I said, taking a bite of my sandwich. "She makes me uncomfortable."

"Why?"

I shrugged as I pulled the Performance Band Festival information sheet out of my binder. "Did you read this?" I asked, stabbing the sheet with my egg-salad-soiled fingertip. "It says here that it's going to cost two hundred dollars per student to go on that trip. You never told me it was going to cost that much to go away for two days!"

Holly was the only reason I was in band. At the beginning of ninth grade, everyone who was in band was put into one homeroom, and everyone who wasn't was put into another, and since we wanted to be in the same homeroom, and since Holly wanted to continue studying the flute, I'd agreed to take up the clarinet so we could stay together. I'd almost dropped out in my second week when I realized that my lack of musical ability was probably going to drag down my entire grade-point average, but Holly had convinced me to stick it out so we could go on this trip together.

"I had no idea it was going to cost that much money," said Holly, eyeing me anxiously. "What are you going to do?"

"Well, asking my parents is out of the question," I said as I reread the note to make sure I hadn't missed anything. "So I guess I'll just have to save every penny I make from my baking and keep my fingers crossed that sales don't slow down."

"They won't," said Holly, "because you are totally awesome. Plus, I'm going to come over this weekend and help you make posters to put up around the neighborhood to make sure everyone knows about the Great Francie Freewater, Baker Extraordinaire."

Holly pretended to sound the trumpets. I tried not to look too pleased.

"The real question is what products I should focus on," I murmured, setting my half-eaten sandwich to one side. "My carrot zucchini muffins have been selling well these days, but the price of zucchini has climbed so high since winter set in that I don't know how much longer I'm going to be able to turn a profit on them. Banana is a decent fallback muffin, I suppose, but it's so *pedestrian*. I mean, who can't make a banana muffin?"

"I can't," said Holly, sucking salt off her fingers one at a time.

"My cheesecakes and dainties are always popular, of course," I continued. "But the ingredients are so expensive. Nana says I'd save a bundle if I started using artificial vanilla extract, margarine and generic brand semi-sweet chocolate squares, but I say get *real*. I mean, what self-respecting baker uses artificial vanilla extract? My god, it's like using chalk dust instead of flour."

"Who does that?" asked Holly, looking vaguely revolted.

"Exactly!" I cried, flinging my arms into the air. It was such a nerdy display of enthusiasm that I immediately blushed and sat on my hands. "The bottom line," I continued in a low voice, "is that I'm going to have to think through my product offering very carefully and then make sure I pace myself, because if I give in to the temptation to do too much too fast, I'm going to burn out, you know? It's always been one of my biggest challenges in the kitchen. That, and the fact that I'm *really* hard on myself. If a batch of cookies isn't baked to absolute perfection I won't put them out. I'll throw them in the garbage, or feed them to Nana's idiot bird, Rory. She doesn't like when I do that — says it gives Rory an attitude of entitlement, and also cramps — but I think she's missing the point. The point is that it's a symbolic gesture."

"I know *exactly* what you mean," said Holly eagerly. "When I'm practicing a piece on the flute, I won't settle for anything less than flawless execution."

"Which is why, when you finally turn pro, people are going to pay thousands of dollars for the privilege of hearing you perform," I said confidently.

"Ooh, do you sincerely think they will?" breathed Holly.

"I sincerely do."

"You're a good friend, Francie."

"Yes, I am," I agreed, reaching for the nearly empty chip bag. "And don't you forget it."

⚬⚬⚬

Darlene reappeared after lunch without offering any explanation as to where she'd been, even though I made a point of telling her exactly where I'd been. She matter-of-factly pointed out that I had a blob of egg salad on my T-shirt, offered me a cinnamon breath mint and then led me through the halls to geometry class, smiling at cute boys and greeting older girls the whole way. It was like hanging around with a beautiful, popular strain of infectious disease, and I couldn't decide whether I wanted to be infected or vaccinated.

I was still mulling over this dilemma later that afternoon when Mr. Simmons — who taught last period Life Skills in addition to disrespecting me and my fellow Student Social Committee members every second Wednesday at lunch hour — announced that our second term project was going to constitute eighty percent of our grade.

"What!" I cried, my voice rising above the sudden murmur of protest that filled the room. "Mr. Simmons, that's insane! Isn't that insane?" I asked the girl beside me. She nodded. "Isn't that insane?" I swiveled to ask Darlene, who was sitting in the seat behind me.

"Not really," she said, looking up from the fancy jar of lip balm she held in the palm of one hand. "At the last private school I attended, we wrote exams that were worth a hundred percent of our final mark. And that was in every subject."

"*That* is insane," I whispered, my jaw dropping.

Mr. Simmons hammered his fist against the blackboard several times. "Oh, stuff a sock in it, people. This is Life Skills class, not Free Ride class. It's time you got with the program. You think life hands out crappy little pop quizzes and gives gold stars for coloring in the lines? Well, think again."

I was so affronted by this condescending speech that I could hardly breathe.

"Excuse *me*, Mr. Simmons," I said, my voice practically dripping with dignity. "I think what my classmates and I meant is that — "

"Can it, Freewater. Not interested," he interrupted. "Now, pigeons, do you want to know what your little project is going to be about? Or do you want to guess and hope for the best?"

Pigeons! It was almost beyond endurance!

"Well?" he barked.

No one said a word. So, not knowing what else to do, I swallowed my pride and asked Mr. Simmons what the project was going to be about.

"Pigeons, you're going to tell me what you want to be when you grow up."

A chorus of groans rose up in the classroom.

"Shut it! Shut it this instant!" he bellowed, waving his meaty arms at us as the vein in his forehead began to throb. "I'm not talking about those lame pieces of drivel you scribbled in second grade about how you wanted to own a beauty parlor or become a fireman someday. I'm talking about serious research into educational requirements, salary expectations and lifestyle considerations. I'm talking about careers that are real and attainable. I'm talking about projects presented in a format that will *blow my mind*."

I raised my hand and asked if he could possibly be a little more specific as to what, exactly, he was looking for and how it would be marked.

"No," he snapped. "Now, I have to step out for moment, so sit quietly and work on your project outlines." Patting the inside pocket of his shabby sports jacket to make sure he had cigarettes, he headed for the door. Halfway there, he stopped and pointed a thick, tobacco-stained finger at us. "Quietly," he repeated. "Don't jerk me around on this, people. In case you haven't noticed, I'm not the most patient man that ever lived."

❧❧❧

Most of us spent the rest of class complaining — quietly — about the project. What did he mean he wanted us to write about careers that were "real and attainable"? Not many people became famous rock stars or Nobel Prize–winning scientists (or world-renowned bakers with their own TV shows, best-selling cookbooks and monthly magazines), but *some* people did. Did that qualify those occupations as "real and attainable"? Somehow, we didn't think so.

When the bell finally rang, I said good-bye to Darlene and made a beeline for my locker. Usually, Holly and I met there after last class to take the bus home together, but she'd gotten out of school early that day for a dentist appointment, so I just grabbed my coat and left. When I got outside and saw that the bus was nowhere in sight, I decided to run home. I had exactly seventeen minutes until the start of my favorite television program, and I didn't want to be late because it was hosted by none other than the *other* love of my life — internationally acclaimed celebrity baker Lorenzo LaRue.

In addition to having a weekly show called *Getting Baked with Lorenzo,* my darling had lush, dark curls that cascaded down his back in direct violation of the health codes of every major city in North America. I was deeply attracted to this rebellious streak of his, and also to his lush, dark curls.

As I ran along through the biting cold, I distracted myself from the stitch in my side by fantasizing about someday taking the place of the Lovely Lydia, Lorenzo's faithful assistant. As far as I could tell, her sole contribution to the show was giggling whenever Lorenzo licked something off her index finger. In my fantasy, I was so much more than that: I murmured encouragement and suggestions; I handed over ingredients with grace and efficiency. Lorenzo could hardly keep his eyes on the pecans he was chopping in preparation for the flour-based crust of his Lemon Layered Delight, so entranced was he with both the shimmering perfection of my hair and my fantasy breasts, which were so large and full that they required an underwire bra. In my mind, I'd just whispered something ingenious about setting aside a tablespoon of chopped pecans for later use as a garnish, when Lorenzo smiled wickedly and indicated that I should dunk my index finger into a nearby bowl of lemon pie filling. Instantly, the fantasy fizzled. The idea of being slobbered on — even by Lorenzo, even in my fantasy — was enough to make me vomit.

With mere seconds to spare, I burst into the café and planted a brief, chilly kiss on my mother's cheek before hurrying to the kitchen. Here, I paused just long enough to snatch two pieces of crisp bacon off Marguerite's griddle and half a chicken sandwich out from under my father's nose before barreling on up the back staircase. Flying into our apartment, I sprinted across the worn hardwood floors to my nana's closed bedroom door and skidded to a halt with my nose an inch away from the peeling white paint. Breathing hard, I pounded on the door.

"Nana!" I hollered. "Nana! Are you in there? Come quick! It's time for Lorenzo!"

Nana used to have a thing for this TV evangelist named Raoul. Then, three months ago, when she was in the hospital being treated for a blood clot she'd gotten following hip surgery, I introduced her to Lorenzo, and she'd been hooked ever since. I didn't really mind sharing him with her, I guess, except that she never even *tried* to pretend she liked him for anything other than his looks, and I didn't really think it was appropriate for her to have those kinds of feelings for a man I cared about.

I heard the clump of Nana's cane as she crossed the bedroom floor. Suddenly, the door flew open and she stood before me, tiny and severe, her snow white hair sticking out in all directions.

"Nana!" I cried. "Were you napping?"

"No," she lied, thumping her cane on the floor for emphasis. The cane was a temporary thing, just until her hip was completely healed. She liked to complain that it made her feel like an invalid, but I think she secretly enjoyed being able to thump it at me whenever she felt I was being cheeky.

"You shouldn't lie, Nana," I admonished with a broad smile as I stuffed the two pieces of bacon into the sandwich and took a big bite. "And you shouldn't feel bad about getting caught napping, either. After all, you recently went through a terrible medical ordeal. You need to build up your strength."

"Don't talk with your mouth full," she snorted, thumping her cane at me again. "Now, stand aside. You did say it was time for Lorenzo, didn't you?"

"Not that I recall," I sang as I skipped after her into the living room. "Maybe it came to you in a dream. While you were napping."

Nana pursed her lips at me and plopped down on the couch. Stuffing the last of my sandwich into my mouth, I leaped onto to my father's favorite recliner and flung aside old newspapers until I found the remote. Clicking it on, I turned to the right channel and settled back just as the opening credits faded and the spotlight shone down on Lorenzo.

"'Allo, ladies," he said, looking deeply into the camera with eyes the color of warm chocolate. "'Ave you all missed me as much as I've missed you?"

I sighed audibly. Oh, he was so good-looking! And when he stared into the camera that way, it felt as though he was staring *right* at *me!*

"Do you know, it feels as though he is staring *right* at *me!*" exclaimed Nana in a hushed voice.

"He isn't," I assured her.

On cue, the Lovely Lydia glided onto the set wearing a seamless white gown. I shook my head in disbelief. Good lord, didn't this woman know how staggeringly silly it was to wear white in the kitchen? One dribble or splash and that gown was history! For the life of me, I couldn't understand what someone like Lorenzo saw in someone like her. Sure, she was pretty enough, I guess, if you liked her kind of blond bimbo look, but I'd never heard her make one single suggestion of value during the baking process. Not *one*. Lorenzo deserved to be assisted by someone more substantial — by someone who shared his passion.

By someone like *me*.

Coming to a languid halt in front of Lorenzo, Lydia extended one slender hand toward him. With the kind of chivalry generally reserved for my True Romance novels, he bowed deeply and bestowed upon it a heartbreakingly gentle kiss.

Then he cast a sideways glance at the camera and gave me a sly wink. The studio audience went wild.

"Oh, what a tease!" cried Nana delightedly, flapping her fingers toward the TV screen.

"He wasn't winking at you, Nana," I informed her.

Now Lorenzo strode manfully over to his baking counter and held up a picture of a woman named Hildegarde Kunkle, who was organizing an upcoming charity bake sale in the basement of her local church. After explaining how his book *Life in the Emotional Bundt Pan* had helped Hildegarde conquer her pastry demons and get over her pathological fear of strudel, Lorenzo warmly encouraged everyone who lived in the same city as Hildegarde to get out and show their support.

I started to imagine what this kind of exposure could do for my little business, but my visions of clamoring crowds and rave reviews vanished when Lorenzo clapped his hands, tossed his luxurious mane over his shoulders and got down to work. The *Recipe Del Giorno* (that means "Recipe of the Day" in some foreign language, I think) was a pumpkin cheesecake with a gingersnap crust. Lorenzo got so overheated with the effort of grinding up those gingersnaps that he had to take off his shirt. Nana cheered. My mouth went momentarily dry at the sight of the deep brown nipples that punctuated his broad, hairless chest. Then, knowing what an insult it would be to a master baker like Lorenzo to focus on his looks instead of his talent, I tore my eyes away from his nipples and forced myself to concentrate on his clever tips for ensuring a light and fluffy texture to all my cheesecakes.

Twenty-six glorious minutes later, Lorenzo, still shirtless, shoveled a forkful of fresh pumpkin cheesecake between the eager lips of the Lovely Lydia, who damn near swooned at the taste of it. The studio audience cheered again, and so did Nana. I rolled my eyes, then waited for the most exciting moment of the show.

"And now, ladies, I 'ave an important contest announcement," said Lorenzo, seductively fingering the thick gold chains around his neck. "To the woman who can intoxicate me with a dessert that dazzles all my senses, a copy of my latest cookbook, *Baking Love by Candlelight.*"

For some reason, Nana found the title of Lorenzo's latest cookbook so hilarious that she couldn't stop laughing, so I missed hearing the rest of the contest details. Luckily, I had the show's Web site tagged as a favorite. All the details would be posted there; they always were. I lived for Lorenzo's contests. Sometimes the prize was something small (but fabulous!), like one of the autographed pictures in his exclusive collection (ten poses, all with his shirt off), but sometimes it was something big, like backstage passes and VIP seating in his studio audience. Technically, I wasn't supposed to enter the contests because I wasn't eighteen years of age or older, but I always did anyway. After all, this wasn't some smarmy chat room where middle-aged perverts tried to lure unsuspecting girls to say and do disgusting, dangerous or embarrassing things — this was a corporate Web site run by professional people who would probably all have heart attacks if they knew underage girls were sneaking in under the radar. Besides, the way I figured it, if I ever actually won, it would be fate's way of telling me that I shouldn't worry about the age difference between Lorenzo and me, no matter what the rest of society thought.

As the closing credits rolled over sweeping camera shots of Lorenzo shaking hands with overwrought members of his studio audience, I flopped back onto the recliner and closed my eyes.

"Isn't he something?" sighed Nana.

"He's too young for you," I said without opening my eyes. "And, anyway, what would Mr. Darnell say if you took up with another man?"

Mr. Darnell was Nana's gentleman friend. They started dating a couple of years after Poppy died, around the same time my parents bought the café and asked Nana and Rory to move in with us so there'd be someone to take care of me when they were working downstairs. Their moving in was supposed to have been a temporary thing — just until the café got off the ground — but no matter how hard my parents worked, it never got as far off the ground as they had hoped and, after a while, I guess we all got used to the arrangement.

"You leave Mr. Darnell out of this," ordered Nana sternly. Then she smiled. "Did I mention that he's taking me out for a fancy dinner on Friday evening to celebrate four years enjoying each other's company?"

"That's nice," I said. Then I snuggled deeper into my dad's chair and let my thoughts drift to Friday night. The day had been so busy that I hadn't thought about the Dive into Winter event since that morning on the bus, but as I now looked back on the way Tate Jarvis had acted toward Darlene in chemistry class, I realized with a jolt that it was no longer a question of simply wanting to attend.

For the sake of my heart, which would surely shatter into a million tiny pieces if Tate Jarvis got a chance to spend barely dressed quality time alone in the pool with Darlene, I *had* to be there.

∼∞∼

For the rest of the week, in order to get my parents to think that I'd given up hope, I didn't say one word to them about the pool party. Then, the minute I got home from school on Friday, I locked myself in the café bathroom, waited until I heard my mother walk by and then loudly pretended to barf my guts out while pouring big, sloppy glugs of water into the toilet for added realism. The plan I'd come up with was simple. Step 1: Get my parents thinking about how bad it would be to have me spewing highly contagious vomit all over their customers. Step 2: Let them figure out a way to cover my shift at the café. Step 3: Experience a miraculous, last-minute recovery. Step 4: Go to the pool party and let Tate drool all over me in my daring new bathing suit.

Unfortunately, my mother completely derailed my plan by insisting that she take me to the hospital for tests, observation and possibly an intravenous drip to replenish the staggering volume of fluid I'd apparently lost. Alarmed by the certainty that any ER doc with half a brain in her head would nail me as a fraud and possibly report me to the authorities, I tried to tell my mother she was overreacting, but she was so adamant that, in the end, the only way I could get her to back off was by tearfully blurting that I'd experienced a miraculous, last-minute recovery and was heading upstairs to change into my work clothes.

∼∞∼

I was so devastated by the fact that my plan had failed that the minute I set foot in the apartment, I ran to call Holly. As I passed by the kitchen, however, I noticed Nana hovering worriedly around Rory's cage.

"What's wrong?" I sniffled, wiping my eyes.

"It's Rory," she said. "The darn fool got loose again. As far as I can tell, he ate a bar of soap, half a roll of toilet paper and every last bristle on your toothbrush. I found him an hour ago, lying on the bathmat looking sick as a dog. I called Dr. Peterson right away, of course, but he said the best he could do for poor Rory was to prescribe something to make it all pass through more comfortably."

"POOR RORY," squawked the bird, trying to claw me with his scratchy toes.

I took a step back from the cage and shook my fist at him.

"The doctor said it wasn't a necessity, especially since Rory always seems to recover nicely after these kinds of incidents, but I feel obligated, seeing how it was me that left the cage door open," continued Nana fretfully, giving her freshly coiffed hair a scrunch. "The problem is, Mr. Darnell will be here in fifteen minutes and it just doesn't seem right to keep him waiting while I run off to pick up stool softeners for my bird."

In order to teach Rory a lesson about eating people's toothbrushes, I was about to agree with Nana that she should forget about the stool softeners, when I was hit by another one of my brilliant ideas.

"Nana!" I cried. "Why don't *I* go pick up Rory's medicine for you?"

I threw a loving look at Rory, who summoned the last of his strength in order to lift up his tail feathers and show me his bum.

"I thought you were supposed to help out in the café tonight," said Nana.

"That's true. But this is *Rory* we're talking about, Nana," I gushed. "What could be more important than seeing that your dear feathered friend gets the medicine he so desperately needs?"

Nana eyed me suspiciously.

"You seem pretty excited about spending your Friday

night running medical errands for a bird you don't even like," she finally observed.

Realizing that I was in jeopardy of overplaying my hand, I tried to look hurt. "How can you say that, Nana?" I mumbled. "I'm only trying to help."

Nana was silent for a long moment. She was no dummy, and I knew she knew something was up, but I also knew she'd feel very rude ruining Mr. Darnell's carefully planned evening with a trip to the vet on behalf of her idiot bird. So I wasn't altogether surprised when she finally said, "Well, you'll have to ask Marguerite, since she's the one you'll be stepping out on. If it's all right with her, I guess it's all right with me."

"Oh, THANK YOU, NANA, THANK YOU! THANK YOU! THANK YOU!" I cried, forgetting all about my plan to ratchet down my enthusiasm.

"For what?" she asked, eyeing me suspiciously again.

"Well, uh, for giving me a chance to help, of course," I mumbled, reaching for the phone. "Now, if you'll excuse me, I have to go give Holly a call."

3. The Naked Truth

There is nothing so alluring to a real man as the sight of a barefoot woman with a plate of blueberry turnovers in her hand and a wanton look in her eye.

From Baking Love by Candlelight *by Lorenzo LaRue*

Marguerite wasn't at all keen on the idea of covering for me at the café while I ran out to fetch avian stool softeners as a favor to Nana. However, Marguerite was an animal lover, and when I pointed out the agony Rory was likely to face if he tried to pass those toothbrush bristles unaided, she reluctantly relented. With a whoop of joy, I vowed to be back as soon as humanly possible, grabbed my knapsack and flew out the door.

I was so exhilarated by the way things had turned out that I ran the whole way to the recreation center and arrived just in time to see Holly's mother drive up with Holly and Tabitha in the backseat, scrapping like a pair of caged weasels. As I stood there trying to catch my breath, Holly delivered one final swat and leaped from the car, slamming the door so hard it made *my* teeth rattle. Then she waved merrily at her infuriated sister, turned and skipped toward me. Laughing uncontrollably, we linked arms and skidded across the slippery sidewalk to the entrance of the rec center. Yanking open the door, we tumbled inside and ran for the changing room, where Holly immediately kicked off every last stitch of clothing and, humming happily to herself, began rooting through her swim tote for her bathing suit.

Not wanting to look like an immature dolt in the face of my best friend's unnatural ability to be comfortable prancing around completely naked in front of total strangers, I resisted the temptation to barricade myself into a personal change cubicle and slowly peeled off my own clothes.

Unfortunately, just as my panties hit the floor, disaster struck.

"Well, hell-*o!*" came a perky little voice.

Horrified, I looked up to see Darlene leaning against a nearby locker. Her little arms were folded across her fully clothed chest, and her glossy rosebud lips were curled up in a knowing smile. With a cry, I tried to fold in half, spin around, cover myself with my hands and grab for my towel, all at the same time.

"Are you having some kind of spasm, Francie?" asked Darlene curiously as she peered at me even more closely. "Because, if you are, I should tell you that I once knew a man who swallowed his own tongue during a spasm. Would you like me to stick something into your mouth to make sure that doesn't happen to you?"

I was so traumatized by my own nudity that instead of trying to take control of the situation by saying something cool or clever, I just snatched up my bathing suit and collapsed to the bench. Holly immediately leaned over and whispered that according to her mother, sitting in public places without underwear on was a good way to catch a venereal disease. I was up like a shot, hopping around on one leg while I struggled to get the other one through the maddening tangle of crisscrossing straps on my expensive new one-piece. I'd put my left foot in and out several times when, without warning, Darlene burst into a high-spirited rendition of the Hokey Pokey, startling me badly. I slipped on a section of wet tile, crashed into my locker and toppled to the floor at her feet.

Holly gasped. Darlene stopped singing.

"Are you okay?" she asked. "I mean, other than the fact that you're lying on that disgusting floor without any clothes on?"

Before I could reply, Sharon and Jody, the two tallest girls in our grade, came flopping up like a pair of oversized puppy dogs.

"Holy moly, you're completely naked," observed Sharon, staring down at me with her hands on her hips.

"So?" I said, tugging at my bathing suit, which Jody was now clutching with her very long, ugly simian toes. "Who cares if I'm naked? I don't care. Why should I care? I'm not some immature *dolt*, you know. I'm completely comfortable with my own fudging nudity," I babbled, feeling completely unhinged. "Is that the crime of the century or something? Huh? Well? IS IT?"

A strange silence followed my outburst. I looked up.

"Not at all, dear," smiled a nervous-looking elderly woman in a turquoise bathing cap. "But you're lying in front of my locker and I need my shampoo."

Jody dropped my bathing suit like a hot potato and skittered behind Sharon. The two of them dissolved into fits of silent laughter when the elderly woman nodded at me proudly and then dropped her towel as if to say that she, too, was completely comfortable with her own fudging nudity. Darlene grinned as though I was the star attraction in her own personal freak show, then bounced off in the direction of the private change cubicles. When she was gone, Holly helped me off the floor and steadied me while I worked my way through the tangle of straps and shakily pulled on my bathing suit.

The pool party turned out to be a complete bust. The hot tub was off limits due to a problem with the chlorine level, the sauna was off limits due to the fact that Mr. Simmons refused to leave it and no one wanted to sit beside him when he was sweaty, half-naked and in a foul mood about having to waste a Friday evening on good-for-nothing punks like us, and the lifeguards closed the high diving board after Randy Newton nearly belly-flopped himself to death trying to impress Holly with his backward somersault skills. Worst of all, as I cruised around the shallow end trying to have fun without getting my hair wet, I overheard Randy tell Greg Podwinski that Tate Jarvis wasn't coming on account of some stupid hockey game. I was so crestfallen at the news that I could hardly summon the energy to slug Randy when he later snuck up behind me and dumped a pail of water over my head.

"Don't worry, I'll get him for you!" shouted Holly as she excitedly leaped onto his back. Wrapping her arms around his neck and her legs around his waist, she grunted and threw her weight around like a pink-bikini-clad cowgirl trying to take down a particularly mulish bronco.

Randy looked ready to pass out, and not from the effort of trying to defend himself, either, I might add.

I watched them tussle for a moment, then waded over and tapped Holly on the shoulder. "I think I'd better get going now," I said, pushing my sodden bangs out of my eyes.

"All right!" she replied breathlessly, her cheeks pink from exertion. "I'll come by tomorrow around four to help make posters — and to let you know exactly how long it took me to dunk this jerk," she said, putting a fake choke hold on Randy, who struggled and grimaced but made no serious effort to get her off his back.

"Okay," I said, drifting away before she had a chance to add that the posters were to let the world know about the Great Francie Freewater, Baker Extraordinaire. That sort of thing always sounded flattering and glamorous when she said it to me, but if she ever said it in front of anyone else, I knew I'd have no choice but to change my name, move to Antarctica and spend the rest of my life trying to figure out how to turn penguins into cupcakes.

❧❧❧

Back in the locker room, I grabbed my stuff and made a beeline for the private change cubicles. A short while later, I heard someone pad silently into the cubicle beside me. Next thing I knew, Darlene was asking if I wanted to join the chemistry study group she was starting.

"I don't know. I've always done just fine in chemistry without a study group," I said as I dragged the towel back and forth across my bare shoulders. "Why would I want to join one now?"

"Because," came Darlene's voice from high above me, "Tate Jarvis wants to join one."

I shrieked and clutched the towel around myself at the sight of Darlene's little elf head poking over the top of the cubicle divider. Shooing her away, I swallowed the lump in my throat and said, "What makes you think I'd care whether or not Tate Jarvis wants to join one?"

"Because," came Darlene's voice from down at my feet, "you're the third person at our desk in chemistry class. I thought you might feel left out if you discovered that Tate and I were studying together without you."

I shrieked again, this time at the sight of Darlene on her hands and knees, peeking up at me from under the cubicle door.

"Plus, I heard a rumor you'd eat four pounds of broken glass for just one slow dance with him," she added with a grin as she ducked her head from side to side in order to avoid being poked in the eye by my jabbing foot.

Though I tried not to show it, a wave of panic washed over me — my god, if that broken-glass comment got around, I'd be the laughingstock of the entire school. I had to do something, fast! "Well, that is just the silliest thing I ever heard, Darlene," I said. "The fact is that I wouldn't slow-dance with Tate Jarvis if he knelt on four pounds of broken glass and *begged* me to."

"Oh," she said, pulling her head out of my cubicle. "My mistake."

Heart pounding, I waited until I heard her start to walk away before stuffing my damp towel into my knapsack and reaching for my underwear. Suddenly, a hammering fist on my cubicle door caused the lock to pop and the door to bang open.

I shrieked for the third time.

"Listen," said Darlene. "I just wanted to apologize for laughing earlier, when you slipped and fell." She paused, then, with a chuckle, added, "Of course, you've got to admit it was pretty funny. You being naked and all."

I ignored her in favor of frantically struggling to tug up my underwear with one hand and cover my meager breasts with the other.

"You *did* think it was funny, didn't you?" asked Darlene, cocking her little head to one side. "Because I have to tell you, Francie, I don't think much of people who can't laugh at themselves."

I wanted to tell her the only thing that would have made me laugh harder was if she'd ripped off my arm and started clobbering me over the head with it while I lay naked and shivering on the slimy floor at her feet, but I just knew if I did she'd run around telling everybody I was a big, stupid crybaby, so instead I told her I thought it was the funniest thing ever.

"Now, uh, do you mind giving me a little privacy, please?" I asked as I struggled to adjust my underwear, which had somehow gotten uncomfortably twisted while being dragged up over my damp rump.

"Oh, sure. No problem," she said, backing away.

Relieved, I tried to close the cubicle door.

She abruptly slapped it open again. "Just one last thing, though," she said, poking her head back into my personal space.

"What!" I cried in exasperation.

"I think you've got your underwear on backward."

∽∾∾

I headed for home much later than I'd originally planned, and as I hurried along listening to the snow crunch quietly beneath my feet, I felt the first flutterings of panic in my belly. Prior to this, the sneakiest thing I'd ever done was to tape-record the sound of me practicing my clarinet so that on days when I just couldn't bear to practice a minute longer, I could play the tape and Nana would think I was practicing when I was really reading or whispering on the phone with Holly. This was way WAY sneakier than that. And I'd risked it all for what? Nothing! I'd been *so* counting on Tate to gasp at the sight of me in my sexy new swimsuit and to be struck dumb by the sudden recognition of his own true feelings for me. And not only did he not even bother to show up, but I find out he's been making plans behind my back to study chemistry with *Darlene*. I just didn't understand how he could do this to me! Wasn't I the one who'd spent months dropping subtle hints that I'd be more than happy to curl up in front of a roaring fire somewhere and explain acids and bases to him? And just where did Darlene get off referring to me as the third person at our chemistry table, anyway?

I was still brooding over this when I slipped in the alley door of the café and was hit by a smell so horrible that my eyes began to water.

I knew this couldn't be a good sign. Marguerite never burned as much as a piece of toast. If she'd burned enough liver and eggs to make this stink, it either meant she was so sick with worry about me that she was having a dangerously difficult time concentrating at the griddle, or she was so busy trying to handle both the kitchen and the dining room that the whole place was falling to pieces.

Either way, I was in big trouble.

Trying not to panic, I hurried to the kitchen to offer Marguerite my sincerest apologies, and also a plausible explanation for the fact that my hair reeked of chlorine and was plastered to my head in dripping rattails.

When I flung open the door, however, the person I found hovering over the smoking griddle was not Marguerite, but Ricky, whom I hadn't seen or thought about since we'd shared *full frontal body contact* on the bus last Monday.

"Francie!" he blurted, lifting his head so fast that he smacked the back of it against the exhaust fan that hung above the griddle.

His face was flushed and greasy and he was wearing an apron and a hairnet. It was such a shocking sight that I couldn't think of a thing to say.

"Where have you been? Are you okay?" he asked, his thick, dark brows crinkling with concern.

"Fine," I said as I stared at the remains of a charred sausage in order to avoid further eye contact. "Uh, what are you doing here, Ricky?"

"It's Rick now, remember?"

I tried not to grimace. Or blush.

"About an hour ago, Marguerite called over to our place looking for a way to reach your mom," he explained. "She was really furious."

"Furious?" I said weakly. "Are you sure she was furious and not just terribly worried?"

Ricky chuckled deeply. "I'm positive. Apparently, a tour bus full of geriatric gamblers broke down in front of the café right after you left, and the ones that didn't have complicated dietary considerations needed fresh napkins and ice water refills every two seconds. Marguerite ranted for a while about how you'd taken advantage of her generous heart and about the fact that your mom's crappy cell phone had died again. Then she asked for my mom's cell phone number so she could call my mom and ask to speak to your mom to find out if it was all right to close the café early, but I wouldn't give it to her."

"You wouldn't?"

"No. I told her I'd come over and cover for you."

"You did?" I asked faintly.

Ricky nodded eagerly.

I started to feel woozy and wondered if I'd gotten hypothermia running home with wet hair. I wanted to ask Ricky why he'd done this, but feeling suddenly afraid of what his answer might be, I settled instead for asking why he was working the griddle if he was supposed to be covering for me.

"Well ... I was working out front at first, but after a couple of cheeseburger platters sort of accidentally ended up on the floor, Marguerite sent me to the kitchen and took over the dining room."

"Oh," I said, peeking through the short-order window at Marguerite, who was blowing around the dining room like a tropical storm. "Well, thanks for pitching in, Rick ... y."

He smiled. "Oh, don't thank me. Thank my band."

"Your *band?*"

"Uh-huh. We were right in the middle of jamming when Marguerite called."

"You were?"

Ricky nodded eagerly. "Yup, but don't worry — the guys were totally cool with calling it a night when I told them you needed me."

I was completely taken aback by the bizarre direction this conversation had taken. It seemed like only yesterday that Ricky had shaved three of his mother's cats bald on a dare. When had he gotten old enough to have a band?

"We're called Minus Zero," he explained as he hacked off a piece of greasy burned egg and dragged it across the sizzling griddle. "It's kind of a joke because there is no such thing as minus zero, of course, but at the same time, it's also sort of a statement, you know? Like, when you feel as though you're worth *less than nothing?*"

He sounded very passionate and tortured and deep. I tried hard not to stare at his hairnet.

"We play mostly cover stuff, but I've also written a few tunes," he continued. "My songs are very personal — if you know what I mean." He paused to adjust his hairnet, and as he lifted his arm I saw a tuft of dark armpit hair poking out of the short, tight sleeve of his black T-shirt. "Anyway," he said, dropping his arm back down and giving me a quick, embarrassed grin, "I guess after tonight you owe me one, hey?"

The sight of Ricky's armpit hair had shocked me so completely that I just stood there gaping at him like some sort of ninny until I heard a noise behind me. Turning quickly, I saw Marguerite's face looming in the short-order window.

She looked ready to kill me.

"Good luck," whispered Ricky, his lips so close to my ear that I could feel his warm breath on my bare skin. Too startled by his unexpected nearness to act casual, I lurched forward in order to put some distance between us and accidentally touched my nose to the outside of the heat lamp. With a cry, I stumbled backward into his waiting arms.

"You okay?" he asked as he gently pushed me to my feet.

I wanted to tell him I was fine, but for some reason I was suddenly having trouble catching my breath. So instead I nodded once, gave him a slug in the arm to thank him for covering for me, then scurried out front to face the music

_{∂∂∂}

As a punishment for taking advantage of her generous heart, Marguerite made me stay after the café closed in order to scrub out the toilets — twice — while she sat in the dining room soaking her feet and calling for me to get her another ice water every two seconds.

By the time she finally let me go upstairs, I was dog tired. The apartment was quiet and still, and dark except for the thick wedge of dim yellow light that spilled from the kitchen doorway. I walked over and found Nana sitting alone at the kitchen table, feeding bits of bran muffin to Rory through the thin wires of his gilded birdcage. When she saw me, she set the muffin down and reached for her cane.

"There you are!" she said, pretending not to notice that Rory had begun tearing up the newsprint at the bottom of his cage in a blind rage the minute she'd stopped hand-feeding him. "I was beginning to worry."

"Why?" I asked cautiously, wondering how much she knew.

"What do you mean 'why'?" she snorted, thumping her cane at me. "Because it's part of the job description, that's why."

I smiled — partly from relief that she didn't seem to know I'd been sneaking around, and partly because I knew she really *did* think worrying about me was part of her job description.

Feeling suddenly famished, I reached down and broke off a big piece of muffin.

Rory froze.

I hesitated just long enough for him to think I might actually be planning to feed it to him, then smiled happily and crammed it into my own mouth.

He went berserk.

"So," asked Nana, over the squawking din, "did you make it all right to Dr. Peterson's office?"

For a minute I just stood there, chewing and staring and wondering what on earth she was talking about. Then it hit me.

Rory's medicine. I'd forgotten all about it.

I swallowed my mouthful of muffin with difficulty.

"Oh," I said as the sweat began to bead on my brow. "*Oh.* Well, the thing is ..."

Nana set her cane to one side and jammed both hands on her hips. "You tread mighty carefully here, young lady," she warned severely.

In that moment, she didn't look like a tiny old woman recovering from hip surgery and blood clots. She looked like a *warrior.*

"Oh, Nana!" I cried, collapsing before her. "I'm so, so sorry! I meant to go get Rory's medicine tonight — truly I did! — but ... but then I went to my pool party — "

"The one your parents expressly forbade you to attend?" she interrupted in a terrible voice.

"Yes. No!" I cried. "Not exactly — I wasn't told I couldn't go, I was just told I had to do something else instead. There's a difference! There really is! And, anyway, I would never, *never* have done it if the circumstances hadn't been extraordinary. I'm one of only two ninth-grade representatives on the Social Committee, Nana — it wasn't *right* that I miss an event I'd organized just so Mom and Dad could have slave labor for their café!"

"It's your café, too," said Nana through pinched lips.

"No, it isn't," I said quickly. "It was their dream to own a café, not mine. My dream is to live in a world where people get to attend events that were their ideas in the first place."

Nana reached up and tugged at the glittering bauble on her left earlobe — a sure sign that she was softening.

"Oh, Nana," I pleaded, throwing my arms around her. "Please don't tell Mom and Dad. Please! They'll be so upset — they'll think I'm turning into one of those troubled kids who lies and has sex and does drugs and lets her grades slide and doesn't make it into college and never gets a good job and ruins her whole life because of a few bad choices at the start of it all. But that isn't me, Nana. I swear it isn't!"

I clung to her fiercely in the hope that she might feel through my very skin the strength of my desire that she not tell my parents.

"Well," she finally said.

"Yes?" I breathed.

"Since Dr. Peterson did say the stool softener wasn't a necessity ..."

"Yes? Yes?"

"And since poor Rory will probably get the same measure of bowel comfort from the bits of bran I've been feeding him ..."

"POOR RORY," he squawked, strutting back and forth across the bottom of his cage like small, feathered dictator.

"... I might be able to see my way clear to keeping this between you and me on one condition."

"Name it!" I cried, almost unable to believe my good luck.
"Give me the tape."'
"The tape?" I asked.
"The clarinet tape."
My heart skipped a beat. "What clarinet tape?" I asked, trying to sound innocent.

Nana's eyes flashed, and her lips pinched together so hard that they practically disappeared.

"Oh," I said, flushing. "You mean the one I put in the cassette player when I'm supposed to be practicing. Sure. No problem, Nana. I'll go get it for you right now."

"You do that," she said, reaching for her cane. "Oh, and Frances?"

"Yes?" I said.

"About those troubled kids who make bad choices at the start of it all ..."

"I won't become one of them, Nana," I assured her.

"See that you don't."

4. A Nasty Shock

Life without you
is like a dog without relish
You know what I'm saying?
It's totally hellish.

From "Frying My Heart on the Griddle of Your Love" by Rick Skametka

The next morning when I awoke, I pulled my favorite True Romance novel from my bedside table and flipped to the part where the dashing army commander risks his life to rescue the rival king's daughter from the turbulent river and then attempts to revive her while she lies limp in his arms, the thin fabric of her wet dress clinging to her youthful curves like a second skin. In my mind, the army commander slowly morphed into Tate Jarvis, I became the princess with the perky breasts and the turbulent river turned into the dangerously overcrowded pool at the recreation center. Closing my eyes, I sighed deeply and tried to imagine what it would feel like to be held tight in my rescuer's arms while he performed mouth-to-mouth resuscitation on me, but then I noticed I was drooling on my pillow, so I wiped my lips with the back of my hand, tossed my book aside and got out of bed.

Padding to the bathroom in my bare, chilly feet, I took a pee, checked for pimples in my hand mirror and was just trying to decide if it was too soon to shave my armpits again when the door flew open and my mother walked in.

"Hey, ever heard of a little thing called *privacy*?" I complained as I tried to pretend that I hadn't been assessing the length of my pit bristles.

"Sorry, honey, I didn't realize you were up," she said. "So, how was it last night?"

I almost blurted out that the pool party had been a complete disaster, but caught myself in the nick of time. "You mean at the café? Oh, it was pretty busy. A busload of old people showed up and kind of took the place by storm," I said truthfully.

My mother smiled. "Well, that's good news. Busy beats the alternative. Speaking of which, are you planning to do some baking this afternoon?"

"Of course," I replied. "I'm starting to get regular customers — what would they think if they showed up on Sunday morning and I had nothing to sell to them? Besides, I've been working on a white chocolate raspberry scone that is practically a religious experience and I really want to nail it." I smiled at the thought of Mrs. Watson from down at the beauty parlor praising Jesus for me and my scones. "Which reminds me ... I'm going to need a bit more counter space over the next few months. I'm trying out for the school Performance Band and if I make it, there's a big band festival in Portage la Prairie that I'll be expected to attend." I hesitated before continuing in a rush. "It's going cost two hundred dollars, not including spending money, but I should be able to make all that and more if I push hard with my baking between now and then."

My mother frowned and leaned against the door frame. "Two hundred dollars?" she said in a voice that made it sound like even more money than it was.

"Don't worry — like I said, I can earn it myself. Every last penny."

"I know you can," she said. "That's not what I'm worried about. I'm worried that the extra work is going to take time away from your studies."

"I'm doing fine in school."

"Dad and I expect you to do better than fine," she reminded me gently. "Your education is the one thing we've never stopped saving for, but it's up to you to get the top marks you're going to need to get into a good college."

"I'll get them. I promise," I assured her. "So, can I do the extra baking?"

"You bet," smiled my mother.

I thanked her and waited for her to leave the bathroom, but she hesitated for so long that I finally asked if she had something else to say.

"Only that if you're planning to shave your armpits again, be sure to use a squirt of Dad's shaving cream and plenty of water this time," she whispered. "Dry shaving can give you a terrible rash."

⟋⟍⟍

As soon as I heard my mother head downstairs to the café, I hurried to the kitchen, pulled an ice tray from the freezer, popped out a cube and pressed it against the fresh pimple I'd spied in the hand mirror.

"What are you staring at?" I asked Rory, who was perched on his ridiculous little swing looking as fit as ever. "Haven't you ever seen a person ice down a zit before?"

"HAVEN'T YOU EVER SEEN A PERSON ICE DOWN A ZIT BEFORE?" he squawked.

I flung a few melted drops from my ice cube at him, then used my free hand to drag a chair over to the counter so I could retrieve my cookbook from the top shelf of the cupboard. It was my most prized possession. It had started out as a thick, empty notebook with a beautiful lavender cover, and every time Nana and I had baked something new together, we'd carefully copied the recipe into it. When I was very small, she'd done the writing and I'd added illustrations, mostly in purple crayon. When I got a little bigger, I'd done the writing *and* the illustrations. These days, the heavy, cream-colored pages were rumpled and sticky and streaked with flecks of batter, and it had been years since I'd illustrated a recipe *or* baked with Nana.

But whatever else may have changed, one thing had stayed the same: the thrill I felt when my own personal cookbook lay open before me and the flour was flying fast and furious. The way my mouth watered at the sight of brown sugar castles dissolving in seas of melted butter, and the pride that swelled within me when people marveled over something *I'd* created. There was a nameless comfort to be found in a kitchen redolent with the delicious smells of my own fresh baking, and for as long as I could remember, the feeling had tugged at me, like a destiny calling.

Then, when I was around twelve, two things happened that took it to another level entirely.

First, my parents told me I was old enough to start earning my own spending money. In the months that followed, I did a little baby-sitting, mowed a few lawns and occasionally washed dishes in the café. Then one blustery Saturday afternoon in December, I baked a batch of walnut chocolate chip cookies I'd promised to contribute to the bake sale my class was organizing in order to raise money for our foster child in Guatemala. Half an hour later, my mother phoned up from the café to say that customers were clamoring to know what smelled so heavenly. With a hammering heart, I'd hurried downstairs with a plateful of cookies still warm from the oven, and the response had been so overwhelming that my parents had immediately suggested I begin operating a weekend business selling assorted baked good at the café. And just like that, baking was no longer just some little hobby of mine. It was a bona fide business venture.

The other thing that happened, of course, was the miracle of inspiration known as Mr. Lorenzo LaRue. He encouraged me to try new things — to step out there and be my own person. Having always been a meticulous recipe-follower, I was afraid at first, but then one day I suddenly found myself beating eggs instead of whisking them, adding a dash of this and a sprinkle of that. Lorenzo called it "feeling the recipe" — tapping in to the intuitive gift that each woman possesses to make her strudels and cupcakes more than the sum of their simple ingredients.

My confidence in the kitchen soared, and I began to expand my horizons — not just making minor changes to other people's recipes, but creating brand-new recipes of my very own!

Rapidly flipping through my cookbook, it was these recipes that I scanned in the hopes of finding a dessert that would dazzle *all* of Lorenzo's senses. A copy of *Baking Love by Candlelight* would go to the winner of his latest contest, and I wanted that winner to be me! Selecting one of my personal favorites — No-Bake Coconut Caramel Chocolate Chews — I booted up my computer and navigated my way to the contest page on Lorenzo's Web site. I quickly input the recipe and, in a flash of inspiration, added an emotional description of how Lorenzo had inspired me to start a baking business, finishing off with a heartfelt plea that he issue a televised call for support for me just like he'd done for Hildegarde Kunkle. I clicked YES when the site asked if I was eighteen years of age or older, YES when it asked if the recipe being submitted was one of my own creation, and YES when it asked if I acknowledged the fact that by submitting the recipe, I was irrevocably conferring all rights of ownership to Lorenzo LaRue Incorporated. Then I hit SEND. A video clip of Lorenzo suddenly appeared, in which he tossed his glorious hair around for a while before seductively thanking me for entering the contest and reminding me to tune in to next week's show. When the clip ended, I sat dreaming I'd the won the contest and that Lorenzo had been so intoxicated by my recipe that he'd insisted on personally presenting his latest cookbook to me. I imagined his surprise when he discovered I wasn't *quite* eighteen yet, and then the melting look in his eyes when he realized that inside the shy but beautiful young girl who stood before him was the woman he'd been waiting for his whole life.

Then I turned off my computer, put back my recipe book, tossed the ice cube I'd been using to ward off further development of the pimple and headed to the bathroom to take a shower.

❦

Half an hour later, I pulled on my jacket and purple high-tops, grabbed my knapsack, ran down the back stairs two at a time and skidded to a halt at the swinging door of the café kitchen. Peering through the small, round window in the door, I was relieved to see that Marguerite was nowhere in sight. I was almost positive she wouldn't mention last night to my parents, since she *had* given me permission to go out in the first place, but I figured it couldn't hurt to avoid her for a few days. Smiling at the sight of my father whistling to himself while he artfully sprinkled icing sugar on an order of French toast, I shoved open the door, ran over and gave him a hug. Then I asked him to make me a fried-egg sandwich and told him that unlike some people, he didn't look completely gruesome in a hairnet.

"Thank you," he smiled, cracking a couple of farm-fresh eggs onto the griddle.

"So, have you decided whether I can get my ears pierced for my birthday?" I asked, hoisting myself up to sit on the counter behind him.

"No," he replied.

"You promised you'd decide," I reminded him, reaching for a dill pickle. "My birthday is in seven days, you know."

"I know," he said, putting a couple of thick pieces of rye bread into the industrial toaster.

"You said yourself that your reluctance to give me permission was unreasonable," I pointed out, crunching away.

"I know," he said, flipping the eggs.

"Especially since your own wife has had her nose *and* her eyebrows pierced."

"She let those holes grow over a long time ago," he reminded me with a nostalgic sigh.

"Still. I'm practically the only girl in school who doesn't have her ears pierced," I said. "It's embarrassing, and it's affecting my ability to fit in."

"What are you talking about?" he said. "You fit in just fine."

"But I'd fit in *better* if I had pierced ears," I insisted. "Keep that in mind when you make your decision, all right?"

"All right," he said, handing me my sandwich, which he'd drenched in no-name-brand ketchup, just the way I liked it.

We chatted about this and that for a few minutes more, then I slid off the counter, grabbed another pickle and headed for the door.

ফ্ফ্ফ্

As I hurried out into the crisp morning air, I went over my plans for the day. Even before my mother had agreed to give me more counter space, I'd decided to make two kinds of muffins, two kinds of cookies, a double batch of scones and, time permitting, an upside-down apple cheesecake. With that much additional inventory, not only would I make at least fifteen dollars more than I usually made, but I'd blow my customers' minds. As I cut across the street and turned the corner toward the grocery store, I smiled and let my eyes glaze over as I imagined my father opening the café doors the next morning and nearly being trampled to death by the crush of people racing to get to my baked goods display. Maybe somewhere in the crowd there would be a talent scout of some kind who would taste genius in my work and stop at nothing to get me a recipe book deal and my own syndicated baking show!

I'd just started fantasizing about Lorenzo LaRue entering one of *my* contests when I walked past the front window of a discount electronics outlet about a block from the grocery store and noticed Ricky and a couple of other guys inside checking out amplifiers. I immediately crouched down and waddled until I was past the window. I couldn't bear the thought of facing Ricky again so soon. What if he suddenly blurted out that the reason he'd covered for me was that he had *feelings* for me? What if he swept me into his big, hairy-pitted arms and told me to pucker up because I owed him one? My god! I would simply die!

Bursting with nervous energy, I ran the rest of the way to the grocery store, where I zoomed through the aisles loading my cart with ingredients and nearly mowing down less enthusiastic shoppers. When I finished paying for everything, I packed what I could into my knapsack and was just struggling to hoist the rest of the bags into my arms when someone sidled up beside me. He was so short I could barely see his thickly lashed gray eyes over my grocery bags.

"I know you probably get this all the time," he murmured as he stared deeply into my eyes without blinking once, "but you are by far the most stunning creature I have ever seen."

I wanted to break eye contact with him and flounce away in order to show him I wasn't in the habit of talking to peculiar boys who paid goofy compliments to strange girls, but I couldn't. I tried to say something witty, like "What planet are you from?" or "How long have you been legally blind?" but the words just wouldn't form.

Somewhere in the grocery store, an annoyed-sounding woman hollered a name, but I missed it.

"I have to go now," the boy whispered in a voice so low I found myself leaning forward to hear him better. "But I have a feeling we'll meet again."

സ

I was so distracted by my encounter with the mysterious little weirdo with the big gray eyes that I completely forgot Ricky and his friends were in the discount electronics store until the door flew open as I was walking past and I accidentally ploughed face-first into Ricky's chest. After he recovered his balance and saw it was me, he smiled and asked in his icky deep voice if I was okay. Immediately, his friends started grinning and elbowing each other in the ribs.

"Don't let them get to you," Ricky murmured as he reached out to steady my bags.

I was just about to tell him that I wouldn't when I felt the back of his hand brush against my breast. Well, not

exactly against my breast — more like against the front of
my ski jacket. But underneath the spot on the jacket that
he touched there was nothing but T-shirt, bra and *breast*,
and when he reached for the bag of groceries in my arms,
I felt him touch it.

"I've got to go now," I said breathlessly, skittering
backward.

"Okay," he nodded.

My heel hit a hidden ice patch and I nearly went down.

Ricky *leaped* to my assistance. His friends snickered.

"I'm fine," I assured everyone as I scrambled beyond reach.

"Are you sure?" asked Ricky worriedly.

"Positive," I squeaked. "Good-bye!"

⁄৩৩৶

After I left Ricky, I wondered why he'd asked me if I was
okay. Was he *trying* to embarrass me in front of his friends?
And what was that back-of-the-hand groping business all
about? It was hard to believe this was the same boy who'd
once spun me so fast on the old tire swing under the apple
tree in his mother's backyard that I'd thrown up all over her
prize geraniums. That boy was fun and easy to talk to. This
boy was turning me into a nervous wreck.

⁄৩৩৶

My nerves were still jumping like live wires when I got
home, but I started to calm down the minute I set the
grocery bags on the kitchen counter and got to work hauling
out mixing bowls, measuring spoons and muffin tins.
Whistling cheerfully, I took down my recipe book and put
on the slightly soiled chef's hat I'd found at a vintage
clothing boutique two years earlier. I washed my hands with
the thoroughness of a surgeon and even held them up in
front of me as I walked across the kitchen to dry them on
the only thing available — the quilt that Nana used to cover
Rory's cage. Rory immediately tried to peck me in the side

of the head as a punishment for taking liberties with his cage covering, but I ignored him except to say that he'd better be a good studio audience today or else I wasn't going to give him any samples. He settled down nicely after that, so I headed back to the counter to organize my work space and mentally run through my plan of action.

Finally, after double-checking to make sure I was truly alone in the apartment, I put on the same music I put on every time I started to bake — the same music I planned to use as the theme for my own syndicated television show one day. It was an ultimate rock medley, music so powerful and inspiring that my arm started making whisking motions at the very sound of it. Cranking the volume to the max, I lowered my head and waited for the first notes to sound. When they did, I took a deep breath, lifted my head and smiled brilliantly at my studio audience.

It had begun.

As I packed a cup of brown sugar only slightly out of synch with the thumping bass line, I could feel the familiar fire beginning to burn deep within my belly. I did a half spin with one hand held high and removed some melted butter from the microwave oven with a flourish. Pivoting, I poured the butter into the mixing bowl. Then I gave my studio audience a wicked smirk and slid across the kitchen in my stocking feet to grab the cinnamon. Back at the mixing bowl, I didn't even bother to measure it out, I just gave one firm shake, and then another. Then I buried my nose in the bowl, sniffed deeply and pronounced it intoxicating.

My studio audience went wild.

But I didn't stop there. I was poetry in motion! I danced around the kitchen with a mixing bowl in one hand and a wire whip in the other, beating eggs until they begged for mercy. I told amusing little anecdotes as I expertly shredded carrots and zucchini; I pretended to conduct a symphony orchestra with my spatula. I was charming, I was funny, I was informative! My current audience lacked kitchen facilities, arms and brains, but if he'd had those things, he would have been able to copy what I was doing, no problem. As I scraped batter into my muffin cups with practiced ease, I imagined the baking community abuzz with gossip about the beautiful young baking prodigy who'd come from nowhere to take their world by storm. Why, people who'd previously shown no interest whatsoever in baking were suddenly finding themselves lingering in the baking aisle at the grocery store, or sifting flour and white sugar together for no reason at all. It was a phenomenon.

I was a phenomenon!

The day sped by. Rory was on the top of his game, squawking with excitement every time I slid something into the oven and gobbling up still-warm samples with the fervor of an addict. When Nana came home about mid-afternoon, I turned down the music so she could hear herself think, and when my father came upstairs to catch a bit of the ball game on TV before the dinner crowd wandered in, I turned it off altogether. I also took off my chef's hat and stopped talking to my studio audience. It took a lot of the fun out of it, but that just couldn't be helped, because although I believed that baking in front of millions of TV viewers was my destiny, the idea of anyone except maybe Holly seeing me in my groove was completely mortifying. It was one thing for Lorenzo LaRue to gyrate his hips in time to the music as he rolled out pastry crust for his deep-dish peach pie. *He* was a star — people expected him to bake with flair. *I* was just an almost-fourteen-year-old who baked as a way to earn spending money. People would think I was a freak if they saw me dancing around the kitchen in my stocking feet shouting baking tips to a parrot with anger management issues.

I was taking the last batch of cookies off the cooling racks when my dad stood up, stretched and said he was ready to go back to work, so I asked him to give me a hand bringing my trays downstairs. Piled high with mouthwatering treats and covered with plastic wrap to seal in freshness until the next morning, these trays created quite a stir when we marched into the dining room and set them down on the back counter. Pretending not to notice the attention, I was just about to start fantasizing that I was unveiling my latest top-secret creations in my own world-renowned Baked Goods Emporium when the door behind me opened and I heard a sound that made the hair on the back of my neck stand up.

Whirling around, I gasped as I saw Holly and *Darlene* tumble into the café, red-faced with cold and laughing like they'd been friends forever. Holly gave Darlene a playful shove in the direction of the bathroom, then ran over to where I stood with my mouth hanging open.

"What is *she* doing here?" I blurted.

"I invited her," explained Holly breathlessly. "Last night after I finished dunking Randy Newton, she swam over and asked me what I was doing this weekend, and when I said I was coming over here tonight to help you make posters advertising your baking, she asked if she could tag along. I wasn't going to say yes at first, but then she told me how lonely it was being the new girl and I kind of felt sorry for her, you know? I mean, you and I have each other, but she has no one. You're not mad at me, are you?"

I was more shocked than angry, but even if I had been angry, what was I going to say? That she shouldn't have been nice to the poor, lonely new girl? There was just no good way to phrase something like that, so I ignored her question and instead asked how long it had taken her to dunk Randy Newton.

"Quite a while," she replied with a grin. "I was surprised when he finally went down, too, because I wasn't even touching him at the time. I was too busy trying to retie my bikini top, which had come loose in all the thrashing."

I pictured Randy lying at the bottom of the pool in an almost-exposed-breast-induced state of catatonia. "I'm surprised he didn't drown."

"He almost did, I think." Holly giggled. "Honestly, he was under the water for *ages*. Can you imagine if I'd had to give him mouth-to-mouth resuscitation?"

I wanted to freak her out by telling her that just that very morning I'd pictured Tate Jarvis giving *me* mouth-to-mouth resuscitation. Instead I said, "Why would you have had to give him mouth-to-mouth resuscitation? Weren't there any lifeguards on duty?"

"There were, but *still*. You just never know," said Holly with a delicious shiver. "Darlene said she once found a little boy floating facedown in a ditch and the only way she was able to keep him alive until the paramedics arrived was by giving him mouth-to-mouth."

"And you believed her?" I asked.

"Why wouldn't I?"

"Because she's weird, that's why."

"She's not weird," said Holly.

"She is so," I insisted. "Last night when I was leaving the pool party, she followed me into the locker room and kept peeking into my private change cubicle."

"What!"

"It's true!"

Holly looked uncertain. "Well, I still think we should give her a chance," she said as she lifted the plastic wrap from the edge of one of my trays and pulled out the biggest peanut butter chocolate chip cookie she could find. "Do you realize she's gone to four different schools in the last six years?"

"Yeah. So?"

"So?" cried Holly through a mouthful of cookie. "Can you imagine how hard that must have been on her?"

Just then, Darlene bounced back into the dining room looking pretty and perky and *perfect*.

"Well, what about how hard it was on *me* seeing her sit down next to Tate in chemistry class?" I whispered fiercely as Darlene skipped over to us.

I waited with confidence for Holly to agree that I'd

probably suffered way more than Darlene, but to my surprise she didn't say anything. It was the first time she'd ever refused to automatically agree with me on something important, and as the silence between us stretched, I began to grow uncomfortable. So, feeling flustered and not knowing what else to do, I changed the subject.

5. The Worst Week Ever

This is BOGUS.

**Barely legible scrawl found on the incomplete chemistry
assignment for which Tate Jarvis received yet another failing grade**

The next morning I sold all my baking by ten-fifteen. In the
cheery warmth of the pleasantly crowded café, my mom
bustled from table to table, smiling, pouring coffee and
telling anyone who'd listen that in addition to being
gorgeous and handy in the kitchen, I was an honor student
who would someday cure cancer or run the country. When
they heard this, several of my elderly customers shuffled
over and dropped another dollar in my tip jar. Meanwhile,
Mrs. Watson from down at the beauty parlor practically
fainted when she tried the raspberry white chocolate scones,
and her reaction nearly caused a stampede. I had so many
disappointed customers that I had to promise to make a
triple batch the following weekend.

I felt like a star.

After my baking sold out, I snatched a piece of toast from
the industrial toaster in the kitchen, gave my dad a buttery
kiss on the cheek and bolted back upstairs to put my
earnings into the empty baking powder jar in my night table.
Humming happily to myself, I grabbed the phone and
started to dial Holly's number, eager to tell her how much
money I'd already made toward the Performance Band trip
to Portage la Prairie.

Then I stopped. Slowly, I put the phone back down. Last
night, after helping me make posters, Holly and Darlene had
hung around for a while, but it wasn't nearly as much fun
as it usually was with just Holly and me. When I tried to
bring out the Ouija board so we could ask it questions about
our love lives, Darlene had burst out laughing and said she
hadn't played with Ouija boards in years. Then, in a hushed

voice, she'd told us that she'd once spent eight weeks in the care of an old immigrant woman from Romania who'd taught her how to read palms and tea leaves, so I spent the next forty-five minutes listening to Darlene predict a glorious, hunk-filled future for Holly and tell me I had the shortest, thinnest, sickliest-looking love line she'd ever seen in her life.

I wasn't mad at Holly for bringing Darlene over and ruining what could have been a perfectly nice evening, but I thought it was only fair that she should call me instead of the other way around in order to make up for what she had done.

I spent the day loafing around the apartment waiting for the phone to ring. That evening — after I finished studying for an upcoming geography test and doing a little hard time on my clarinet — I pulled out my Life Skills binder and took another stab at beefing up the outline for my term project. I'd done a lot of thinking about it since it had been assigned, but every time I sat down to write it, I got stuck.

"You've talked about becoming a lawyer," reminded my mom when I wandered downstairs to the café in search of inspiration and a grilled-cheese sandwich. "Why don't you write about that? You're so bright, honey, and your grades are so good — getting into law school would be a cinch for you."

"I suppose," I shrugged, dipping the corner of my sandwich into the fat blob of ketchup I'd squirted onto my plate. "Only ... I don't even really know what lawyers *do*."

"I guess that's why your teacher wants you to do some research," smiled my mom as she wiped a smear of ketchup off my chin with the corner of her work apron.

"I guess it is," I agreed, stuffing the last quarter of the sandwich into my mouth. Picking up my plate, I headed to the kitchen to talk to my dad about it, but Marguerite said he was taking out the garbage, so I settled down on the rickety three-legged stool in the corner to wait for him. While I waited, I watched Marguerite at the griddle — swaying her hips and moving her arms as though in time to music only she could hear. She made flipping burgers seem so much like dancing that after a few moments of watching her, a question popped into my head.

"Marguerite, did you always want to be a short-order cook?" I asked

"No," she replied, wiping the back of her hand against her glistening forehead. "When I was a little girl in Jamaica, I dreamed of being a photojournalist. You know, traveling the world taking marvelous pictures and writing stories for important magazines."

"Sounds neat," I said, as I had a sudden vision of Marguerite, her woven straw purse and her camera all squashed into the back of a camouflaged Jeep in hot pursuit of a pride of genetically engineered man-eating lions.

"Neat," she agreed with a smile, deftly flipping a pair of minute steaks onto a plate heaped with steaming shoestring potatoes.

"So why didn't you do it?" I asked. "Why didn't you pursue your dream of becoming a photojournalist?"

"Because I wanted other things more," she explained as she slung the plate under the heat lamp and rang the bell. "I wanted to be a good wife to my husband, and a good mother to my children. I couldn't have done those things if I'd been gone half the time, putting myself into dangerous situations and never knowing where my next paycheck was coming from."

I thought about this for a minute before asking, "Does it ever make you sad to think about the life you might have lived?"

"No, because I like the life I'm living. Besides, I still practice my photography and writing every chance I get, so who knows what might happen? When my babies are all grown up, perhaps I'll hang up my hairnet for good and hit the road in pursuit of stories that will change the world. Now, run along before you ruin my current dream: the dream of being able to fry up my next order in peace and quiet."

"That's a pretty insulting dream, Marguerite."

"Well, soon as I finish my shift, I'll be sure to write to Amnesty International about your troubles," she chuckled, giving my cheek an exuberant pinch. "Meantime, get out of my kitchen."

∽♥♥

After leaving the kitchen, I tracked down my dad, told him I was thinking of researching a career in law and confirmed that he'd never heard of a successful lady lawyer who'd reached the age of fourteen without having her ears pierced. Then I headed back up to the apartment. When I saw that there were no phone messages, I brushed my teeth, changed into my pajamas and climbed into bed with my latest True Romance novel. After reading the same paragraph over three times without absorbing a single word, however, I jumped up, ran over to the phone and dialed Holly's number. She was my best friend; there was no reason to play this silly waiting game with her!

As it turned out, Holly wasn't even home. I almost laughed aloud when I realized that she had a perfectly good excuse for not calling me, then her mom wrecked everything by adding that she was out with a friend and wouldn't be back until late.

"Would you like to leave a message?" asked Mrs. Carleson.

"No, that's okay," I said slowly. "I guess I'll just see her at school tomorrow."

∽♥♥

Holly was waiting for me at the bus stop as usual the next morning. I was tempted to ask her where she'd been the night before to see if she'd tell me the truth, but I didn't want to infect our time alone together talking or even thinking about Darlene, so instead I tentatively asked if she was still coming over after school to help me put up the posters we'd made on Saturday night. When she crossed her eyes and said, "Duh!" I hugged her hard enough to crush to smithereens the bag of chips in her knapsack.

I was so looking forward to hanging out with Holly after school that the day seemed to fly by, with the exception of the interminable three minutes Mrs. C kept me after last class to go over the rhythm of the clarinet piece I was working on, and also to torture me with her perfect hair. As soon as I was dismissed, I bolted down the hall and rounded the corner to my locker so quickly that I nearly tripped over Darlene.

"Her dad is working late tonight and she didn't want to have to spend all evening by herself, so I told her she could hang out with us and help put up posters," explained Holly when I gave her a questioning look.

"That's okay, isn't it, Francie?" asked Darlene, fixing me with her wide eyes.

I wanted to tell her to get stuffed, but once again, there was no good way to say it. I looked at Holly to see if she was purposely doing this to upset me for some reason, but she seemed completely oblivious.

"Yeah, it's okay," I finally said. "Let's go."

✑✑✑

When we got back to my place, our plan was to grab the posters and get to work right away, but while she was in the kitchen rooting around for something to eat, Holly noticed a letter propped up against the canister of rolled oats.

"It's for you," she said, wandering back into the hall and handing it to me.

"Who's it from?" asked Darlene, leaning closer to get a better look.

"I don't know," I said, edging away from her. "There's no return address."

"Then you should be careful when you open it," she advised. "A cousin of mine once received an envelope without any return address and it turned out to be a letter bomb sent by his psychotic ex-girlfriend."

"I don't have a psychotic ex-girlfriend," I said, tearing open the envelope with such ferocity that I dropped the card inside. It hit the floor and fell open, and when it did, the microchip inside suddenly burst into song:

> 'Appy Birthday to you!
> 'Appy Birthday to you!
> 'Appy Birthday beautiful lady!
> 'Appy Birthday to you!

Mortified, I snatched up the card. On the front was a picture of Lorenzo LaRue holding an elegantly decorated chocolate cupcake in front of his glistening bare chest; inside was a verse about how he would be thinking of me on my special day.

Darlene was in stitches. "Who ... the *hell* ... is that from?" she asked, in between gasps of hysterical laughter.

"It's from the guy on the front of the card," said Holly before I could stop her. "He's a celebrity baker."

"Well, he's also a pervert," giggled Darlene. "What kind of a man sends a card like that to a thirteen-year-old child?"

"I'll be fourteen in six days," I said tightly. "And Lorenzo isn't a pervert. For your information, he thinks I'm eighteen."

"Why does he think that?" she asked.

"Because whenever I enter his on-line contests, I say that I am so I won't be disqualified."

At this, Darlene burst out laughing again. Suddenly, I was so angry I decided to give her a piece of my mind no matter how mean it made me look in front of Holly.

"What's so funny?" I snapped.

Darlene smiled. "Oh, I just remembered my father once did some consulting work for the company that produces this guy's show," she said, daintily tapping two-dimensional Lorenzo on the left nipple.

"Lorenzo LaRue Incorporated?" I blurted.

"Yes, that's the one," said Darlene offhandedly. "Remember

how I said my dad is a management consultant whose firm specializes in taking over failing businesses? Well, he once spent six weeks working side by side with the producers to keep that show afloat."

Holly looked excited. "Do you think your dad would put in a good word for Francie? She's such a big fan, she'd give anything to meet that guy or even just to hear her name mentioned on his show. Isn't that right, Francie?" she asked, giving my arm a squeeze.

"That's right," I babbled, bobbing my head up and down so fast I felt dizzy.

"Anything is possible, I guess," murmured Darlene, leaning over to tug a loose thread from the hem of her jacket.

Without meaning to, I clasped my hands beneath my chin. "I ... I would really appreciate ... I mean ... it would mean so much to me if — "

"I'll talk to my dad and see what he says," interrupted Darlene with a wave of her little hand. "Now, if you'll excuse me, I have to go to the bathroom."

ᵒᵒᵒ

After Darlene got out of the bathroom, she asked if I'd mind looking over her chemistry homework before we went out to put up posters. Unfortunately, she only had half of the assignment completed, and by the time she'd finished the rest of it and I'd corrected it for her, it was time for Holly to get going. Darlene decided to leave with her, so I walked them both to the front door of the café and watched as they headed off down the snowy sidewalk together. When they were about halfway down the block, Darlene suddenly turned and waved at me. Then she linked arms with Holly, and the two of them were swallowed up by the night.

ᵒᵒᵒ

The next day at lunch, Holly couldn't stop talking about how exciting it was that Darlene's dad might contact Lorenzo's producers on my behalf, and how incredibly lucky it was that of all the high schools Darlene could have attended, she ended up attending ours.

"Yeah, that was super lucky," I said shortly. "Now, don't forget you're coming over Saturday night to celebrate my birthday."

At the mention of Saturday night, Holly's mouth dropped open and her face turned beet red.

"Is something wrong?" I asked.

"No. Well, uh, maybe," stammered Holly, glancing over my shoulder at something. "I'm not sure. I mean, I'll have to see."

"What do you mean you'll have to see?" I asked.

Instead of answering me, Holly busied herself with the contents of her chip bag. Then — almost as though she couldn't help herself — she snuck another peak over my shoulder.

"What on earth do you keep looking at?" I cried, swiveling around in my chair to follow her sight line.

In the back corner of the cafeteria, I saw a bunch of the girls from our grade — including Darlene — huddled in a corner whispering about something. When they noticed me staring at them, they all fell silent.

I felt the blood drain from my face. Turning, I looked at Holly.

"I'm not looking at anything," she mumbled as two bright spots of color reappeared on her cheeks. "Here — have some chips."

I was so upset by the events of lunch hour that in gym class it took me fourteen tries just to hit the rim of the basket from the foul line. Sharon and Jody, the two best basketball players in our grade, kept murmuring encouragement and slapping me on the back after each air ball, but it didn't make me feel any better, especially when Darlene stepped up to the foul line right after me and sank three baskets in a *row*.

Later, in the changing room, she grinned and told me the important thing was that I'd done my best.

"Thanks," I said uncertainly.

I turned away then, to continue getting dressed, so it was only out of the corner of my eye that I saw Darlene lean over and whisper something to Sharon and Jody.

Both of them nodded and smiled.

~∂∂∂~

For the rest of the week, I couldn't shake the feeling that people were staring at me and talking about me behind my back. Worse, I suspected Holly of being behind it all. I'd never known her to act so weird. Tuesday after lunch, for example, she told me she'd forgotten something in the cafeteria, but five minutes later I spotted her in the north stairwell whispering to Randy Newton and Greg Podwinski. Wednesday morning I thought I heard her giggling with Darlene by the water fountain outside the Language Arts classroom, but when I asked her about it later she said I was being paranoid. Thursday afternoon she was even late for band class, despite the fact that it was her all-time favorite class *ever*. When I asked her where she'd been, she blushed and said she didn't know.

~∂∂∂~

That week was the most miserable, awful week of my entire life. I kept waiting for Holly to mention my birthday again, but she didn't say one word about it until the very end of the day on Friday, when she casually asked if I wanted to hang out with her Saturday afternoon.

"I thought it would be fun to go shopping for something to wear to the dance next Friday," she said, giving the big oaf who'd just trampled on her foot an elbow in the ribs. "Then, afterward, we could head back to your place for birthday cake or whatever."

I stood rooted to the spot in the middle of the noisy, crowded hallway, not at all sure how I should respond. Part of me couldn't help wondering if she only wanted to get together because her mystery plans had fallen through, but the other part of me badly wanted to believe I was the victim of my own overactive imagination and that things between Holly and me were the same as ever. I had other girls I was friendly with, but Holly was my only best friend. She was the only one I spent time with and talked to outside of school. If I didn't have her, I didn't have anybody.

"Um, who else will be coming shopping with us?" I finally asked.

"No one," said Holly, giving me a puzzled look. "Why?"

"Just curious," I said, so relieved I couldn't stop smiling. "It sounds like loads of fun, Holly. The thing is, I've got baking to do on Saturday, so we'll have to make it a little later in the afternoon, okay?"

"Okay, or else why don't I just come over early and help?" she said, sticking her foot out to trip the guy who'd just shouldered past her. "I could pass you the ingredients or something."

I thought about the last time Holly had come over to help. She'd spent fifteen minutes throwing raisins into the air and trying to catch them in her mouth, fifteen minutes belting out filthy, made-up lyrics to the tunes of my most cherished rock classics and three hours watching TV and shouting for me to hurry up and finish so we could hang out.

"Come over around ten," I told her. "I can't wait."

❦

The next morning, something woke me early. I sat up slowly, rubbing my tired eyes and wondering what it was. Then I remembered: today was my birthday! I was officially fourteen years old! Tossing the covers aside, I leaped out of bed and hurried to my vanity mirror to see if I looked any older. I'd just started squeezing my breasts between my biceps in the hopes of discovering a newfound ability to produce cleavage, when I smelled cinnamon.

Shoving my feet into my purple bunny slippers, I hurried to the kitchen.

"Good morning, Francie," said Nana.

"GOOD MORNING, FRANCIE," squawked Rory.

"What are you making, Nana?" I asked, ignoring Rory completely.

"A couple of pans of cinnamon buns," she replied, giving me a peck on the cheek. "For your birthday breakfast!"

Grinning, I poured myself half a glass of pineapple juice and sat down to watch her work on the next batch of buns. She wasn't as flamboyant as I was, but she had a rhythm as timeless and comforting as the slow rocking seas. I listened to the winter wind howling in the early morning darkness beyond the window and settled deeper into the warmth and coziness of our small kitchen. After a while, I found myself telling Nana all about Holly's strange behavior that week. Nana listened intently without saying a word, and when it was clear I was done talking, asked how long I'd been friends with Holly.

"Forever," I said.

"And has she ever given you a reason to mistrust her?" asked Nana without looking up from the yeasty dough she was kneading.

"No," I said.

"Why don't you think on that while you're finishing up this second batch of buns?" she suggested, pushing the mixing bowl toward me. "It'll give me a chance to go down and fetch some eggs for our omelet."

I quickly offered to go get the eggs in order to save her the trip downstairs, but she thumped her cane at me and stalked out of the kitchen without a word, so I turned my attention to the cinnamon bun dough.

"You know what, Rory?" I said as I set a nine-by-twelve non-stick baking pan down on the table next to the mixing bowl. "Nana is right. Holly is my best friend and she's always been loyal. And do you know what that means she deserves?"

"AVIAN STOOL SOFTENERS," he squawked, spitting a sunflower seed at me.

"No," I said. "It means she deserves the benefit of the doubt, you disgusting excuse for a parrot."

Leaning over, I was just about to give him a little jab with the handle of my spatula when Nana reappeared in the doorway.

"What are you doing?" she asked suspiciously.

"Uh, thanking Rory for wishing me a happy birthday," I said, quickly tucking the spatula behind my back.

Nana beamed at Rory as though he was the most brilliant, thoughtful bird on the planet. Rory gazed back at her with a vacant expression, then pooped in his food dish.

"Amen to that!" laughed Nana, thumping her cane with delight.

I rolled my eyes as I measured out a heaping teaspoon of cinnamon.

"Be nice to my bird," Nana warned, giving my ear a sharp tweak.

The unexpected tweak made me jump, causing the teaspoon to fly out of my hand and hit Rory's cage, covering him in a thick dusting of cinnamon. Screeching and flapping his wings in a startled panic, he sent cloud after cloud of cinnamon wafting through the kitchen. Sneezing and coughing, Nana hurried to the cage to try to calm her idiot bird, while I laughed and danced around behind her in my purple bunny slippers, excitedly shouting at Rory that everything tasted good with cinnamon — even parrots!

Later, as we were sitting down to breakfast, Nana scolded me for telling Rory he'd taste great with cinnamon.

"You're right, Nana," I agreed in a subdued voice as I tore off a piece of warm, sticky cinnamon bun and shoved it into my mouth. "No matter how he was spiced, Rory would still taste like a dog's breakfast."

✉✉✉

I did my grocery shopping and was back home and up to my elbows in mixing bowls by the time Holly showed up, yawning and bleary-eyed, at eleven-fifteen. Wordlessly, she poured herself a tall glass of soda and plopped down in a chair beside Rory's cage to watch me work. At first, I held back a little because sometimes it's not an easy thing to let people — even your best friend — in on your most private, personal fantasies. Holly was so exactly like her old self, however, that after a while I loosened right up. Dancing back and forth in front of the counter, I used my best TV voice to explain how to roll perfectly sized cookie-dough balls every time, and added extra splashes of vanilla extract to my recipes with reckless abandon. In between chattering nonstop about everyone at school, Holly cheered and stamped her feet. For a while she leaned way back and played mind-blowing riffs on her air guitar every time something came out of the oven. Then she jumped up and marched around the room playing the rock'n'roll air flute with such enthusiasm that Rory nearly squawked himself to death with excitement.

Just as I was carefully setting the last lemon square into my baking tray, my mother called to tell me to leave the cleanup for her, and also to say that I should hurry downstairs because she and my dad had a surprise for me. Suddenly bursting with birthday excitement, I slammed down the phone and shouted for Holly to follow me. Grabbing our coats, we pounded down the stairs to the café, stormed into the dining room and ran over to my mother.

"Where's my surprise!" I shouted, bouncing up and down and tugging at her shirt like a two-year-old. "Where is it? Give it here! Come on, cough it up!" I demanded as I tried to stick my hands into her pockets.

Laughing, she slapped my hands away and called for my dad. He emerged from the kitchen holding an envelope. Opening it carefully (on the off-chance that the card inside contained a microchip capable of belting out embarrassing birthday greetings), I found three crisp twenty-dollar bills inside.

"For me?" I squeaked, so surprised by the sight of so much money that I was only a tiny bit disappointed I'd received money instead of pierced earrings.

"For you," smiled my dad.

My mom leaned over and gave me a hug. "Happy birthday, Francie. Have fun shopping."

Holly and I spent almost four hours tromping through the mall. I ended up with an outfit I didn't even like because I was too weak to resist her insistence that I buy clothes that made me look my age. The skirt was so short you could practically see my underwear when I sat down, and the top was so tight I had to keep my arms crossed at all times unless I wanted my breasts to stick out like a pair of mismatched grapes. Holly didn't find anything until the very end of our shopping extravaganza, when she discovered a pair of truly hideous platform shoes at the bottom of the bargain bin at the discount shoe outlet. After admiring them on her feet for several minutes, Holly tentatively asked what I thought of them. Not wanting her to go home empty-handed, I raved on and on about how awesome they were and how jealous I was that she'd found them first. Thrilled by my reaction, Holly skipped to the front counter, paid for them, then turned and tried to thrust them into my unsuspecting arms.

"What are you doing?" I asked in alarm.

"Giving you your birthday present, silly," she laughed. "I only *pretended* I was buying them for myself so I could trick you into telling me what you truly thought of them. Aren't I a genius?" she asked, giving me a jolly poke in the stomach. "Well, don't just stand there with your mouth hanging open. Try them on!"

Slowly, I kicked off my beloved purple high-tops, peeled off my grubby sweat socks and slipped the shoes onto my bare feet.

"Oh my god," Holly breathed rapturously as I straightened back up again. "They are just so *perfect*. Between those shoes and that skirt, your legs look about a million miles long!"

I smiled and tried to ignore the fact that the glitter on the faux fur was already starting to make my feet itch.

"Just *wait* until Tate Jarvis gets a load of you in this outfit," said Holly as I shuffled unsteadily after her, feeling dizzy and disoriented on account of my new three-inch heels. "If he's the drooling Neanderthal I know he is, he'll be all over you like stink on pigs."

ೲ

The thought of Tate Jarvis lusting after my million-mile legs sustained me during the long, frigid walk home. By the time I reached the café, however, my feet and back were aching so badly it took me a moment to notice the CLOSED sign on the front door.

"I don't understand," I said slowly. "The only time my parents ever closed the café on a Saturday evening was when Nana had to be rushed to the hospital because of blood clots." My mouth suddenly went dry. "Holly," I stammered, "you ... you don't think Nana — "

"Don't be ridiculous," she interrupted. "Look — the blinds in the front windows of the café are drawn. Why would your parents have taken the time to do that if your nana was having a medical emergency?"

I stared at the closed blinds for a long moment. "You're right," I said at last. "There's nothing wrong with Nana — *the café is being robbed!*"

"*What?*"

"There's no other explanation!" I insisted. "Don't you see? My parents never close those blinds. Never! The only reason they'd be closed is because some lunatic wants privacy while he herds my parents and their customers into the meat cooler."

"You don't have a meat cooler."

"You know what I mean!" I cried. "Oh, Holly, what are we going to *do?*"

"The only thing we *can* do, Francie," she replied grimly as she gave the air in front of her face a series of vicious karate chops. "Charge in there and give that creep a taste of his own medicine."

Horrified, I lunged forward to stop her from opening the door, but it was too late. As if in a slow-motion nightmare, I saw the doorknob turn and the door begin to open. Opening my mouth in a silent scream, I was just about to throw my body in front of poor Holly to shield her from the crippling firepower of the meat-cooler lunatic when she cried, "You first, Francie!" stepped to one side and shoved me through the open door.

6. Surprises and Other Mixed Blessings

When confronted by the tasty evidence of your abilities in the kitchen, ladies without baking skills will almost certainly lash out at you in a jealous rage. Coat your heart in Teflon so their ugly words won't stick, and remember that I think of you, always.

**From Teflon and the Lady:
A Love Story by Lorenzo LaRue**

Clattering forward in my brand-new three-inch heels, I stumbled over the threshold of the café, lost my balance and instinctively grabbed for the first thing I could get my hands on.

Ricky Skametka.

For one terrible instant the thought flashed through my mind that *he* was the lunatic robbing the café, then I looked past him to see my family, my classmates and even my nana's idiot bird all grinning at the sight of me clutching Ricky like he was the last life preserver on board the *Titanic*.

"Surprise!" they shouted.

"SURPRISE!" squawked Rory, releasing a splatter of poop.

Everybody laughed. Blushing furiously, I skittered away from Ricky, then blinked up at the pink and white streamers that radiated outward from the giant cluster of balloons dangling from the center of the ceiling.

"What is this?" I asked uncertainly as clouds of tiny bubbles began to issue forth from a contraption near the cash register. "Is ... is this some kind of party?"

Holly clapped her hands and hooted in delight. Someone at the back of the room belched richly; someone else cranked up the volume of my favorite song.

"Is it a party for *me?*" I asked in a teeny-tiny voice.

"WELL, DUH, SILLY!" shouted Holly, giving me an exuberant one-arm hug around the neck. "Your mom and dad have been planning it for *ages* ..."

"It's true," interjected my dad.

"We have," added my mom.

"... and then last week," continued Holly, seemingly oblivious to the fact that my parents had spoken, "I went around and secretly invited everybody. Honest to gosh, I've never done so much sneaking around in my entire *life*! You must have thought I was up to no good at all."

"Are you *nuts*?" I cried, giving her a two-handed shove that knocked her backward into Randy Newton, who just happened to be lurking nearby.

Holly wriggled away from Randy, who looked as though he'd just had an atomic bomb dropped on his head. "So, were you surprised?" she asked, grinning from ear to ear.

"Surprised?" I said as I caught sight of Tate Jarvis *himself* shot-gunning a root beer in preparation for another belch. "Oh, Holly," I sighed. "You don't know the half of it!"

☙☙☙

Almost to the last tiny bubble, it was a magical evening.

Along with an only half-joking speech about the perils of bodily mutilation and growing up too fast, my dad gave me a gift certificate to get my ears pierced, which my mother followed up with a pair of genuine diamond-chip earrings. Nana got me a snow white baker's hat that fit like a dream but that I hurriedly shoved to one side when Greg Podwinski loudly asked if the Pillsbury Doughboy knew I was wearing his headgear. The girls in my class got me a giant stuffed teddy bear, Vivian and Ricky got me gift certificates for the movies, and Marguerite waved an expensive-looking camera around and promised to put together an album of party pictures for me.

The boys in my class got me nothing, of course, but the very fact that they'd shown up at all was gift enough. I could hardly believe that Tate Jarvis was attending a social function in my honor. Why, he was practically standing in my very own living room! And he'd met both my parents — he'd even spoken to my father at length! Never mind that the discussion had centered on how my dad didn't appreciate that Tate and the other boys had stuffed paper towel down the toilet in the men's washroom, causing it to overflow — the point was they'd *spoken!* Man to man!

Knowing there'd never be a better time to make my move, I spent four hours working up my nerve and then, just as people started getting ready to leave, I sidled over to where Tate was feeding giant chunks of carrot cake to Rory, who was gulping them down so fast he looked to be on the verge of choking.

"That could give him diarrhea," I blurted, after racking my brains for a good opening line.

"So?" said Tate without looking at me.

"Yeah. Right. Good point," I said breezily, giving my bangs a fluff.

Something about this gesture caught Tate's attention in the most spectacular way. Dropping the carrot cake, he reached over and pushed my bangs out of my eyes.

Rory immediately began gnawing on the wires of his gilded cage in an effort to escape so that he could exact revenge on Tate for cutting off his carrot-cake supply, but both Tate and I ignored him.

Tate studied my face as though seeing it for the first time.

I held my breath and wondered if I was about to get my first kiss.

"How come you never get any pimples on your forehead?" he finally asked.

Only slightly disappointed that he hadn't managed to phrase this spine-tingling compliment about my complexion in a more romantic way, I opened my mouth to modestly give the credit to good genes when Rory suddenly screeched, "HAVEN'T YOU EVER SEEN A

PERSON ICE DOWN A ZIT BEFORE?"

"I don't know what that stupid bird is talking about!" I said quickly. "He's a complete moron. Even other *birds* think he's a moron."

"HE'S A COMPLETE MORON," agreed Rory, flinging some birdseed in Tate's direction.

Tate looked extremely insulted.

"Shut up!" I hissed at Rory.

"SHUT UP!" he squawked back at me.

"No, you shut up!" I raged, shaking my fist at him.

"NO, YOU SHUT UP!" he cried, flapping his wings in excitement.

I was so angry I could have killed that stupid parrot on the spot. However, some deep-seated feminine instinct told me that the sight of me ripping the head off a live bird might tarnish Tate's view of me as a delicate flower worthy of his love. So, instead, I took a long, cleansing breath and turned to apologize to the boy of my dreams for the disgusting manners of my nana's demented parrot.

But Tate was gone.

✿✿✿

"So he just up and left without even saying good-bye?" asked Sharon as we were cleaning up after the party.

"Well, I wouldn't exactly put it *that* way," I confided in low tones. "I think he probably did say good-bye, but I was just too distracted to notice."

"Who cares anyway, though, right?" piped Darlene, who was suddenly standing behind us. "I mean, it's not like you've got a thing for that goofball or anything."

I felt my face get red. "Tate isn't a goofball, Darlene," I said, feeling very noble to be defending my soul mate's honor at the expense of my own personal dignity.

"Oh, no? Well, you might think differently if you'd seen him at the Chip Factory last weekend," she laughed. "Unscrewing the caps from the salt and pepper shakers, ripping open all the little sugar packets, drinking half a bottle of ketchup on a dare. Holly said he was worse than a two-year-old!"

I rolled my eyes, not believing a word of it. I mean, I knew that kind of behavior was right up Tate's alley, but there was no *way* Holly would have seen Tate outside of school and not mentioned it to me.

"It's true," continued Darlene cheerfully. "A bunch of us went out after the pool party last Friday night and when Tate and some of the guys from his hockey team showed up, we pushed two tables together and ordered three plates of fries with gravy on the side."

If I hadn't known it was impossible, I would almost have said it sounded like Darlene was telling the truth.

"Is there a point to this story?" I asked, smiling slightly at Sharon and Jody to show them I believed in giving my best friend the benefit of the doubt.

"Only that the Chip Factory is where Holly and I got to talking and discovered how much we have in common." Darlene smiled. "Do you know we both have middle names that begin with the letter *L*, we both received our first kiss on a beach and we both have second toes that are just slightly longer than our big toes?"

"Holly and I have big toes that are exactly the same shape," I blurted, feeling sick with the sudden, terrible certainty that Darlene was telling the truth.

"Neat!" she chirped, scraping a cake plate off so carelessly that crumbs flew everywhere. "Anyway, the next day, Holly came over to try out my new karaoke machine, and after we'd sung 'I Got You, Babe' for, like, the millionth time, my dad took us out for dinner. We got to sit at our very own booth and order virgin piña coladas that tasted exactly like coconut-flavored Slurpees, only better." Darlene paused and cocked her little head at me. "You seem surprised, Francie. Didn't Holly tell you any of this?"

"She probably did, but I was just too distracted to notice," I mumbled.

Sharon nodded solemnly. So did Jody.

Darlene ignored them.

"You get distracted an awful lot, don't you?" she said, reaching up to toy with a shimmering lock of hair. "You know, you might want to get that checked out. I once heard of a guy who had that problem and after he died they discovered that some kind of disease had eaten holes *right through his brain!*"

"My brain is fine."

"I'm sure it is," she said. "Anyway, just before Bruce came to pick Holly up —"

"Bruce?" I interrupted.

Darlene looked at me quizzically. "Holly's dad."

My mouth dropped open. "You call him *Bruce?*"

"That's his name, isn't it?" she laughed. "Anyway, just before he came to get her, we agreed it would be super fun if we had dinner at my place before the dance next Friday night, and I just want you to know that you're more than welcome to tag along!"

I nodded — not because I appreciated her offer, but because I was so stunned by it that I was having difficulty maintaining control of the muscles in my neck. Satisfied, Darlene turned and skipped off in the direction of the kitchen, where Holly was busy helping my mom with the dishes.

For a minute, Sharon and Jody just looked at me. Then, as though not sure what else to do, Jody leaned over and gave me a few of the back slaps that had so encouraged me during my epic attempt to sink a basket in gym class.

"Holy moly," added Sharon, with feeling.

I nodded once — for real this time — then hurried to the bathroom so they wouldn't see me start to cry.

കൈ

The next morning, I awoke from a dream so sexy that I lay in bed blushing for almost a whole minute before the memory of Holly's betrayal came back to me in a terrible rush. Rolling over, I pulled my pillow over my head and decided never to get up again. I imagined my parents' anguish as I lay there day after day in a lethargic stupor; I pictured Holly — hysterical with remorse — struggling and screaming as she was dragged from my sickroom. I saw Tate Jarvis, the very picture of stony masculine reserve, refusing to leave my side — his large hands tirelessly clasping my small ones, the agony of heartbreak and love lost etched in every one of his totally awesome features.

It was such a pathetic and tragic image that after picturing it several dozen times, I began to sob uncontrollably.

When was I finished, I got up, took a long, hot shower and went downstairs to sell my baking. Later that afternoon, Holly called to talk about the party and to see when we were going to the mall to get my ears pierced. She sounded so happy and excited and oblivious to the hurt she had caused me that I suddenly didn't see the point of bringing it up and making myself look like a big, boring drag.

"Why don't we go to the mall right now?" I suggested, trying to sound at least a little bit perky. "I think it would be super fun."

⤜∂∂∞

"Don't worry. You're going to be fine," Holly assured me as we circled the mall for the third time.

"How do you know?" I asked, wondering why on earth I'd ever been so excited about having holes punched through my flesh. "You've never had your ears pierced."

"I know because Darlene has had hers pierced twice and she says she'd never bother to get them pierced professionally again. She says it's a waste of money because it's just as easy to do it yourself with an ice cube and a potato."

"And how, *exactly,* do you pierce your ear with a potato?" I asked waspishly.

"You don't, silly," said Holly, stopping at a hat display to try on an ugly pink fedora. "The potato just keeps your earlobe from wobbling around. Darlene says after you ice the lobe down, you position the potato behind the ear, take a deep breath and shove the pointy part of an earring through."

"That sounds painful," I said. *And stupid,* I thought.

"Darlene says you can also use a special kind of hoop earring," continued Holly, giving the brim of the fedora a jaunty tug. "She says you just keep squeezing it into your earlobe until the front and back parts meet and, voilà, your ear is pierced."

"Or else, voilà, you're bleeding like a stuck pig and on the road to a gruesome skin infection," I said, rolling my eyes.

"I'm just telling you what Darlene told me," laughed Holly, popping the fedora back onto the head of the armless mannequin from which she'd swiped it. "Now, are you ready to get your ears pierced, or what?"

☙☙☙

After only two more laps of the mall and a pit stop at the food court for a plate of onion rings, I decided I was ready. For one thing, I was feeling so emotionally drained by the events of the past twenty-four hours that I figured I'd have nothing left to give toward a punctured-flesh-induced anxiety attack, and for another thing, there was no way I was going to let Holly think I was afraid of something *Darlene* thought was no big deal.

As it turned out, I grossly underestimated my emotional reserves and, in fact, had plenty left to give toward an anxiety attack. I also discovered that I possessed keen reflexes when it came to avoiding personal mutilation — at one point, the technician told me that if I didn't stop jerking my head right before she was about to squeeze the trigger of her piercing gun, she was going to turn me away and refuse to cash my gift certificate.

Holly stood by my side the entire time — holding my hand, murmuring encouragement and making faces behind the back of the crabby technician. In the end, however, it was the vision of Darlene juggling bloody potatoes and laughing like a hyena that gave me the strength to see it through.

☙☙☙

The next morning, I got up early in order to give myself the kind of extra-special hairdo that would show off my newly pierced ears to their best advantage. Unfortunately, this took so long that I missed the bus and had to walk to school through a blustery snow squall. By the time I arrived, I was ten minutes late, my high-tops were soaked, my feet were freezing and my hair was a soggy, stringy mess of congealed hair products. Luckily, Holly took my mind off my troubles by bursting out of homeroom, running up and jumping on my back with such force that I slammed into a nearby bank of lockers.

"Guess what?" she hollered, holding on to my neck and kicking her feet excitedly. "Mrs. Cavanaugh just announced she's holding tryouts for the school's Performance Band tomorrow after school!"

"So soon?" I grunted, spinning in circles in an effort to dislodge her.

Holly gave me a noogie on the top of my damp, sticky head and jumped down. "The festival in Portage la Prairie is only a month away," she said, her cheeks aglow with band-nerd fever. "We're going to need some time to practice together unless we want to march up on that Performance Band stage and make complete idiots of ourselves."

"I don't really care if we make idiots of ourselves," I admitted. "But I will absolutely die if I don't get to go on the trip."

"Then go home tonight and practice," said Holly. "And I mean *really* practice. Don't just sit in your room talking to me on the phone and playing that tape of yours."

"Nana took away the tape last week," I confessed. "And I have been practicing — *really* practicing — every day since. And do you know what?"

"What?" asked Holly.

"I still sound like a constipated dog trying to go to the toilet."

Across the hallway, Sharon and Jody burst into loud guffaws.

Holly grabbed me by the front of my shirt. "Well, go home tonight and practice harder," she ordered sternly, shaking me like a rag doll. "I want you on that trip with me. Understand?"

With a feeling of happiness so intense I almost started to cry, I flung my arm across her shoulders and fervently said, "I understand. Now would you please be so kind as to come to the bathroom and help me fix my hair? In case you haven't noticed, it looks like something that got pulled out of a clogged bathtub drain."

Tuesday after Performance Band tryouts, Mrs. C dismissed us all with a promise to post the names of the successful candidates on the band-room door the following week. Chattering excitedly, Holly and I got our jackets out of our locker and had just started walking toward the bus stop when I felt a tap on my shoulder.

It was Ricky Skametka. He'd been at the auditions as well, hoping to get a spot in the band on the basis of his saxophone performance, which had been so soulful I'd started blushing even before he'd started sweating.

He gave a quick, embarrassed smile to Holly. "Uh, Francie, could I talk to you for a minute?" he asked in his low, rumbling voice. "In private, I mean?"

I gave Holly a wide-eyed look, then followed Ricky to a spot some distance away. He turned to me and, after a nervous look over his shoulder, said, "I want to talk to you about the dance on Friday."

My heart nearly stopped. Oh, no. He wasn't going to ask me to go to the dance with him, was he? Yes, he was! I could see it in his eyes! Oh god, how could he do this to me? Didn't he realize that I didn't think of him in *that* way? This was hideous. In all the many hours I'd spent pondering my dating future, I'd never imagined having to face something like this. My mind raced as I tried to think of the perfect thing to say to keep from hurting Ricky's feelings while at the same time letting him know I'd rather have all my fingernails ripped out than go to the dance with him.

"The thing is," Ricky continued. "I was wondering —"

"YOU SHOULD KNOW THAT I'M GOING TO BE VERY BUSY AT THE DANCE, RICKY!" I practically shrieked. "I'M ON THE SOCIAL COMMITTEE AND THERE'S JUST NO TELLING WHAT KINDS OF LAST-MINUTE ISSUES ARE GOING TO ARISE THAT WILL REQUIRE MY IMMEDIATE ATTENTION! HONESTLY, IT'LL BE A MIRACLE IF I HAVE TIME TO BREATHE, LET ALONE DANCE!"

When I was done, Ricky got a very strange look on his face. I wondered if he was going to cry; I decided to scream if he tried to kiss me.

"Okay," he said uncertainly, after a moment of dead silence. "What I was wondering, though, is if you could maybe talk to Mr. Simmons about letting my band perform a set at the dance. We're looking for gigs in order to get some experience playing live, and I just think we'd have a better chance if the request came from someone on the Social Committee."

"Oh."

"Would you do that for me, Francie?" he asked, hunching his rather broad shoulders against the cold, damp wind that had suddenly begun to blow in earnest. "As a friend?"

✿✿✿

"As a *friend?*" cackled Holly later that evening when she called to discuss the Ricky situation for the ten-millionth time. "Who is he kidding?"

"He *is* a friend," I insisted, dangling my head over the side of the bed.

"Gimme a break," said Holly. "What I don't get is why you don't go for it. He's cute, he's tall, he's in a band, he's a grade ahead of us and, according to you, he's got armpit hair."

"Don't be gross." I gagged.

"I'm not being gross," said Holly. "Armpit hair means he's not some little boy, Francie. It means he's mature — capable of having a relationship."

Holly's enthusiasm was so contagious that I tried to imagine myself slow-dancing with Ricky. For a fleeting moment it almost worked, but then Imaginary Ricky hunched over and started whispering sweet, warm nothings into my ear with his icky deep voice.

"No!" I shuddered, giving my suddenly itchy earlobe a vigorous scratch. "No way. Ricky will never be anything more than a friend, Holly. Never."

✿✿✿

When I awoke the next day, my itchy earlobe was red and tender. That night, it looked a little swollen. By Friday morning, it was oozing a foul-smelling yellow discharge. It was so obviously infected that my mother wanted to take me to see a doctor. I told her she was totally overreacting, then ran all the way to the bus stop to show Holly how gross my ear looked. After agreeing that it looked disgusting, she warned me to be careful because Darlene had once known a girl whose piercing infection had gotten so bad it had traveled to her brain and killed her.

"One more person who knew Darlene and then died a horrible death," I muttered under my breath.

"What was that?" asked Holly, shoving a fistful of shredded bubble gum into her mouth.

"Nothing," I said loudly.

∞∞∞

Ten minutes later, while we were sitting in homeroom waiting for the first bell, the world's leading authority on infected-earlobe fatalities reminded us that she was having people over to her place that night before the dance. Holly grinned and said she couldn't wait. Then she darted off to the bathroom to pick the remains of an exploded bubble out of her hair, leaving me alone with Darlene.

"I have to tell you, Francie, my dad is really pleased that I'm having people over tonight," she informed me. "He's not surprised, of course, because I've always done a good job fitting in quickly, but it's still nice for him to see me succeed socially in a new place, you know?"

She sounded like such a little twerp that I would have rolled my eyes if I hadn't just then remembered something very important. Clearing my throat (and feeling slightly guilty for having thought of her as a little twerp), I said, "So, um, speaking of your dad, Darlene, did he ever get a chance to put in a good word for me with Lorenzo?"

"With who?" she said blankly.

"With Lorenzo," I repeated, lowering my voice. "You know — the celebrity baker."

"Ohhhh," she said, smiling slightly. Then she frowned. "Yeah, no, Daddy hasn't had a chance to do anything about that yet, Francie, and frankly, I'd appreciate it if you wouldn't mention it tonight when you're over. He's been under a lot of pressure lately, and I wouldn't want him to have to deal with anything that might give him another heart attack."

"No problem," I said hastily, embarrassed for having brought up such a sensitive subject.

"Thank you," she sighed, reaching for her fashion magazine. "You're a good friend."

❦❦❦

That night, Holly and I showed up at Darlene's big house shortly before six o'clock. Her dad greeted Holly at the door as though she was his long, lost daughter, then led us through a dim hallway stacked with unpacked moving boxes to the kitchen, where Sharon, Jody and Darlene were already stuffing their faces with two-for-one pepperoni pizzas. Holly immediately tucked in beside them, but I stood rooted to the spot, dumbstruck by the endless counter space, the vaulted ceiling, the oversized stainless steel micro-convection oven and the strategically placed spotlights that shone down like *magic*. It looked exactly the way I'd always dreamed the studio kitchen on the set of my syndicated TV show would look. Why, I could practically see myself behind the gorgeous granite countertop, my chef's hat perched upon my head, my lusciously painted lips widening in a dazzling smile as the camera zoomed in to give my worldwide audience a closer look at —

"Why are you just standing there?" interrupted Darlene. "And what are you smiling at? You're not in some kind of fugue state, are you? Because I once read about a guy who slipped into a fugue state and then butchered his entire family with a Philips screwdriver. He was later sentenced to death by electrocution, by the way."

"I'm not in a fugue state," I stammered, blushing hotly.

"She just likes your kitchen," explained Holly, lifting a slice of pizza high above her head in order to lower the dangling strings of melted mozzarella into her open mouth.

"Likes my *kitchen?*" said Darlene. Her expression made it clear she'd have preferred to hear that I was a screwdriver-wielding mass murderer.

Sharon and Jody lifted their faces out of their plates long enough to cast curious glances in my direction, then went back to their feeding frenzy.

"I don't know what Holly is talking about," I said, ignoring the faintly puzzled look on Holly's face.

"Whatever," shrugged Darlene, turning back to her pizza.

Jody lifted her impossibly long foot and kicked the chair beside her halfway into the middle of the kitchen floor.

"Sit," she commanded though a mouthful of cheap pizza. "Eat!"

❧

After dinner, we went upstairs to Darlene's room, where we spent almost an hour getting ready for the dance. I changed into my skimpy new outfit, including the platform shoes Holly had bought for me. When I put them on I was almost as tall as Sharon and Jody, and I towered over Darlene, which secretly pleased me until I overheard her whispering to Holly that she liked being small because boys almost always preferred to slow-dance with girls shorter than themselves. The logic of this hit me like a punch in the gut as I got a sudden vision of myself hunched over a dwarfed Tate Jarvis, straining to rest my gigantic head on his tiny little shoulder. If we'd been at Holly's place, I would have immediately kicked off my wretched, romance-ruining shoes and borrowed a pair of her flats, but we were at Darlene's place, and even though she had about a million pairs of shoes, I just couldn't bring myself to ask her to lend me a pair.

"You don't think these shoes make me look freakishly tall, do you?" I asked Holly later, when it was just the two of us in the bathroom trying to figure out how to use Darlene's high-tech eyelash curler.

"Of course not," she replied absently as she unsteadily tried to catch my lashes in the curler.

I shrieked with pain as the jaws of the contraption clamped down on the tender flesh at the edge of my eyelid, then composed myself so Holly could try again.

"Are you sure?" I panted, wondering if curled eyelashes were really worth it. "Because I would just *die* if I ever found out that the only reason Tate Jarvis didn't ask me to dance was because I looked like a giantess."

"Giantesses are hot," murmured Holly as she waved the contraption in my face again. "And so are you. And if that moron Tate Jarvis doesn't ask you to dance tonight, I think you should use your big fat heels to stomp him like the cockroach he is."

"Oh, Holly," I cried, ducking away from her. "I could *never* do that!"

"No?" she said. "Well, don't worry. I think bug spray would work just as well."

7. Betrayal

"Oh, Randall! How could you deceive me like that?
You have torn my very soul asunder, and as tender
flakes of croissant are swept away by brisk morning
breezes, so shall pieces of me be lost to the
wind forever."

Excerpt from The Cad Who Loved Me by Ima Dormatt

At first, the dance was everything I'd hoped it would be. The guys hung out on one side of the gymnasium, the girls hung out on the other, everybody moved around in reassuring little clumps and nobody danced. Then the DJ pumped up the volume and people spilled onto the dance floor — slowly at first, then faster and faster as it got crowded enough to hide in the middle. The temperature in the gym began to rise as the thumping backbeat seeped into our bloodstreams, and things reached a fever pitch when the Chicken Dance song came on full blast and three hundred screaming teenagers jammed their hands into their armpits and wriggled around like brain-damaged poultry.

Then the music slowed down and we all fled the dance floor in a panic.

I'd made contact with Tate Jarvis shortly after the girls and I had arrived. Not wanting to be so obvious as to look for him myself, I'd sent Holly out on a top-secret reconnaissance mission. When she'd returned with his exact coordinates, she'd nonchalantly suggested to Sharon, Jody and Darlene that we all go for a little walk, thereby giving me the perfect opportunity to strut my stuff past Tate. To my great joy, the minute he'd seen me, he'd shouted, "Nice legs!" and given a wolfish whistle. Blushing hotly, I'd tossed my chin at him and carried on.

It had simply never *occurred* to me that he could have been talking about someone else's legs, so when the DJ slowed things down and I saw Tate walking toward us, I just assumed my dream was about to come true. I was so excited that I started to feel dangerously dizzy, and it was while I was standing with my head down to keep from passing out that I heard Tate say, "Wanna dance?"

Heart pounding, I looked up only to find that he was *looking at Darlene!*

Anyone with half a brain could see how I felt about him, so I waited for Darlene to say that she had a broken leg or that she never danced with broad-shouldered, good-looking, first-string hockey players or that it was against her religion to dance, period. I waited for her to say something — anything — that would prove she was really and truly the dear friend she claimed to be. What she said, however, was: "Sure, Tate! I'd love to."

I couldn't believe my ears. As I watched them walk away — hand in hand! — I felt sick. And stunned. And *furious.* Not to mention completely humiliated to be left standing against the wall by myself like some lame duck while practically every other girl on the planet had been asked to dance.

Then I remembered Ricky. His band was going on in less than half an hour, so I knew he had to be around somewhere. He was a year older and at least four inches taller than Tate, and I figured that if a girl like me was seen dancing with a guy like him, a guy like Tate just might start to wonder what he was missing.

With this in mind, I began desperately scanning the room for Ricky. As I did so, I noticed a very short, very weirdly dressed guy standing all by himself, eagerly gazing out over the dance floor and snapping his fingers in time to the music. He looked no older than eleven, and I was just wondering what a kid his age was doing at a high school dance, when he suddenly noticed me noticing him, pivoted on one foot and started strutting toward me like a player with *all* the moves.

Hastily, I turned the other way and made a big show of examining my fingernails. Thirty seconds later, I snuck a peek over my shoulder to see if my quick thinking had gotten rid of the little guy.

He was standing right behind me.

"Yo. My name is Harold Horvath," he said, lazily toying with the collar of his form-fitting electric blue dress shirt. "Would you like to slow-dance with me?"

"Um ..." I let my voice trail off and looked away, hoping he'd get the hint.

"Well? Would you?" he asked, pulling a comb out of his back pocket and carefully smoothing back his hair.

I shrugged apologetically.

"Was that a yes?" he persisted. "I sure hope it was a yes because, you know, it took a lot of courage for me to come over here." He turned and marched out onto the dance floor. "Hurry up!" he called back to me. "I really dig this tune!"

Like a person under the power of an evil hypnotist, I inexplicably found myself following Harold Horvath out into the middle of the dance floor.

"Oh, yeah," he breathed, closing his eyes and wrapping his arms around me.

Mortified, I laid my hands on his thin shoulders and concentrated on keeping as much distance between our bodies as humanly possible. Harold swayed provocatively and softly sang along as "Stairway to Heaven" played on and on and on. A million years later, when the song finally ended, he gave me a weirdly sexy smile, stood on his tiptoes and leaned close. He was just about to whisper something into my infected ear when he pulled back sharply.

"You really should get that checked out," he advised, staring at my earlobe with a mixture of concern and revulsion.

"What?" I asked distractedly as I caught sight of Tate giving Darlene's perky little backside a two-handed squeeze.

Harold said something in reply, but I didn't catch what it

was, because just then Darlene pulled away from Tate and skipped over to where Harold and I were standing. I could tell she was bursting to share all the gory details of her dance with Tate, and since I knew for a fact I would drop dead of a broken heart if I was forced to listen to them, I told her to go away.

"Yeah, beat it!" said Harold, glaring fiercely at her as he surreptitiously tried to get me to hold his sweaty hand.

I tucked my fingers into my armpits and waited for Darlene to leave before telling Harold to go away, too.

"Fine, but you don't know what you're missing," he complained.

After he strutted off in a huff, I decided to hide out in the bathroom until the dance was over. The place was crammed with girls trying to cry without ruining their eye makeup, and I'd just found a free space by the wall next to the hand dryer when the door of the bathroom burst open.

It was Holly.

"Oh, Francie," she cried, running over and flinging her arms around me. "How *are* you?"

"Horrible!" I blurted tearfully. "Tate asked *Darlene* to dance."

"What a jerk," fumed Holly through clenched teeth.

"I know!" I said, almost weak with relief that Holly understood the truth about Darlene at last. "I couldn't believe it when she said yes —"

"No," interrupted Holly. "I mean *Tate*. How could he ask Darlene to dance right in front of you when he knows perfectly well you have feelings for him? What kind of monster is he, anyway?"

I gripped her arm hard enough to leave fingerprints. "You've got it all wrong, Holly," I said fervently. "*She's* the monster. Darlene is. She should have refused to dance with him!"

"Why?" asked Holly, sounding genuinely puzzled. "I mean, how was she supposed to know you liked him? You told her you wouldn't slow-dance with him if he knelt in four pounds of broken glass and begged you to."

I felt my insides turn to ice. "So," I said softly, after a moment of dead silence, "the two of you have been talking about me."

"What?" asked Holly, looking confused.

"Did you tell her you thought Tate was a cockroach?" I asked bitterly. "Did the two of you have a good laugh over the fact that I had feelings for a big, ugly bug?"

"Francie ..." cajoled Holly, reaching for me.

"Don't 'Francie' me," I snapped, pushing her away. "Do you have any idea what it feels like to have my heart stomped on and then to find out that my so-called best friend has been gossiping about me behind my back with the *stomper?*"

Holly was starting to get angry. "You're being completely ridiculous," she said. "I would never, never be disloyal to you."

"Oh, sure," I muttered "That's what you say *now*."

"It's true!" she said loudly, stamping her foot.

I believed her — at least, I wanted to — but everything was suddenly such a mess. With the arrival of Darlene, a thread had come loose in the fabric of our relationship. Things were unraveling at an alarming rate, and I somehow had to show Holly that she was going to lose me as a best friend if it continued on in this way.

With this in mind, I folded my arms across my chest, stuck my chin in the air and abruptly turned my back on her.

It would have been a very powerful gesture if Sharon and Jody hadn't walked over at that very moment and started drying their armpits at the hand dryer. With my face averted, I waited in silence for them to leave and then snuck a peek over my shoulder at Holly to see what she thought of my gesture.

As it turned out, she didn't think much of it.

"You know what, Francie?" she said, sticking her own

chin in the air. "If you want to believe that I have nothing better to do with my time than sit around with Darlene talking about *your* personal life, BE ... MY ... GUEST!"

And with that, she turned on one heel and flounced out of the bathroom without a backward glance.

✐✐✐

After I got my crying under control, I told Mr. Simmons I wouldn't be able to work my shift at the canteen because I'd gotten food poisoning from the cheap pizza Darlene had served for dinner. Then I called my mom and asked her to pick me up. As soon as I got into the car, I could tell she could tell something was wrong, but she knew enough not to ask what it was — unlike my dad, who greeted me at the door of the café with such a concerned look on his face that I burst into tears, ran up to my bedroom and sobbed myself to sleep.

✐✐✐

Saturday morning, after rereading the most heartbreakingly tragic passages from my three favorite True Romance novels, I let my mother drag me to the walk-in clinic to see a doctor about my ear infection. When I was done there, I headed for the grocery store, where I shuffled up and down the aisles filling my cart with over-priced zucchinis and raspberries past their prime. Back at the apartment, I dropped my shopping bags on the floor of the kitchen and slumped into the nearest chair.

"Hello, Rory," I sighed, laying my head down on the table. "How are you today?"

Rory stared blankly at me for a moment, then leaned over and began gnawing at the wires of his gilded cage.

Hauling myself out of my chair, I walked over to his cage.

"I know just how you feel," I soothed, stroking his hard little beak with one finger. "Trapped and alone. Do you realize I'll probably never leave this apartment again, Rory?"

My eyes welled with fresh tears. "I'll never go to another movie, never go to another sleepover party. Never walk through the mall getting talked into buying clothes I don't even want." I laughed shakily and brushed away a few tears. "And do you know why, Rory?" I continued, my lower lip trembling. "Because I have no friends. None. I never needed other friends before because I always had a best friend. But now she's got a new friend and I have no one at all."

Rory stopped gnawing. He cocked his head to one side as though listening carefully to me. Then he jammed his beak between the wires of the cage and gave my finger a painful chomp.

"Ow!" I shrieked, jerking my hand away. Furious, I reached out with my other hand and gave Rory's cage a good rattle. He fluttered around in a noisy panic, wearing the bewildered expression of someone who just couldn't understand why this terrible thing was happening to him.

"You'd like Darlene," I informed him as I gave his cage one final shake. "Darlene is a jerk, just like you."

"DARLENE IS A JERK," he squawked.

"That's right," I nodded, turning to unpack my shopping bags.

"JUST LIKE YOU," he added.

"No, like *you*," I corrected.

"LIKE *YOU*," he insisted.

"You don't know what you're talking about," I snapped. "I'm not a jerk. I'm a victim."

"I'M A VICTIM."

"In your *dreams*," I scoffed. "Now, would you please shut up and let me get organized?" I put on my baker's hat and tilted my face to allow my phantom makeup artist to powder my nose. "I've suffered so deeply and on so many levels in the last twenty-four hours that it's not even funny, but I am a professional baker with a wildly popular syndicated TV program and my worldwide viewing audience is counting on me. And do you know what that means, Rory?"

"I'M A VICTIM."
"No. It means the show must go on."

◌◌◌

The hustle and bustle of baking and selling took my mind off my fight with Holly for a while, but by Sunday afternoon there was nothing left to do but think. I hung around the apartment in the hopes that she might call, but she didn't. I thought about calling her, but I couldn't. What if we got into another fight? What if she hung up on me? What if she said she never wanted to speak to me again and that our friendship was over? I didn't know what I'd do if she said those things, so I did nothing at all.

Until shortly before four o'clock, that is, when I decided I couldn't take it a minute longer. Rolling off the couch, I grabbed my jacket and headed for the door. I was going to go over to Holly's place and work things out, once and for all. If she tried to slam the door on my face, I'd stick my foot in the crack — or maybe even my hand. It didn't matter if my fingers got crushed — I hoped they *did* get crushed, so that she'd see how far I was willing to go to make everything right again.

Full of renewed vigor, I flew out the apartment door and barreled into my dad with such force that I nearly sent him toppling backward down the stairs. After he recovered, he said there was someone waiting to speak with me downstairs.

"Who is it?" I asked, grabbing the front of his shirt. "Is it Holly?"

"I don't know who it is," he said, wincing as he extricated his chest hair from my clutches. "Your mother just asked me to pass along the message. Go ask ..."

I bounded past him down the stairs and flung open the swinging door of the dining room so hard it rattled on its hinges. Eagerly, I scanned the room, but I didn't see Holly anywhere.

"Where is she?" I bellowed at my mother, who was standing three feet away from me.

"In the bathroom," she replied mildly. "Now would you mind not shouting in the ..."

I sprinted out of the room, my mind brimming with words of apology and devotion and promises to never, *never* again doubt Holly's loyalty if only she would take me back as her best friend.

I skidded to halt in front of the bathroom just as the door began to open, and the smile on my face died a fast, painful death when I saw that it wasn't Holly who had come to see me after all.

It was Darlene.

"You," I said in a hollow voice.

"Yes, me," she replied briskly. "We need to talk, Francie, but before we do, you should let your mother know that the hand soap dispenser in the women's bathroom is empty. That kind of oversight is pretty unsanitary, don't you think?" she asked, marching away before I had a chance to answer.

I followed her back into the dining room and watched as she sat down at my favorite table, in my favorite chair. Then I sat down across from her.

"So, Holly told me all about the fight you two had in the bathroom at the dance," she said without preamble.

"Oh?" I said, anger bubbling up inside of me at the thought of the two of them discussing me behind my back. *Again.*

"That's right," said Darlene, taking a tube of cinnamon breath freshener out of her purse and giving her mouth three quick squirts. "She said you were mad at me for dancing with Tate."

"No," I retorted tightly. "I was upset with Holly for discussing my feelings for Tate with *you* behind my back."

"You told me you didn't have feelings for Tate," observed Darlene.

"Well, Holly knew perfectly well that I did," I hissed, jabbing my finger at her. "And when you told her what I'd told you, she could easily have explained that I'd only said that because I didn't think my personal life was any of your business."

"Maybe she thought it wasn't her place to correct the misinformation you'd given me," said Darlene, looking down her nose at my finger. "Maybe she was afraid you'd get mad at her if she told me the truth."

I think I stopped breathing.

"Except it's kind of funny, isn't it?" she continued, tapping her pointy chin with her perfectly painted little fingernail. "Because you got mad at her anyway."

"I ... I wasn't mad," I spluttered, back-pedaling furiously. "I was hurt. I ... I didn't understand ..."

"And so you turned your back on her without giving her a chance to explain?" asked Darlene incredulously. "*Wow*. If that's the way you treat your best friend, I wouldn't want to see how you treat your worst enemy. But, hey, who am I to judge? I don't even have a best friend. The only real friend I have is Holly, and that's why I'm here. To fix whatever is wrong between you and me so Holly doesn't have to feel like she's caught in the middle."

I was so indignant I hardly knew what to say. Darlene wanted to fix whatever was wrong between the two of us? She was the thing that was wrong! And FYI, there wouldn't even *be* a middle for Holly to get caught in if it wasn't for her! I desperately wanted to tell Darlene to go away and stop wrecking my life, but I knew if I did I'd be forever marked as the mean, selfish ogre who had chased away the perky little ambassador of peace.

I was trapped.

"If it helps any, you should know I only danced with Tate because he asked me to," confided Darlene. "As a person who is so self-assured you don't mind walking around naked in public changing rooms, this might be hard for you to understand, Francie, but regular girls sometimes have difficulty saying no when guys ask them to dance."

"Really?" I said, trying not to shudder as the memory of dancing with Harold Horvath washed over me like a bucket of cold split-pea soup.

"Yes." Darlene nodded. "Now, I won't lie to you — I'm almost certain Tate has feelings for me. However, I can assure you that he is too boorish, dense and self-centered for me to ever regard him as anything other than a friend. So please believe me when I say that under no circumstances should you consider me competition for his affections."

"Oh. Okay," I said, my relief at this bold declaration somewhat tempered by the fact that Darlene had just described the man of my dreams as a troglodyte.

"In fact," she went on, "I'm even willing to use my position of influence to help you get closer to him."

"You are?" I said, feeling rather taken aback.

"Sure. Why not?" she replied. "Anything if it will improve things between us and make the situation easier on Holly."

"Right," I agreed, annoyed with myself for not thinking to mention Holly first.

"Because she's really sensitive, you know."

"I know," I said, even though I knew no such thing.

"Good." She nodded. "Now, I just need to ask you one last thing."

"What is it?"

Darlene frowned deeply. "You're not acting this way toward Holly to get back at me for not getting my dad to use his influence on your behalf with that celebrity baker, are you?" she asked.

"What?" I spluttered. "No!"

"Because I thought I'd explained that my father is under a lot of pressure," she continued, examining her nails. "I'd do almost anything to improve this situation, Francie, but I really think it's a bit much to expect me to put my father's health in jeopardy, don't you?"

"Yes!" I cried. "But I wasn't! I mean, of course it would

have been *nice* if he'd been able to do something, but I never expected —"

"All right, fine. Don't have a cow," said Darlene, waving her little hand at me. "I just needed to make sure. You wouldn't believe how selfish some people can be."

◆◆◆

That evening, I called Holly to apologize for my behavior at the dance. I was humble and sincere and took all the blame for what happened. She didn't hang up on me, but she didn't burst into noisy tears of relief and forgive me, either. Instead, in a rather distracted voice, she just told me not to be silly. Feeling awkward, I started to ask if this meant we were best friends again, but she cut me off abruptly, saying she had to go pound on her little sister for LISTENING IN ON THE OTHER EXTENSION. These bellowed words were followed by the sudden sound of a phone clattering to the floor and several shrieks of terrified laughter. Hastily, Holly said she'd see me at the bus stop the next morning. Then she was gone.

◆◆◆

The next day, I left for school so early my mom wondered aloud if my ear infection hadn't traveled to my brain, after all. I told her, "Ha, ha," then ran as fast as I could to the top of the street. I was thrilled to find Holly waiting for me, and even more thrilled when she wordlessly offered me a stick of Juicy Fruit gum and started telling me how, after hanging up on me the night before, she'd used the business end of a toilet plunger to keep Tabitha pinned behind the bathroom door while she'd repeatedly dunked Tabitha's personal hairbrush into the toilet in order to teach her a lesson about listening in on other people's private conversations. I laughed as though this was the funniest thing I'd ever heard, then joined Holly in feeling totally narked at her parents for making her trade hairbrushes with Tabitha afterward. There was nothing at all unusual about our conversation, which is precisely why it meant so much to me.

Halfway to school, Darlene boarded the bus and squashed in on the other side of Holly even though the seat was only meant to hold two people. When Holly told her about the hairbrush-in-the-toilet incident, she laughed even harder than I'd laughed. Then she asked Holly if she'd heard anything about her Performance Band audition.

"I just can't stop thinking about how much it means to you," said Darlene.

"Me neither," I said quickly.

Holly nodded. "Mrs. Cavanaugh is going to post the results today. I'll just die if I don't make it, won't you, Francie?" she asked, turning to me with wide, nervous eyes.

I was gratified by the fact that Holly had turned to *me* for comfort, but as I opened my mouth to say something reassuring, Darlene suddenly slipped off the edge of the bus seat and fell to the dirty floor with a cry. Abruptly, Holly dumped her knapsack on my lap, turned away from me and hurriedly reached down to help Darlene.

A short while later, when Darlene was dusted off and cozily settled in between Holly and me so that there would be no chance of her falling again, Holly leaned over, smiled and asked for her knapsack back.

Wordlessly, I handed it over.

∂∂∂

That morning, during the break between second and third periods, Holly galloped up to me and breathlessly blurted that the Performance Band results had been posted. Grabbing my arm, she nearly yanked me off my feet in her haste to get to the band room door. When we arrived, we shoved our way to the front of the crowd and anxiously scanned the list for our names. I'd just spotted Ricky's name when Holly started screaming in my ear that she'd made it.

I gave her a gigantic hug and then hurriedly resumed looking for my name. I scanned the list once, twice, three times. Then the pre-scream smile died on my lips.

I ... I hadn't made it. I couldn't believe it. I mean, I knew there was a *chance* this might happen, but I never actually believed that —

"There's your name!" squealed Holly, pointing to the bottom of the page.

My heart gave a wild thump when I saw a handwritten note.

Francie Freewater,

I need to speak with you as soon as possible regarding your participation in the Performance Band. Thank you,
Mrs. Cavanaugh

Holly and I were both mystified as to why Mrs. C would need to speak with me. In a slightly subdued voice, Holly said that maybe Mrs. Cavanaugh wanted me to play a solo at the festival. Every year, one or two people were given this special honor.

"Don't be ridiculous," I scoffed. "If she was going to ask anyone to perform a solo, it would be you, Holly. You're the one with the musical gift, remember? I'm just along for the ride."

∽✸✸✸∾

As it turned out, the reason Mrs. C needed to speak with me was more shocking — and terrible — than anything I could have imagined.

"I'd like you to join the Performance Band in a general percussion capacity, Francie," she explained that afternoon, when I finally tracked her down on her way into the staff bathroom.

"Pardon me?" I said, thinking I must have heard her wrong.

"You know," she replied, tucking a shining lock of perfect hair behind one ear. "Triangle, cymbals, wooden sticks."

"Wooden *sticks?*"

Mrs. C pantomimed holding a block of polished wood in her left hand and smartly smacking it with a second block of wood held in her right hand, all the while making rhythmic clocking noises with her tongue.

"Yes, yes, I know what the wooden sticks are," I said impatiently. "I just don't understand why you're asking me to play them. I'm a clarinet player, for heaven's sake!"

"Yes, you are," she said carefully. "But I'm afraid your audition wasn't quite as polished as it needed to be for you to earn a spot on the band playing that particular instrument."

For a moment I just gaped at her. Then I clasped my hands and bowed my head.

"Please change your mind. Please let me play the clarinet," I begged in a quiet voice. "Please, *please,* don't make me play the wooden sticks. Or the triangle. Or the cymbals."

"One of the pieces I've selected also calls for the tambourine," she interjected with a small smile.

"The tambourine?" I cried, flinging my hands into the air. "Mrs. C, you're killing me! I'll look like a complete loser playing the tambourine while everyone else in the band gets to play a real instrument!"

"The tambourine is a very real instrument," she said firmly. "The rhythm and zest it can bring to a piece can transform it completely!"

I made a noise so despairing it barely sounded human.

Mrs. C looked annoyed. "Francie," she said, "I'm not going to stand here all day trying to convince you that an appropriately timed clash of cymbals can make or break a concert. I went out of my way to find a spot for you on the Performance Band after deciding that your clarinet playing wasn't up to snuff. If you don't like the spot I found for you, don't join the band."

With that, she pushed open the bathroom door and prepared to disappear inside.

"Wait!" I cried in alarm. "I never said I wasn't going to do it. Jeez! Since when is it against the law to discuss options?"

Mrs. C stopped abruptly and swung her head around to face me. Her thick, glossy hair followed a fraction of a second later, coming to rest with a bounce and a ripple.

"So you *do* want to join?" she asked. "In a percussion capacity, I mean?"

I nodded without much enthusiasm, wondering if my hair would ever look as good as hers.

"And you'll practice diligently? And with a positive attitude?"

Sensing that I was still on thin ice, I tore my gaze away from her fabulous hair, nodded more eagerly and even offered to perform a triangle solo if she wanted.

Mrs. C laughed. "If you can shake the maracas with attitude, Francie, that'll be good enough for me."

8. The Contest

The next best thing to baking with Lorenzo! His kung fu grip lets him cling with desire to the edges of your mixing bowls; pull his drawstring to hear him whisper, "'Allo," as only he can. Hair accessories and tiny leather pants sold separately.

From the packaging of the soon-to-be-released Lorenzo LaRue action figure

Over the following few weeks, there were so many Performance Band rehearsals that I started dreaming in four-four time.

Unlike the percussion sections in some schools, which were reserved for super-cool kids who could do things like throw their drumsticks into the air and catch them without missing a beat, our percussion section was clearly the Performance Band garbage dump. Sharon had been assigned to the gong, which she insisted on striking with the solemnity of an Aztec priestess presiding over a human sacrifice, Jody played the snare drum like an overcaffeinated heavy metal head banger and Randy Newton was such a nervous wreck on the tympani that no matter how many times Mrs. C asked him to please close his mouth, his lower jaw hung halfway to his knees. I knew this was mostly because for some reason Holly had started coming to band practice wearing clingy, scoop-necked sweaters that showed off her sparkling 36C personality to its very best advantage. Having suffered for love myself, I tried to be understanding, but Randy's nervousness threw off his timing, and his appalling sense of rhythm slowly started to rub off on me. It was humiliating, particularly because every time Mrs. C stopped the Performance Band to once again tap out the beat for Randy and me, we just got more flustered and more out of synch until eventually, Randy was reduced to hammering upon the tympani in a blind panic while I spasmodically clutched at my triangle and stomped both feet in a futile attempt to keep time. We were so horrendous that halfway through the third Performance Band practice, Mrs. C gently dismissed Sharon, Jody, Randy and me with a promise to hold special percussion section rehearsals. Laying down my castanets with as much dignity as I could muster, I wiped the sweat from my forehead and joined the others in silently filing out of the band room while all of the real musicians looked on with a mixture of pity, distain and amusement — all except Ricky, who raised his saxophone in a silent salute, and Holly, who, from her prime location in the glamorous woodwind section, gave me a warm smile of encouragement, then absently reached into the front of her sweater to adjust the way her right breast was sitting in its C cup and inadvertently destroyed what was left of Randy's brain.

Worst of all, I had a feeling that my banishment to the percussion section wasn't helping my situation with Tate Jarvis, because despite Darlene's assurances that she'd been saying all sorts of good things about me to him, he seemed even *less* interested in me now than he'd been before.

"I swear he's been treating me differently ever since I got demoted," I lamented as I sat eating lunch with Holly and Darlene while we waited for Mr. Simmons to show up for our Social Committee meeting.

This was Darlene's first meeting. I'd been secretly crushed when she'd announced that she wanted to join the committee, because over the last few weeks, in addition to spending oodles of time alone with Holly, she'd also managed to push her way into almost everything Holly and I used to share as best friends. She came shopping with us and hung out with us after school and fixed her hair and lip gloss in the bathroom with us during the breaks between classes. Holly had even invited her to our most recent sleepover party. I'd kept hoping Darlene would fall asleep first — so that Holly and I would be able to whisper together for a while, just the two of us — but I fell asleep first and in the morning, when I went searching for my bra, I found it in Holly's freezer. After I'd drifted off, Darlene and Holly had soaked it in water and then carefully laid it out next to the butter pecan ice cream and frozen mixed vegetables. The two of them had found the sight of my frozen-stiff bra hilarious, but it had taken everything in me not to burst into tears.

Up until today, the Social Committee had been one of the last places where I still had Holly all to myself — where it still felt at least a little like the way things used to be.

"What do you mean when you say Tate's been treating you differently?" asked Holly as she buried her nose in a big bag of popcorn twists. "Differently how?"

I glanced at Darlene, who blinked at me expectantly then slowly reached into her purse and pulled out a small baggie full of raw vegetables.

I took a bite of my messy tuna sandwich in order to give myself time to figure out how to say what I meant without looking like a lovelorn dork in front of Darlene. "Well, last week, for example, during our chemistry midterm, he never once nudged me in an effort to get me to uncover my test paper so he could copy my answers," I explained carefully. "I mean, I've never let him copy off me before, so I realize it's not like he had any reason to hope I'd let him do it this time, but that's not really the point."

"What is the point?" said Darlene, looking very serious but sounding like she might start laughing at any moment.

I felt my face grow warm. "The point is that in the past he's always tried to copy off me, and this time he didn't," I said.

It was so much more than that, of course: it was the way Tate no longer laughed when I pretended to use the Bunsen burner to light my hair on fire, and the fact that he no longer bothered to catch my pencil for me when I threw it into the air and missed it on the way down. It was the way he moved his hand when my fingers "accidentally" brushed against his, and the fact that he never looked up when we passed each other in the hallway even though I always gave him my most piercing stare.

I could have told Holly these things, and she would have understood. With Darlene, it was different.

"Well, Francie," said Darlene now as she bit a snow pea in half with a snap of her little white teeth. "It could be that our little study group has been such a big help that Tate doesn't feel he needs to copy off you anymore." She threw back her head and laughed merrily. "Though I must admit, there were evenings we thought we'd *never* figure out why water expands upon freezing, when virtually every other liquid on the planet contracts!"

Thinking I must have heard wrong, I asked Darlene what on earth she was talking about.

"Oh!" she said brightly. "Well, the way I understand it, when water freezes it does so in a peculiar kind of pattern on account of the ... the *angle* of the bonds between the ... the —"

"Between the hydrogen and oxygen molecules," I interrupted impatiently. "Yes, I know. But that's not what I meant. I meant — what do you mean, 'there were evenings'?"

"Tate and I have been studying together since my second week here," she shrugged, taking a dainty nibble of broccoli. "I told you about it the night of the pool party, remember? I even invited you to study with us."

I stared at her, stunned.

"Well ... I remember you mentioning it," I spluttered, accidentally spraying bits of chewed tuna everywhere. "But I had no *idea* you'd actually gone through with it."

"One thing you should know about me, Francie, is that when I say I'm going to do something, I do it," said Darlene, fastidiously wiping the table in front of her with a wet wipe from her purse. "Now, would you like a stick of celery? I hear it can help kill the smell of tuna."

I could see Holly watching me carefully, as though

waiting for my reaction. So, trying not to completely freak out, I reached into Darlene's baggie and selected a small piece of celery.

"You know, Darlene," I said as I chewed the celery into pulp, "most girls wouldn't arrange study dates with boys their friends have crushes on."

"Is that so?" she said. "Well, another thing you should know about me, Francie, is that I'm not like most girls."

"Which means what?" I asked.

"Which means that I made a commitment to study with Tate until the end of the semester and I'm going to honor that commitment." Leaning toward me, she took a brisk sniff. "You'd better have another stick of celery," she said, wrinkling her little nose. "Maybe even two."

I opened my mouth to say something but she kept right on talking.

"Oh, listen. Don't worry, okay?" she said, sounding exasperated. "I said I'd use my position of influence to help you get closer to Tate and I meant it. In fact, I've been giving it a lot of thought lately, and I think I'm very close to coming up with something so spectacular that he won't be able to maintain his attitude of cool indifference toward you if he tries."

"What is it?" I asked.

Before she could answer, the door of the classroom swung open and Mr. Simmons stomped into the room reeking of cigarette smoke, a Chili Dog Express take-out bag in one meaty fist and an extra-large coffee in the other. Without bothering to have the decency to apologize for being twenty minutes late for our meeting, he shoved half a chili dog into his mouth and announced that Mrs. C had asked him to ask us if we'd consider organizing a pep rally for the Performance Band.

"She wants the band gimps to march into the gym, play a few tunes, then get a five-minute standing ovation from whichever knuckleheads have been able to keep their hormones in check long enough to focus," he explained sourly.

I probably would have barfed at the sight — and sound — of Mr. Simmons talking with his mouth full of chewed chili dog if I hadn't been so mortified by the thought of the entire school seeing me march into the gym playing the triangle. Thinking furiously, I tried to come up with a good reason to kill the whole thing, but before I could, Darlene piped up and said she thought it was a terrific idea. Holly happily seconded the motion, so I was outvoted.

Again.

◦◦◦

I felt a little let down for the rest of the afternoon, but that changed the minute I walked into the apartment and went searching for the TV remote. At the end of the previous week's show, Lorenzo had tantalized us all with the news that he'd be making a major announcement on this week's show. Nana thought perhaps he had a new cooking video coming out, or a new cookbook, or maybe even a new series of bare-chested photographs, but I had a feeling it was something much bigger than that.

"Got it!" I cried. Shoving a book of crossword puzzles, a newspaper and the remains of a stale breakfast bagel off the end table beside my father's recliner, I pounced on the remote and got the TV on without a second to spare.

Lorenzo was standing at the spotlit center of the darkened sound stage with his feet shoulder-width apart and his arms folded across his glorious bare chest. His long, dark curls were blowing back from his face thanks to a wind machine somewhere off-camera, and like the hero in a romance novel, he was staring yonder with a stalwart expression on his noble face. I could hear lute music and the sound of waves crashing in the distance, and the whole effect was so unbelievably amazing that I almost stopped breathing.

"'Allo, ladies," he murmured at last, turning his

languorous gaze toward the camera.

"'Allo to *you!*" cried Nana, flapping her terry-cloth headband at the television screen in delight.

"'Allo," I croaked as the TV remote dropped from my hand and hit the floor with a clatter.

"You look simply fab-oo-lus today," continued Lorenzo, with a knowing smile.

"Why, thank you," twittered Nana. "I just got back from yoga class, don't you know."

I gave my bangs a self-conscious fluff.

"Ladies," he said, striding across the stage with such vigor that I could see his thigh muscles bulging beneath his black leather pants. "Last week I promised you a wonderful surprise."

He came to a halt beside a table covered in a flowing white sheet.

"Maybe it's his own doll," said Nana breathlessly, eyeing the boxy shapes that lay on the table beneath the sheet.

"His own *doll?*" I jeered.

"Yes," clucked Nana indignantly. "These days, all the big celebrities get dolls made to look like themselves. They're genuine collectibles."

My mouth went dry as I imagined myself (played by the incomparable Totally Hair Barbie) and nine-inch-tall Lorenzo LaRue cruising around my bedroom floor in my remote control Barbie Corvette Stingray before retiring to the Barbie Town House in order to rip off our Velcro-tab clothing and assume positions that were probably outlawed in most countries.

"Maybe it *is* a doll," I whispered hoarsely.

Even as I spoke, Lorenzo whipped away the cloth and the camera zoomed in on the mystery boxes. Nana gasped.

"Yes," purred Lorenzo. "Coming soon to a retail outlet near you, 'Sinfully Yours, by Lorenzo.' Baked goods for the woman who has everything but love." He picked up a box and cradled it in his arms. "Conveniently available in single-serving portions, my new line of dessert products will have a non-refrigerated shelf life in excess of two years, and my most tender feelings for you located inside each hermetically sealed cellophane package."

He paused to toss his hair around and blow a lingering kiss at the camera. Both Nana and I reached out to catch it.

"Got it!" she cried, snatching her closed fist to her bony chest.

"Give it here," I ordered, grabbing her arm and pretending to try to wrestle her fingers open.

She shook with laughter and hit me with her terry-cloth headband.

"But wait!" whispered Lorenzo. "There's *more.*"

Nana and I immediately stopped horsing around and leaned closer to the television to hear what he had to say.

"Next week, I will begin a cross-Canada promotional tour in support of the launch of my new product line. In each city, one lucky contest winner will 'ave the once-in-a-lifetime opportunity to stand beside me — shoulder to shoulder! — and assume the coveted role of my devoted onstage assistant."

On cue, the Lovely Lydia glided up behind Lorenzo and draped herself over his well-oiled left shoulder. This time, I *definitely* stopped breathing.

"All you 'ave to do, ladies," murmured Lorenzo as the camera zoomed in for an extreme close-up of his exquisitely pouting lips, "is send me five original recipes, along with a personal poem or short essay describing how I 'ave inspired you in the kitchen, and how you feel 'Sinfully Yours, by Lorenzo' is going to help fill the nameless, aching void in your life."

I barely paid attention to the rest of the show, even though Lorenzo was making a meringue that required him to whip egg whites so fast his well-toned pectorals practically started vibrating. I was consumed with ideas for my submission — and with fantasies of being Lorenzo's devoted onstage assistant. What if I did such a good job that he asked me to take over from the Lovely Lydia on a full-time basis? I imagined pleading with my parents to let me quit school and, when they refused, suing them for the right to become an emancipated minor. I saw myself standing on the steps of the courthouse, tearfully explaining to them that I had to follow my destiny — and then fighting my way through the throngs of reporters to Lorenzo's waiting limousine.

"Can you imagine if I did such a good job that he asked me to take over from the Lovely Lydia on a full-time basis?" asked Nana in a dreamy voice.

"Really, Nana," I murmured distractedly, as Fantasy Lorenzo handed me a chilled goblet of non-alcoholic champagne. "Don't be ridiculous."

ೡೡೡ

All that evening and all the next day at school, I pondered what to write in my submission. I also let myself drift in and out of various Lorenzo fantasies — Lorenzo and I receiving an Academy Award for the Best Baking Documentary, Lorenzo and I signing autographs while a wall of burly bodyguards held back a mob of hysterical fans, Lorenzo and I pushing our mounts to gallop faster as we raced through the surf on a windswept white-sand beach. Several times, I caught myself murmuring Lorenzo's name aloud, and in chemistry I was so spaced out that when Mr. Flatburn asked me a question I didn't even hear him — I just sat staring off into space while he and everyone else waited for me to snap out of it. It was very embarrassing, especially afterward, when Tate leaned over and asked me who this Lorenzo dude was and why we'd been thanking the Academy.

ೡೡೡ

Saturday morning, I was waiting at the door of the grocery store when it opened at eight o'clock. I wanted to get my baking done early so I'd have plenty of time to work on my

Lorenzo essay. The deadline for entering to win the Winnipeg guest spot was the next day at noon, and I didn't want to leave it to the last minute, especially since Nana had already sent her submission in.

"I have no idea what I'll do if she actually wins," I confided to Rory as I dragged his cage over to the island counter and laid out my ingredients. "I mean, I'll *try* to feel happy for her, of course, but inside I'll be dying."

Rory lifted up one of his feet and examined his toes.

Annoyed by his lack of interest in my emotional confession, I pleasantly explained to Rory that it would be like if Nana brought home a mouthwatering vanilla layer cake with whipped-cream-cheese icing and didn't offer him one single bite.

Outraged, Rory flung himself against the bars of his cage and flapped his wings so furiously that he misjudged the rate with which he was gaining altitude, bonked his head on the ceiling of his cage and collapsed into his own food dish.

Enormously satisfied by his reaction, I gave my chef's hat a fluff, hit PLAY on the stereo and spun back to the counter. Now that performing on live TV was an actual possibility, I needed to take my Saturday afternoon baking sessions even more seriously. I had to treat them like rehearsals for the real thing.

Bowing my head, I gripped the counter hard and waited for the music to begin. Suddenly, the first notes of my favorite rock anthem filled the air — catchy, cool and totally irresistible. As I started to move more or less in time with the music, excitement leaped in my belly.

Imagine this is the real thing!

Looking up so quickly that I nearly gave myself whiplash, I flashed a dazzling smile at my studio audience and then started throwing ingredients together and sharing clever tips regarding my one-of-a-kind double-fudge super-chunk nut brownies. As I tossed an egg into the air and caught it behind my back without even looking, I tried to remember that I was only supposed to be a devoted assistant — and to curb my chatter and enthusiasm accordingly — but it felt so unnatural that I gave up almost immediately. If I won, Lorenzo was just going to have to accept the fact that a new era of devoted assistants had dawned — an era in which devoted assistants sometimes took center stage and received thunderous standing ovations for their work in the area of mind-blowing chocolate creations.

"Thank you, thank you!" I breathed, closing my eyes and raising both fists in victory. "And now, for my next recipe —"

Peals of laughter suddenly sliced through the air.

My eyes snapped open and I saw a tiny, elfin figure silhouetted in the kitchen door frame. It was such a startling sight that I accidentally knocked over the vanilla extract.

"Darlene!" I stammered as I fumbled for a dishtowel. "How ... how long have you been standing there?"

"Long enough," she said, still giggling. "And before that I was listening from the living room." She shook her head and wiped tiny tears of mirth out of the corners of her eyes. "I must say, Francie, you put on *quite* a performance. Who knew a person could be so passionate about brown sugar and baking soda?"

I felt my face get hot. "What are you doing here?" I mumbled, tugging off my chef's hat and crumpling it in my hands.

"I dropped by to see if you wanted to come to a movie with me tonight," she explained. "Marguerite said I should feel free to let myself in."

"I see," I said, making a mental note to spit on the tires of Marguerite's car.

But I didn't see, not really. Since befriending Holly, Darlene had never dropped by to see if I wanted to do anything. It was always Holly and Darlene, or Holly and me, or the three of us together, but never me and Darlene.

"How come you're asking me instead of Holly?" I asked suspiciously.

"I did ask Holly," said Darlene, plucking a single milk-chocolate chip out of my cookie dough and popping it into her mouth. "But Bruce is having his birthday party this evening."

"Bruce?" I asked.

"Holly's dad," reminded Darlene.

"Oh, right," I muttered.

"You were my very second choice, though, Francie," she assured me. "And do you know why?"

"Because you have no other friends?" I suggested as I casually slid the bowl of cookie dough beyond her reach.

Darlene laughed merrily. "*No!* Because Tate Jarvis said he's going to be at the movies tonight, and I thought it would be a good opportunity for you to spend some quality time with him."

Blinking rapidly, I shoved the cookie dough back toward Darlene and gestured for her to help herself to another chip. "Tate is going to be there tonight?" I asked excitedly. "Are you sure?"

"Absolutely," smiled Darlene. "I guarantee it. So, do you want to come?" she asked. Her gaze wandered across my legions of cooling racks. "Or are you going to be too busy playing Betty Crocker?"

She laughed when she said this, and I felt my face get hot again. I wanted to tell her that I wasn't *playing* at anything — I was working, and working hard. I wanted to grab her little toothpick arms and explain that baking was my destiny, and ask her if she had any idea what it felt like to know that there was at least one thing in this world I could do better than anybody I knew.

But, of course, I didn't say or do any of those things, because even the thought that it might provoke Darlene into telling Tate she'd caught me blowing kisses to a bored parrot while wearing oven mitts was enough to make me shrivel up and die.

"Of course I won't be playing Betty Crocker," I said lightly, looking down at my beloved mixing bowls as though slightly surprised to find them sitting on the counter in front of me. "What do you think I am, some kind of freak?"

After Darlene left, I returned to work, but without any of the accompanying theatrics. I skimped a little on my output that day, making one batch of scones instead of three and skipping the cheesecakes altogether. I felt a bit guilty about this because I knew I'd have to face disappointed customers the next morning, but if I was going to go to the movie that night, I needed the extra time to work on my Lorenzo essay. It wasn't as easy as I'd expected it to be. When I tried to describe how he'd inspired me, I kept getting distracted by visions of nine-inch Lorenzo floating in my inflatable Barbie Swimming Pool. Naked. And though I racked my brains, the only aching void I could see his new products filling wasn't nameless at all. It was called my stomach.

In the end, I decided to just pour my heart out and hope it was enough. After inputting five of my finest original recipes and hurriedly answering all the contest questions, I sent off my submission, gawked at the short video clip of Lorenzo warmly thanking me for my entry, then turned off my computer and raced to make myself irresistible for my evening out with **Tate** and Darlene.

As luck would have it, Tate never did show up at the theater that night. Darlene was so furious he'd stood me up that she wouldn't stop yammering about it even after the movie had started. It was extremely distracting, and as disappointed as I was by the way things had worked out, I eventually found myself whispering to Darlene that Tate really wasn't worth the heartache she was suffering on my behalf.

9. A Champion French Kisser

Baby, whenever I turn and look at you
It feels like my guts are being ripped in two
My friends say, "Dude, just try to forget her"
But I'd rather feed my heart into a paper shredder.

From "Secret Love Is Totally Tearing Me Apart"
by Ricky Skametka

The following Monday, Darlene made such a point of ignoring Tate in chemistry class that, in a pathetic attempt to get her attention, he repeatedly pretended to blow off his fingers in a Bunsen burner gas-line explosion.

"I'm doing my best to give him the cold shoulder as a punishment for rejecting you so cruelly on Saturday night, Francie," she murmured later, glancing a few feet over to where Tate was lying under a cafeteria table, leg wrestling with Randy Newton. "I just don't know what else you expect me to do!"

I didn't know what else I expected her to do, either. As I watched Tate writhe on the dirty floor with his legs wrapped around Randy's neck, I dejectedly wondered if maybe it was time to give up hope and take my heart elsewhere.

Just then, I felt a heavy hand on my shoulder. Looking up, I saw Ricky Skametka smiling down at me. There were actual bristles poking out of his chin, and he looked so tall that I almost felt dizzy.

"Hello, Ricky," I said, blinking up at him.

"Hello, Francie," he replied. "I was hoping I'd run into you down here. I wanted to know if you were doing anything this Friday night."

I was so startled by his question that I squeezed my grapefruit juice box hard enough to send a stream of juice squirting directly into my eyeball. Dropping the box, I clutched at my badly stinging eye. Ricky bolted from the table so fast that I was sure I'd scared him away, but he returned seconds later and stood behind my chair with a handful of paper towels he'd run under warm water in the boys' bathroom.

"Here," he murmured. "Let me help."

Gently peeling my fingers away from my eye, he tenderly tilted my head backward and pressed the wet towels to my face. It would have been extremely soothing if I hadn't been almost having a heart attack due to the fact that the back of my head was *practically buried in Ricky's crotch.*

"I ... I think I'm fine," I said, when I couldn't stand the proximity of his *thing* a moment longer.

"Are you sure?" asked Ricky, his deep voice filled with concern.

"Yes, I'm sure," I shuddered.

"Okay. Good," he said, sliding into the seat next to me. "So, I can't remember — did you say you were free on Friday night or not?" he asked.

I gaped at him, wondering if I should squirt juice into my other eye. I knew he probably didn't mean to ask me out on a date right there in the middle of the cafeteria, only *what if he did!* The uncertainty of the situation — that's what was killing me. Looking over at Holly's empty seat, I wished desperately that she was back from the vending machine. *She* would have seen how stressed out I was. *She* would have found some way to get Ricky to reveal his true intentions without putting me on the spot. Glancing at Darlene to see if there was any hope of her taking up Holly's slack, I was stunned to see her staring at Ricky with her mouth hanging open.

My own mouth snapped shut in surprise.

"Francie?" murmured Ricky.

"Yes?" I murmured back, unable to tear my gaze away from the dazed expression on Darlene's face.

"Are you free Friday night?" he asked, for the third time.

I turned and looked at Ricky as though seeing him for the

first time. "As a matter of fact, Ricky," I said as I snuck a peek at Darlene. "I *am* free on Friday night."

"Great," he said, flushing slightly. "Because my band is playing at the community club winter carnival this weekend, and I'd really like it if you and a bunch of your friends would come by and help swell the crowd."

"That sounds great!" blurted Darlene, almost before Ricky got the words out of his mouth.

I shook my head and wondered how she could allow herself to be so obvious. "Yes, Rick," I said, feeling very mature and in control. "That does sound great."

"What sounds great?" asked Holly, who had just returned from the vending machine with a bag of chips.

"Going to see Rick's band play this weekend," I said.

"Boy, does it ever!" agreed Holly in a loud voice, ripping her chip bag open with such force that barbecued chips rained down over half the cafeteria. Blushing hotly, she scrambled to her knees to pick them up.

A few feet over, I heard the sound of Randy Newton's head hitting a table leg as a result of a spasm caused by his sudden, unfettered view of Holly's cleavage. Tate unhooked his legs from around Randy's neck, sat up and stared over at our table with an annoyed expression on his face. On the off chance he was annoyed that I was being showered with attention by a boy who was a year older and at least four inches taller than he was, I leaned ever so slightly closer to Ricky and accidentally put my elbow in my egg-salad sandwich.

"Would you like me to get you some more paper towel?" asked Ricky as he stared down at poor Holly, who was still picking chips off the floor.

"No, thank you, Rick," I murmured, glancing over at Darlene as I picked bits of yolk off my sleeve. "You've already done more than you know."

That night, I waited for Darlene to call and confess that she was interested in Ricky so that I could regretfully inform her that I was almost certain he had feelings for me. I didn't want to dash her hopes, but I *did* want to be as honest with her as she'd always been with me where Tate Jarvis was concerned. I owed her that much, especially since I didn't know if I was going to be able to agree to use my position of influence to help her get closer to Ricky. Even though he was just a friend, it didn't feel right trying to encourage him to like anyone but me.

But Darlene didn't call that night, and as I drifted off to sleep beneath the glow-in-the-dark stars I'd Krazy Glued to my bedroom ceiling the year I'd turned ten, I wondered how she was coping with the knowledge that the heart of the boy of her dreams belonged to someone else.

Me.

୬୭

I found out the next day during library period.

"Francie," she whispered. "I have a confession to make."

"Oh?" I asked innocently, setting aside my neatly completed algebra assignment.

Darlene cast a conspiratorial glance over her shoulder to make sure no one in the school library was listening. "I don't think I've been using my position of influence with Tate Jarvis to its maximum potential where you're concerned."

I sighed deeply. "I'm sorry, Darlene, but I'm almost certain that Ricky has feelings for ... Hey, wait a minute. What did you just say?"

"I said I haven't been doing enough to get Tate to like you. But don't worry," she added. "Remember how I once said I was close to coming up with something so spectacular that he wouldn't be able to maintain his attitude of cool indifference toward you if he tried? Well, I did it. Last night, while we were studying at my place, I told him something that just about knocked his socks off."

"What did you tell him?" I asked suspiciously.

Darlene grinned. "That you are a champion French kisser."

I could not have been more shocked if she'd just confessed to having a taste for human livers.

"You did not," I said flatly.

"I did so," she replied, looking very pleased with herself. "I also told him you'd made out millions of times with your tall, good-looking friend from the cafeteria."

"Ricky?" I squeaked, so startled by the thought that I knocked my contraband soda all over my algebra assignment.

"Was that his name?" asked Darlene vaguely.

"You told Tate I'd made out with *Ricky?*" I repeated in disbelief.

"Millions of times," she confirmed.

"Are you insane?" I whispered fiercely as I tried to wipe soda off my soggy assignment without the librarian noticing. "Darlene, you were *supposed* to tell Tate nice things about me ..."

"He seemed to think the thing I was telling him was pretty nice," she chuckled.

"No, no! Nice things like ... like that I have a super sense of humor, or a really warm personality. What were you thinking telling him I was a French-kissing machine who couldn't keep her hands off some other guy?"

"I was *thinking* you wanted Tate to show a little more interest in you," she said.

I glared at her.

"Oh, grow up, Francie," she said, flipping open her algebra textbook. "Do you honestly believe Tate is the sort of guy who is going to like you for your *personality?*"

I didn't know what I was supposed to say to this. I wanted to be liked for my personality, but I also wanted to be liked by Tate, and the whole idea of being liked because I was willing to let guys stick their gross tongues into my mouth made me feel nauseous and icky.

Glancing up from her textbook, Darlene narrowed her eyes at me.

"You know what? Just forget it," she said, sounding more than a little annoyed. "I was trying to do you a favor."

"I know, I'm sorry, it's just that — "

"It's just that I overestimated you," she interrupted, slapping her textbook shut so abruptly it made me jump. "I assumed you were the kind of girl who was cool with getting a little physical once in a while — the kind of girl who was willing to do what it takes to make an impression on a guy like Tate. Obviously, I was wrong. So, don't worry about a thing — the next time I see Tate, I'll be sure to tell him that the French-kissing thing was a lie and that the truth is you're just not ready for that kind of more mature relationship."

"No!" I blurted, so loudly that the librarian shot me a dirty look. "No," I repeated, more quietly this time. "Don't tell Tate anything, okay? I ... I think I just need to think about this for a while."

Darlene shrugged dismissively, then reached for my soggy algebra assignment.

"Please, Darlene," I murmured, resisting the urge to grip her little hand.

"Well," she said, after a long moment of silently copying my algebra answers, "I guess if I told Tate the truth it *would* make you sound like an inexperienced little girl ..."

I felt my face grow hot.

"... and I suppose we wouldn't want that," she continued. Then she paused. "I'm sorry, what did you say your friend's name was?" she asked, looking up from her incomplete assignment as though this was the answer to question number seven.

"Ricky," I said. "I've known him for ages. I could even put in a good word for you with him. If you want, I mean," I added hastily, wondering if I'd gone too far.

In response, Darlene just smiled.

ʚ̃ʚ̃ʚ̃

I spent the afternoon thinking about what Darlene had told Tate about me, and wondering if there was any way I could get her to untell it without making me look like a big stupid dweeb. It wasn't that I was afraid of having a more mature relationship with Tate — in fact, I'd imagined it oodles of times: Tate and I walking hand in hand through a sun-dappled forest; Tate and I waltzing barefoot in the grass by the light of a harvest moon; Tate and I screaming down the highway in his cherry red Corvette convertible. The problem was that Imaginary Me was much cooler than Actual Me, and, in romantic situations involving slimy tongues, much less likely to throw up.

Besides, it was degrading to think of Tate thinking of me like that, and if it ever got back to Ricky that I'd allowed everyone to believe I'd swapped gob with him on countless occasions, it would make me look like a complete nutter.

That night, I called Holly to see what she thought I should do. Tabitha picked up on the first ring and, when she heard it was me, pretended to be Holly. I did a piercing, two-finger whistle into the receiver and then waited patiently for the real Holly to come to the phone. When she did, I told her the whole story.

"But I don't get it," she said at last. "Didn't you explain to Darlene that you've never even kissed a boy?"

I was surprised — and kind of hurt — by the fact that she'd brought up the delicate subject of my lack of experience. We'd both been in the same boat until last summer, when she'd necked with some dude named Leroy in the sand dunes during a family day trip to Grand Beach. Although I'd been truly excited for her having achieved Post-First-Kiss Status, there'd always been an unspoken understanding between us that it had resulted in me feeling a little left behind.

"So what if I've never kissed anyone?" I said gruffly. "How hard could it possibly be?"

Even as I said it, I felt the bottom drop out of my stomach at the thought of Tate's eager lips pressed firmly against mine — his mouth slowly opening, his warm, slippery tongue searching ...

"Not very hard," conceded Holly as I leaned over and put my head between my knees. "Unless you're nervous, of course. If you're nervous, there's a good chance you'll forget to relax your lips."

"There is?" I asked faintly, flopping backward onto my bed.

"Uh-huh," said Holly. "Plus, nervousness can make your tongue do weird things. Like, instead of calmly wiggling around, it might try to hide against the back of your throat, or else it might stiffen up and start jabbing into the guy's mouth like it's trying to win an ultimate fighting cage match with his tongue or something."

I wondered if I was going to throw up.

"So, are you going to talk to Darlene?" asked Holly.

"About what?" I asked confusedly, wondering if I'd ever be able to stave off the dry heaves long enough to French-kiss *anybody.*

"About the lie she told Tate," said Holly. "It would be just like him to blab it all over school, you know."

"It would not," I retorted. "For your information, Darlene said Tate was completely awestruck when she told him I was experienced. She said she'd never heard him speak about me with such admiration and respect!"

"Because he thought you let Rick put his tongue in your mouth," said Holly.

"Exactly!" I said, preparing to defend my ridiculous lie to the death.

"*Would* you let Rick put his tongue in your mouth?" she asked suddenly.

Her question caught me so off-guard that I rolled off the edge of the bed and landed with a thud on the dusty hardwood floor. As I lay flat on my back trying to catch my breath, I remembered the bristles I'd seen poking out of Ricky's chin, and I tried to imagine how they'd feel scraping up against my own chin as he loomed over me trying to shove his strong, masculine tongue halfway down to my kidneys ...

"I don't think so," I said, struggling to control my gag reflex. "Anyway, I'm pretty sure Darlene likes him."

"Darlene?" said Holly, accidentally swallowing the gum she'd been loudly chewing since the beginning of our conversation. "Are you sure?"

"Pretty sure," I said. "She hasn't come right out and said it or anything, but the other day, when she was watching him in the cafeteria, you could have driven a ten-ton truck into her mouth with room to spare."

"I hadn't noticed," murmured Holly. "Do you think he likes her?"

"Are you kidding me?" I hooted. "He barely even said *hello* to her! Which is too bad, of course," I added hastily, not wanting to sound unkind. "But a person can't help the way he feels."

"Or the way she feels," added Holly, with feeling.

"Amen to that," I said, thinking of the long, lonely hours I'd spent pining for Tate. "Anyway, I've got to go check my e-mails now. I entered another one of Lorenzo's contests and I'm expecting a reply any day."

"Another contest, eh?" she said, clacking a fresh piece of gum in my ear. I could hear the grin in her voice. "What's this one for? A tube of the hair-removal cream he uses on his chest?"

"He does *not* use hair removal cream on his chest," I clucked.

"You're right," she agreed. "To get it that smooth, he probably has to wax."

"For your information," I said, "the winner of *this* contest gets to bake with Lorenzo on TV."

"Really?" said Holly, sounding genuinely impressed. "So,

you mean, you'd actually get to meet the guy?"

"Not just meet him," I corrected. "Bake with him."

"Oooh," she breathed. "That's like your dream come true!"

I pictured my face on the cover of *Baker's Digest Magazine* next to a quote from Lorenzo LaRue expressing his amazement at the unprecedented speed with which I'd rocketed to the top of the baking world and commenting on the fact that I was heartbreakingly beautiful, inside and out.

"Not exactly my dream come true," I said with a smile, "but definitely a step in the right direction."

෴

Unfortunately, there was no e-mail from Lorenzo that day, or any other day that week. At first, I figured it was just too early to be looking for results, but then on Wednesday Nana received the bad news that she'd lost. After that I didn't know what to think.

By Friday evening, I was a nervous wreck, but I put it out of my mind in order to get ready for the pre-winter-carnival party I was having. That morning, I'd invited Holly, Sharon, Jody and *Darlene* over to my place to hang out before we headed to the community club to watch Ricky's band play. I was nervous, at first — especially since our apartment was nothing compared to Darlene's gigantic house — but by time the girls had all piled into our little kitchen, I was surprised by how comfortable it felt. For dinner, my dad brought up stacks of thick cheeseburgers fresh from Marguerite's griddle, baskets of homemade fries and ice-cream floats in frosty mugs. Darlene said her stomach would never be able tolerate such rich, greasy food, but Sharon and Jody wolfed back so much, so fast, that a humbled Rory quietly bowed his head out of respect for their awesome powers of consumption.

After dinner, the girls and I pulled on our jackets and tumbled out onto the street in front of the café. In no time we were at the community club, gorging ourselves on candy floss and giant pretzels while we wandered up and down the noisy, crowded aisles playing cheap carnival games. I'd just picked from a white laundry tub of murky water a floating duck with the winning number 3 written on its underbelly, when a voice on the loudspeaker announced that live entertainment was now being offered in the hall next door. Snatching my prize (a purple velvet pencil) from the leering creep behind the table, I hurriedly followed the girls into the hall. As we pushed our way past the adults waiting to get into the dreary indoor beer garden, I could feel my excitement growing. I'd never been to a concert before — and certainly not to one where I'd been *personally* invited by the lead singer.

"Have you had a chance to talk to him for me?" murmured Darlene as we ran to the front of the stage and stared up at Ricky, who smiled down at us before turning to say something to his drummer.

I hadn't had a chance to talk to Ricky about Darlene or anything else, but before I could tell her this, Ricky's deep, icky voice boomed out of the speaker beside us.

Only it didn't sound icky anymore.

In fact, it sounded kind of nice. I looked around at the small crowd that had gathered to hear him sing; I looked over at my friends, who were swaying in time to the music. Then I looked back at the boy I'd once spent the night alone with in a two-man tent under the apple tree in his mother's backyard, and I remembered how we'd awoken the next morning in time to eat Corn Pops and watch the sun rise.

And my stomach did a funny kind of lurch.

"Is something wrong?" asked Holly, leaning over to shout in my ear but never taking her eyes off Ricky, who looked positively *anguished* as he sang the lyrics to his original composition, "Frying My Heart On the Griddle of Your Love."

"No," I said as I tried unsuccessfully to catch my breath, and also to remember exactly what Tate Jarvis looked like. "I ... I think everything is just fine."

⁄᷐᷐

When the set ended forty-five minutes later, Ricky jumped down off the stage with the agility of a panther and walked right over to where the girls and I were standing. Everybody who'd been watching him perform watched him approach me.

I felt like a star.

"Holy moly, you can really sing," declared Sharon, giving Ricky a slug in the arm.

"Thanks," he mumbled, mopping the sweat from his forehead with the grungy white towel that hung around his neck. Turning toward me, he ducked his head at Holly — who was glued to my side — and murmured, "So, um, Francie ..."

"Darlene here can really sing, too," interrupted Sharon, putting Darlene in an exuberant headlock.

"Really?" said Ricky, looking closely at Darlene for the first time.

"Really!" said Sharon heartily. "She can belt out the Hokey Pokey like nobody's business. You should let her perform with your band sometime. I bet she'd really rock."

"I bet she would," said Ricky.

I bet Sharon would have been really surprised to find Ricky's sweaty towel stuffed into her big fat mouth, but before I could find out if I was right, Ricky put his arm around my shoulder and nervously asked if he could speak to me in private. I could feel the heat from his skin through my blouse, and as he led me backstage, I frantically tried to remember everything Holly had told me about French kissing.

"So, Francie ..." Ricky said tentatively as he turned to face me.

"Yes, Rick?" I said quickly, my heart pounding so hard I

could hardly hear myself speak. This was all happening so fast my head felt like it was spinning. Could I really go through with this? Could I actually act on my sudden feelings for Ricky and pretend that all those months I'd carried a torch for Tate meant nothing? Could I ignore my sort-of promise to Darlene to use my position of influence to help her get closer to Ricky? Could I somehow keep myself from power-puking cheeseburger and ice-cream soda all over Ricky at the first slithery sign of his slimy tongue?

Yes, yes I could! I thought wildly as I tilted my head slightly in order to give Ricky easier access to my lips.

Ricky stared at my mouth. "Francie, do you remember that time I covered for you at the café?" he asked.

"Of course," I murmured, slurring slightly because I was trying so hard to keep my lips relaxed.

"And do you remember how we agreed that you owed me one?"

"Uh-huh," I breathed, wondering if I should stand on my tiptoes so he wouldn't have to lean down so far.

"Okay, well, I was wondering if you'd be willing to ... I mean, if you'd consider ... Could you tell me if your friend has ever mentioned me?" he finally blurted.

I gazed at him dreamily through half-closed eyes. "What?" I said at last.

"Your friend," said Ricky. "Has she ever mentioned me?"

For a minute I just stared at him. Then, unable to keep the emotion out of my voice, I cried, "You like *Darlene?*"

"Who? Oh. No," said Ricky with a strained chuckle. "The other one. The one with the big ... um ... eyes," he added, blushing so hard that Marguerite could have fried an egg on his forehead.

"Holly?" I whispered, my mouth dropping open. "You like *Holly?*"

Ricky nodded.

"You like Holly," I repeated.

Ricky nodded again.

"My best friend — Holly," I persisted.

"That's right."

Feeling weak with shock, I leaned heavily on a nearby microphone stand, which promptly collapsed, sending high-pitched feedback echoing through the hall. Ricky instantly leaped to my aid and helped me to my feet with a strong, *friendly* hand.

I cringed, feeling like a fool for ever having thought his tender touches meant anything more than that.

"Listen," he said hastily. "If she doesn't like me, just say so, okay? I can take it. I swear."

He gritted his teeth as though preparing to take the lash against his bare skin. I thought about how it had felt to have everyone believe that *I* was the object of his affection, and how easy it would be to nip this thing in the bud without anyone ever being the wiser.

Then I thought about how many years Ricky and I had been friends before he'd turned into *Rick*. I thought about how he'd run for a warm paper towel when I'd squirted juice in my eye, and how gently he'd held my head against his revolting crotch while ministering to me.

He deserved better than that from me.

And come to think of it, so did Holly.

"I really don't know if Holly likes you, Ricky," I finally mumbled as I tried to conjure up an image of the temporarily abandoned Tate and me locked in a passionate (though possibly tongueless) embrace. "But I'll do what I can to find out."

10. Expect the Unexpected

I like my women the way I like my Bundt cake: simple and well rounded, with an empty space in the middle into which I can insert my love.

From Life in the Emotional Bundt Pan *by Lorenzo LaRue*

Holly and Darlene were both staring at me intently as I emerged from backstage with Ricky. My heart ached with the knowledge that he liked Holly instead of me. I was happy for her, of course, but she already had guys who liked her. I mean, Randy Newton was reduced to the mental capacity of an old sock every time she accidentally dropped a popcorn twist down the front of her shirt. She didn't need another admirer.

I did.

Ricky gave me a gentle nudge, jostling me back to reality. Gazing up into his dark, familiar eyes, I nodded imperceptibly, then turned back to the girls, trying to think of a way to first separate Holly from the group in order to ask her if she liked Ricky — and then to break the news to Darlene that the heart of the boy of her dreams belonged to someone else.

Not me.

Before I could think of anything clever on either front, however, a noise erupted behind us. It sounded as though someone small and fierce was systematically and unapologetically fighting his way upstream through the crowd of people that was headed back toward the carnival.

Just as I turned to check it out, Harold Horvath burst into the open, not twenty feet from where I was standing. Horrified, I quickly turned back around again, but it was too late. Harold had seen me. And with a slow, sultry smile he'd begun to purposefully strut in my direction.

"Hey, do you know that guy?" asked Jody loudly, pointing at Harold with an outstretched arm.

My tongue felt like a giant lump of raw liver. "Ugh ..." I said thickly as Harold Horvath bore down on us.

He came to an abrupt stop directly in front of me and inhaled deeply.

"Ah! It *is* you!" he breathed, languorously smoothing the broad collar of his red satin shirt. "I thought it was you. You remember me, of course. I'm Harold Horvath! We shared a beautiful slow dance last weekend, and then, right after you told that girl to go away" — he flapped his fingers dismissively toward Darlene — "you told me to go away, too. It was very unkind of you and it really hurt my feelings but I've decided to forgive you."

I gaped at him. Sharon and Jody grinned broadly; Ricky leaned over and whispered something into Holly's ear. Darlene folded her arms across her chest.

"I know what you're thinking," continued Harold, ignoring them all in favor of giving his hair a careful comb through. "You're thinking you can't believe I'm willing to give you a second chance after the way you treated me. What can I say? The heart wants what the heart wants, I suppose. What is your name anyway?"

"Francie Freewater," said Jody, elbowing Sharon in the side hard enough to crack ribs. "That's Freewater. F-R-E-E-W-A-T-E-R. It's in the book."

"Francie Freewater." Harold rolled my name around his mouth like a piece of succulent hard candy. "I like it. It suits you. Just like those furry shoes you were wearing at the dance. Where are they, by the way?" he asked, staring down at my purple high-top sneakers with a look of intense disappointment on his face.

"She loaned them to me," said Holly, daintily extending her foot forward.

"They look great on you," blurted Ricky.

Out of the corner of my eye, I saw Darlene's lips tighten.

"They looked great on *her,*" interrupted Harold, staring up at me with a hungry look in his eyes. "I'm not keen on the style myself, but I liked the way they made her look like an Amazon." He slid his cool fingers up and down my bare hand until I recovered my stunned senses sufficiently to jerk away from him. "I know some guys have a problem dating women who are taller than they are, but I like it. The taller the better, I say! Say, speaking of dating, would you like to go to a movie with me sometime, Francie?"

Holly's mouth dropped open. Jody's eyes bulged so far out of their sockets I thought they might fall right out of her head. Sharon gasped, "Holy moly!" and, in a calculated theatrical swoon, Darlene collapsed against Ricky.

Ignoring them all, I smiled uncomfortably at Harold. "Uh, I'm sorry but —"

"Before you answer," he interrupted, "let me just say this: it's only a movie, okay? Try not to overanalyze it. It's just two people sitting together sharing a tub of trans-fat-saturated popcorn and enjoying a little overprocessed, formulaic big-studio entertainment."

"I know, but —"

"I'll even let you pick the movie," he said.

"Well, I —"

"Unless, of course, you don't *like* going to the movies."

If I thought it would have gotten rid of him, I would have claimed I didn't like breathing, but I just knew that any attempt to directly reject this guy was doomed to failure. So instead I settled for clasping my hands hopefully to my chest and giving him a sympathetic look that clearly said that although I did, in fact, like going to the movies, unhappily I just wasn't interested in going with him.

"Oh, I get it," said Harold morosely as he stared fixedly at my clasped hands. "You *do* like going to the movies — you just aren't interested in going with *me.*"

"No!" I blurted, horrified at having the heartless truth flung back in my face. "It's not that!"

Harold started chuckling. "I didn't really think it was," he admitted, running his index fingers along his upper lip as though smoothing an invisible mustache. "How could it be? You hardly know me!"

I was trapped, and unfortunately it wasn't the kind of trap I could escape by chewing my own arm off. Holly gave me the kind of bleak, supportive smile reserved for prisoners being carted off to their own public executions.

Harold eyed the exchange with keen interest.

"Oh, wait," he said suddenly, holding up his hand so fast his poufy satin sleeves billowed behind him. "I see what's going on here!"

"You do?" I blinked.

"Oh, *yes*," he breathed, smoothing his imaginary mustache again. "You don't know me, Francie, and that makes you nervous. Sure, we pressed our young bodies together during one magical slow dance, but that was just animal instincts taking over and we both know it. Technically, I'm a stranger, and while that compels you to view me as dangerous and attractive, it also leaves you feeling just a bit uncomfortable." Harold reached for my hand. "There's no need to look to your friends for support, Francie, because the last thing in the world I want is for you to feel uncomfortable." His voice turned husky. "When we sit together in the darkened theater, I want you to feel —"

"ENOUGH!" I shrieked. Was he trying to *kill* me?

"So you'll go to a movie with me?" he asked.

Mortified beyond words and on the brink of nervous collapse, I nodded.

Harold looked like the cat that swallowed the canary. "All right, then," he purred as he whipped a fancy silver pen and a little black book out of the back pocket of his skintight black leather pants. "Give me your phone number and I'll call you to make arrangements."

I'd never before given out my phone number to a guy for the purposes of setting up a date, so I felt very self-conscious when Harold asked me to speak up, and then again when he loudly repeated the number back to me to make sure he'd recorded it correctly. Harold, on the other hand, didn't seem the least bit flustered by the situation, and as he strutted off into the night whistling "Stairway to Heaven" at the top of his lungs, I found myself wondering exactly how old he really was, and just how often he'd done this sort of thing before.

✐✐✐

After he was gone, Darlene warmly congratulated me on my ability to look past appearances and date whomever I pleased no matter what other people might think. Sharon shared her opinion that Harold was probably going to try to feel me up in the movie theater, and Jody turned away from me, wrapped her long arms around her torso and started groping her own back and moaning in a shockingly realistic impression of two people making out. Trying not to let any of them see the uncontrollable twitch that had suddenly developed in my left eyelid, I grabbed Holly by the arm, dragged her into a nearby portable toilet and locked the door behind us.

"Look at you!" she cried, shoving me with such force that I slammed against the urinal on the side wall and nearly toppled over the entire toilet. "First you go backstage with Rick, then that little guy appears from out of nowhere and practically begs you to go out with him. You are unbelievable!"

"Harold didn't beg," I said, strangely certain he'd never begged for anything in his life. "And as far as Ricky goes ..."

I looked at Holly. She was smiling eagerly in anticipation of hearing that Ricky and I had swapped spit behind the amplifiers, but I noticed that her teeth were gritted as though she was preparing to take the lash against her bare skin.

"He took me backstage to tell me that he likes you," I said simply.

Holly's mouth dropped open as though on greased hinges, and her eyes got very large. "He likes *me?*" she squeaked in the tiniest voice I'd ever heard her use.

"That's right."

"Oh," she said, the word coming out as hardly more than a puff of air.

She sagged against the green plastic wall of the portable toilet, and for a moment, neither of us said anything. Then I said, "So? Do you like him?"

In the weird green light of the toilet, I watched as she clasped her hands to her chest in a gesture that was almost as hopeful as the one I'd used to try to weasel out of going to the movies with Harold.

"I ... I don't know what to say, Francie. I mean, I thought Rick liked *you.*"

"I didn't," I declared, even though I so *totally* did. "I said all along we were just friends."

"Yes, you did say that," said Holly with a teeny smile.

"Which means if you ... you know ... like him, then ..." I took a big gulp of air as an image of tall, tender, sweaty, hairy Ricky singing love songs to Holly flashed through my mind. "Then you should definitely go for it."

Holly bit her lower lip but didn't say anything.

"Seriously," I insisted. "Don't be thinking I'm harboring secret feelings for Ricky or anything crazy like that, because I'm not. I've got Tate Jarvis, remember?"

"I remember," said Holly, nodding slowly. "But I also remember you once told Darlene you didn't have feelings for Tate even though you really did and it caused a big ugly mess."

"Oh, please." I rolled my eyes. "That situation was *nothing* like this one. You and Ricky are my friends. The only thing in the world I want more than to see the two of you happy is to wake up one day and find Tate Jarvis and Lorenzo LaRue dueling for my love on a windswept cliff overlooking the crashing waves of an angry sea."

"Really?" said Holly.

"Well, that and to have my own syndicated baking program in the coveted four-to-six P.M. time slot with fifty percent of the profits from all related merchandise being deposited directly into one of my many offshore bank accounts," I grinned.

Holly laughed aloud and then abruptly covered her mouth with both hands.

"Oh, Francie!" she whispered, shaking her head from side to side. "You don't know what it means to me to hear that you feel this way! The truth is ever since we started Performance Band rehearsals, I've liked Rick so much that I've hardly been able to think straight when he's around. And just now? When you told me he liked me? I swear on my guinea pig Petunia's grave I thought I was going to have a heart attack."

"You did?" I gasped.

"Yes!" she cried, before sighing as though it would have been a marvelous way to die, indeed.

"Holly, I had no idea you felt this way," I said, shaking my head. "How come you never said anything?"

"Because you had dibs on Rick and I respected that," she explained solemnly.

"But ... but what if I'd suddenly decided I liked him as more than a friend? What if he'd suddenly decided he liked me as more than a friend?" I flung my hands into the air. *"What if we'd suddenly started dating?"*

"Well, then, I guess I'd have had to bury my feelings forever," she shrugged.

We were silent for a moment, each of us thinking about how tragic it would have been for Holly if Ricky hadn't been mature enough to take me aside and ask me if I thought she liked him. Someone pounded on the door and shouted for us to hurry up; I hollered that this wasn't Communist China and that we were free to spend the entire evening in the portable toilet if we wished. Then I gave the door a resounding kick to emphasize my devotion to democracy, and turned to Holly.

"You really would have made a sacrifice like that for me?" I asked.

"Yes," she said.

"Even though it would have broken your heart?"

"Absolutely."

"And you never would have let on how much you'd suffered on my behalf?"

"That's right."

"But *why?*" I asked, knowing the answer but suddenly wanting to hear her say it.

"Because I'm your best friend, silly!" grinned Holly, flinging her arms around me. "And that's what best friends do!"

✐✐✐

When we finally emerged from the portable toilet, we found Darlene and Ricky sitting side by side on the stage. Darlene had her little hand on his knee and even from a distance I could tell she'd turned on the charm full blast. Ricky was hunched over, listening attentively to whatever she was chattering about, but the minute he spotted Holly — who was practically floating with happiness — he sat up very straight, slid off the stage and started toward us. Darlene seemed so startled and hurt by the speed with which she'd been abandoned that I felt almost as sorry for her as I'd felt for myself on the many occasions Tate Jarvis had snubbed me. So, after giving Ricky a knowing smile that caused him to immediately trip over his own feet, I left him and Holly to make awkward, stilted conversation together and headed over to lend moral support to Darlene.

Strangely, however, by the time I reached her, Darlene seemed to have recovered completely.

"There you are!" she said brightly, hopping down from the stage. "Come on, let's go find Sharon and Jody! They took off in search of the Mr. Juicy hot-dog man about ten minutes ago and I've been bored silly sitting here waiting for you to get back."

It was such a pathetic lie that I felt sorry for her all over again. But she was smiling in such a dementedly perky manner that I didn't know what to say. I *wanted* to comfort her, and to explain that I'd in no way used my influence with Ricky to get him to like Holly instead of her. It's what I would have done for Holly if the situation had been reversed.

But it wasn't reversed, and Darlene wasn't Holly, and I knew in my gut that if I did anything other than pretend that Ricky had just dropped off the face of the earth, Darlene would give me a shoulder so cold I'd have icicles dripping from the tip of my nose.

Which is why, when she gave me a friendly punch with her wee fist and asked what I was waiting for, I said, "Nothing at all, Darlene. Let's go."

Over the next few hours, I caught only passing glimpses of Holly, but Darlene and I were having such a great time that, to be honest, I hardly missed her. After abandoning our search for Sharon and Jody, we spent a while hanging around with a group of older kids from school who all seemed to know Darlene and who treated us not like puny little freshmen but like actual equals. Then Darlene pulled a twenty-dollar bill out of her pocket and suggested we go spend a little of her dad's hard-earned money. I was reluctant at first — because it didn't seem right to spend money that didn't belong to me — but Darlene insisted that she had a right to spend her money any way she pleased, and that hanging out with someone who was broke was no fun at all, so eventually I gave in and for the next two hours, we ate caramel apples and popcorn and played so many carnival games we each ended up with enough velvet pencils to trade up for stuffed frogs.

When it was time to leave, Holly found me and excitedly whispered in my ear that Ricky was going to walk her home, so Darlene and I were left to walk by ourselves. The night was cold and the dark was so deep that the stars in the sky stood out in sharp relief. I was about to tell Darlene how much I loved the sound of the hard-packed snow crunching beneath my sneakers when she suddenly stopped and turned to face me.

"You once asked me about my mother," she said.

Blinking in surprise, I nodded.

"She used to take me to the grocery store and let me hang out in the floral department while she did the shopping. I loved to smell the flowers, you see," she said in a low, quivery voice. "Anyway, one day, exactly two weeks before my eighth birthday, she never came back for me. I waited next to a bucket of fresh-cut lilacs for almost four hours before anyone noticed I was alone. Later, a review of the security tapes revealed that after dropping me off in the floral department that day, my mother had walked out the front door of the store without so much as a glance in my direction. I haven't seen or heard from her since."

I gaped at Darlene, not knowing what to say.

"You're my friend, Francie," she said softly, putting her little gloved hand on the sleeve of my bulky ski jacket. "I just thought you ought to know."

❧

The next day, after carefully dead-bolting the front door in case Marguerite decided to give someone else permission to break into the apartment and spy on me while I was baking, I dragged Rory to his place of honor in front of the counter, hit the music and threw myself into my work. I had a lot to do — I'd promised to bake an extra batch of white chocolate raspberry scones for Mrs. Watson to take to her niece's baby shower, and my regulars were eagerly anticipating the introduction of my new cranberry lemon muffins. I was still selling out every weekend, so it's not like I needed to keep introducing new products — I was just so full of ideas I couldn't seem to help myself.

Rory seemed a little listless at first — no doubt feeling the aftereffects of having escaped from his cage the day before and eaten Malibu Barbie's hair, three shoelaces and the left sleeve of my mother's favorite blouse before being recaptured — but he perked right up when he saw me accidentally drop a small ball of peanut butter cookie dough on the floor.

"Oh, I'm sorry, Rory. I'd like to let you have it, but I can't," I said regretfully as I picked it up and solemnly carried it over to the garbage pail.

"I'D LIKE TO LET YOU HAVE IT!" he screeched, beating his wings against the cage in a desperate attempt to get at the dough ball — and me.

"It's a shame, really," I sighed. "Such a waste of a perfectly good blob of dough. But I've decided not to feed you any treats for the next little while." I paused to let this terrible news sink in before continuing. "Just so you know, my decision has nothing to do with the fact that you scalped Malibu Barbie and everything to do with the fact that I would never forgive myself if I allowed you to eat something that could make you sick."

Slowly, I opened the lid of the garbage pail. Rory carried on as though I was about to drop his best friend into a vat of boiling oil.

Then the phone rang.

My heart gave a giant thud. I'd been waiting all morning for Harold Horvath to call — not because I *wanted* him to, of course, but because I wanted to get the ordeal over with. Tossing the dough ball at Rory in order to shut him up, I turned off the music and hurried to the phone.

"Yes?" I asked, nervously wiping my sweaty palms on my apron.

"Francie?"

"Oh," I said, feeling an unexpected pang of disappointment. "Hello, Darlene."

"What are you doing?" she asked.

"Nothing much," I said. Last night, as I'd lain in bed, I'd thought of some nice, supportive things I could have said in response to Darlene's shocking account of how her mother had abandoned her. On the phone now, however, she sounded so completely different from the quiet, emotional girl who'd opened up to me the night before that I decided to keep my comforting words to myself.

"Do you want to come over?" she said.

"You mean now?" I asked, looking around my messy kitchen.

"No, two weeks from now, dummy. Of course, now! I got a new classic rock CD for my karaoke machine and there's a song I think you'd be just perfect for. Afterward, my dad said he'd take us out to lunch somewhere nice."

I glanced at the old cuckoo clock that hung above the kitchen sink. I had at least four hours of work ahead of me, and that was assuming I got the cranberry lemon muffins right on the first try. Besides that, there was the guest spot on Lorenzo to rehearse for. I hadn't received word that I'd won, but I hadn't received word that I *hadn't* won, either, and I'd decided that assuming the worst was a waste of mental energy. I mean, for all I knew, Lorenzo had been so touched by my submission that he'd been spending every hour of every day agonizing over the perfect response. I pictured my darling slumped over the keyboard, battered by exhaustion, despairing of ever finding exactly the right words to express the depth of his love for me and my recipes.

"It sounds great, Darlene," I said slowly. "Only —"

"Oh, wait," she interrupted. "I forgot. You get off on spending your weekends slaving over a hot stove."

"I do not," I said, feeling my face grow warm. "I just ... it's just something I do for spending money."

"Whatever. It's weird," she said. "Couldn't you skip it just this one time? I really want you to come over. It would be fun."

"I know, but —"

"Did I mention I want to discuss the Tate Jarvis situation with you? I have an idea that could take things to a whole new level."

For some reason, I didn't like the sound of that. "It doesn't have anything to do with me being a champion French kisser, does it?" I asked worriedly.

"As a matter of fact, it does," she laughed.

I frowned. "I don't know, Darlene. I've been doing a lot of thinking about that whole thing and I'm sorry, but it just doesn't feel right. Plus, Holly thinks Tate is probably going to tell everybody what you told him, and if he does I'm going to look like a complete idiot — or worse."

"Well, I don't know what business Holly has judging *you*," said Darlene severely. "What do you think she and that overgrown hairball friend of yours were doing last night when they took off to be alone together? *Praying?*" Darlene snorted. "Here's a news flash for you, Francie: they most definitely were not. Now, do you want to warm up the cold soup with Tate, or do you want to be stuck with guys like Harvey for the rest of your life?"

"His name is Harold."

"Whatever," she snapped. "Are you coming over, or are you so stuck on what other people think of you that you're willing to give up a chance to get Tate — the guy you supposedly care about — to finally see you as something other than the nerdy little twerp who sits next to him in chemistry class?"

When she put it that way, refusing to at least *listen* to her plan sounded almost selfish on my part. Slowly, I reached up and pulled off my baker's hat.

"I ... I guess I'm coming over," I said as I told myself I could finish my baking later. "I'll be there in half an hour."

☙☙☙

Darlene's plan was ridiculous and degrading and totally out of the question, but I told her I'd think about it so as not to seem ungrateful and nerdy and stuck on what other people thought of me. After that, it was really fun hanging out with her. We discovered that we had identical hairlines, and also that our mothers' maiden names both started with the letter *M*. Her dad insisted that I call him Gary, and Darlene set up a video camera in front of the karaoke machine so we could videotape ourselves singing. I sounded awful and looked like I'd been dead for three days, but Darlene said I did much better than Holly had done her first time and that cheered me a little, even though I knew it shouldn't.

After we got bored with singing, we went for a late lunch with *Gary* at a restaurant that was so fine and fancy that I felt a twinge of embarrassment when I recalled Darlene's comments about the rich, greasy food my parents served at our little café. Gary sat by himself working on his laptop computer and making phone calls while Darlene and I sat in a booth and ordered appetizers and frothy drinks in sugar-rimmed glasses. I ate and drank so much that by the time I got home I felt too sick to even think about baking, so I set my alarm for five o'clock the next morning. Unfortunately, when I got up I was so tired I dozed off after putting my cranberry lemon muffins into the oven and didn't wake up until the smoke detector started wailing, and this left me feeling so jangled that I forgot to put flour in my cheesecakes and they didn't set properly. In the end, all I managed to get done in time for the café opening were Mrs. Watson's scones and one sorry-looking batch of cookies. I'd never before had such a measly product offering, and I was so embarrassed by it that I couldn't bear the idea of having to face my regular customers. So, tiptoeing down to the café kitchen, I shoved the half-filled baking tray at my father and whispered that he should tell anyone who asked that I'd been temporarily stricken with a grotesquely disfiguring life-threatening illness. Then, before he could say a word, I fled back up to the apartment, climbed into his recliner and watched Lorenzo LaRue reruns until I was sure that the last of my disappointed regulars had departed.

11. Date with Destiny

*You are so wise when it comes to baking and life that I am
pretty sure I would find you inspiring even if you weren't
good-looking.*

**From Francie Freewater's submission to Lorenzo LaRue's
"Sinfully Yours" Contest**

The following Monday, the percussion section was allowed
to rehearse with the rest of the Performance Band for the
first time since our disastrous debut. When I entered the
band room, the first person I saw was Ricky. He was
sprawled in a chair near the back of the woodwind section,
wearing his black leather jacket and a pair of sloppily laced
combat boots. He looked cuter than I'd ever seen him look,
and I felt a pang of regret that lingered even after he smiled
and waved at me in front of the entire band. His attention
didn't mean anything anymore.

I was just a friend.

He belonged to Holly.

At least, I assumed he belonged to her. I hadn't spoken
with her in private since Friday night — she'd called on
Saturday when I was out with Darlene, and every time I'd
tried to call her back after that the line had been busy. I'd
been hoping to talk to her on the bus or at school, but
Darlene hadn't given us a moment alone together and I
hadn't wanted to bring up the subject of Ricky in front of her.

Tapping her tiny conductor's baton against a metal music
stand, Mrs. C called the Performance Band rehearsal to
order. The first thing she did was ask the rest of the band to
give the percussion section a warm welcome back. Holly
grinned over at me and clapped with such enthusiasm that
her whole body started to jiggle, causing Randy Newton to
very nearly put his fist through his tympani drum. The next
thing Mrs. C did was tell the class that Mr. Simmons had

kindly agreed to help chaperone the band trip to Portage la Prairie. At this news, I let out such a strangled cry of protest that Sharon immediately threw down her gong mallet and tried to give me the Heimlich maneuver.

"Everything all right, Francie?" asked Mrs. C, raising her eyebrows at me.

After wriggling out of the death grip Sharon had on my torso, I gave Mrs. C a rather breathless thumbs-up and indicated that she should feel free to continue.

Smiling, she made her final announcement. "As you all know, I've been considering asking one or two of our more exceptional student musicians to perform solo pieces at the festival."

I felt a thrill of excitement when Mrs. C said this. I was not so deluded as to think that she might be talking about me or any of the other worms in the lowly percussion group, but I knew that she could be talking about Holly. Next to Ricky, no one tried harder in band than she did.

Crossing my legs, my arms, the fingers on both hands and all of the toes I could manage inside the cramped, sweaty canvas of my dirty purple high-tops, I looked toward the woodwind section, hoping to catch Holly's eye so that I could let her know how hard I was rooting for her.

Unfortunately, she was looking behind her.

At Ricky.

Luckily, before this fact had a chance to really sink in and hurt my feelings, Mrs. C announced that Holly — and Holly alone! — had been selected to perform a solo piece at the festival.

I was so proud and happy that I gave a whoop of laughter, snatched up my cymbals and crashed them together as hard as I could, over and over again. Inspired by my enthusiasm, Jody let loose on the snare drum and Sharon pounded on the gong and rolled her eyes as though she was only moments away from ripping the heart out of a live victim. Randy Newton was the only percussionist who didn't respond.

And I think that's because when Holly leaped up with excitement, the top two buttons of her blouse popped open, accidentally revealing the lace of her lovely tea-colored bra and rendering Randy incapable of doing anything much beyond breathing.

And maybe, I thought as I watched his entire face turn a rather alarming shade of purple, *not even that.*

◦◦◦

After rehearsal was over and I'd finished jumping up and down being excited with Holly, I headed for home. When I got there, I found Nana waiting for me at the door of the apartment. In one hand she was holding Rory, and in the other hand she was holding a letter.

A letter!

"Special Delivery," she informed me. "From Lorenzo LaRue Productions. Rory and I have been waiting half the afternoon to find out what's inside, haven't we, Rory?"

"HALF THE AFTERNOON," he confirmed, trying to peck her hand.

Without taking my eyes off the oversized envelope, I dumped my knapsack on the floor and shrugged out of my jacket.

"Who is it for?" I asked tentatively.

"The Queen of England," replied Nana. "Can you believe they delivered it here by accident? My goodness, but someone down at the post office is going to have some explaining to do."

"I just meant ... are you sure it's for me?"

"Of course I'm sure it's for you," she cried, swatting me over the head with it. "Don't just stand there. Open it!"

"OPEN IT! OPEN IT!" cried Rory, struggling to free himself of Nana's grasp.

With shaking hands I took the envelope from Nana and walked over to the couch. Pushing some old newspapers to the floor, I slowly sank down. For a moment, I just sat there, unable to believe what I was holding in my hands. Then, almost without meaning to, I ripped open the envelope and snatched out the letter inside.

"Well? Well?" asked Nana anxiously, squinting as though it might help her read the letter upside down from across the room. "What does it say?"

Wordlessly, I handed it to her.

Dear Ms. Freewater,

I am delighted to inform you that you were one of just ten finalists for our Winnipeg contest! Unfortunately, you didn't win.

Normally, we would have been pleased to provide you with two tickets to our studio audience as a consolation prize. However, due to an unfortunate capacity miscalculation by our staff, we have no seats left for the Winnipeg show. Instead, please find enclosed a Lorenzo LaRue desktop photo calendar, coupons for the "Sinfully Yours" Strawberry Cream Hazelnut Meal Replacement Bar, and an information pamphlet regarding Lorenzo's current cross-country tour, should you wish to resubmit your essay for consideration in a different locale.

Lorenzo asked me to thank you for taking the time to enter his contest, and to remind you that in the great cheesecake of life, dreams are the flour that holds it all together.

Sincerely,
L. Barnes (BA, MBA) President, Lorenzo LaRue Incorporated,
Executive Producer, "Getting Baked with Lorenzo"

"One of just ten finalists," said Nana, eyeing me carefully. "That's pretty good, don't you think?"

"What's so good about it?" I retorted darkly. "The fact that I don't get to meet Lorenzo or the fact that I don't get to bake on TV?"

"The fact that out of all the people who entered the

contest, your entry was one of the very best," said Nana mildly. "Why, for all we know, you came in second place."

"Second place is nothing more than the first *loser,* Nana," I said, flopping over to one side in order to bury my face in the couch cushions. "So, whoopee! Congratulations to me. I'm king of the losers."

Nana started to say something, but as she did, Rory chomped down on her thumb so hard she accidentally let go of him. He immediately flew to the top of the dish cupboard across the room and began strutting back and forth.

"I DON'T GET TO MEET LORENZO!" he squawked sarcastically. "I DON'T GET TO BAKE ON TV!"

I sat up and shook my fist at him. "You be quiet!" I hollered.

"Now, now," chided Nana as she attempted to shoo him from the top of the cupboard with a broom. "No need to take your disappointment out on poor Rory."

"POOR RORY!" he sang as he ducked the broom and settled down to eat the leaves of the dusty plastic ivy beside him.

Shaking my head in disgust, I got up, grabbed the phone and headed for my room.

"Francie?" called Nana, just before I shut my door. "Try to remember one thing."

"What's that?"

"I'M KING OF THE LOSERS," declared Rory, puffing out his chest proudly.

"He's *not* king of the losers," said Nana, wagging her finger at him. "And neither are you."

∽∾∾

Flopping down on my bed, I dialed Holly's phone number, eager to share my horribly disappointing news with her. *She* wasn't going to tell me I wasn't a loser. She was going do much, much better than that. She was going to tell me that Lorenzo's people were the losers for not picking me as the winner. In a voice quivering with outrage, she was going to describe how they were going to live to regret letting me slip through their fingers and how someday, when I was rich and famous and powerful and capable of crushing them all, they were going to look back and realize it was the worst mistake of their puny little careers.

I was going to feel like a *winner* by the time Holly got through with me.

Unfortunately, Holly's line was busy, and it stayed busy for so long that I finally decided to call Darlene instead. The instant she picked up the phone she asked me why I was calling.

"Uh ... I don't know," I said lamely. "To talk, I guess."

"Well, something you should know about me, Francie, is that I'm not one of those girls who likes to waste time on the phone talking about nothing at all."

"Oh."

"Plus, I'm kind of busy right now."

"Okay," I said.

As I hung up, I wondered how she could have missed the fact that my voice was practically dripping with despair. With a sigh, I dialed Holly's number again. She answered on the first ring.

"What do you want *now?*" she giggled.

"Huh?" I said.

"Oh, it's you," she laughed. "I'm sorry! Rick and I were talking earlier and neither one of us wanted to be the first to hang up, you know? But then I tricked him into hanging up and he felt so bad that he called right back again, and we'd just hung up from that phone call when you called, which is why I assumed that you were him!"

"Oh," I mumbled. "Well, I'm not."

"I realize that now, silly! Oh, Francie," she sighed. "I never imagined that Rick could be so easy to talk to. And can you believe that I was picked to play a flute solo at the festival? It's like all my dreams are coming true at once."

"It's totally awesome," I agreed, sniffling as I wiped

away the tears that had suddenly begun pouring out of
my eyes.

"Hey, are you crying?" asked Holly in alarm.

"No," I blubbered.

"Yes, you are," she insisted. "What's wrong? Tell me!"

There was nothing in the world I wanted more than to
spill my guts to Holly at that moment (except possibly to
open my front door and find an emotionally ruined Lorenzo
LaRue begging for my forgiveness while smearing handfuls
of melted milk chocolate all over his bare chest). However,
as I opened my mouth to do it, I remembered how she'd
been willing to bury her feelings for Ricky when she thought
I liked him. And I thought about the fact that friends
sometimes make sacrifices for one another. And I realized it
was my turn to do the sacrificing.

"Holly, there *is* something wrong, but I'm not going to tell
you about it right now," I said nobly. "This is your night. You
received a major honor today and also had a terrific time
being goofy on the phone with your new boyfriend. Why
don't we get together for a sleepover Friday night and I can
tell you about it then?"

"I can't," said Holly reluctantly. "Not this Friday."

"Why not?"

"Well ... because Rick already asked me to spend Friday
evening with him."

"Oh," I said as fresh tears began to fall.

Holly spent the next few minutes suggesting alternative
sleepover dates and trying to cajole from me the source of
my grief, but I refused to give an inch. After we hung up, I
took a deep breath and was about to start sobbing my heart
out when the phone rang.

Instantly, my tears vanished. I just knew Holly wouldn't
abandon me in my hour of need!

Laughing, I snatched up the phone and cried, "What do
you want *now*?"

There was a dignified pause.

"What do I want? What do I want?" asked a voice.

The blood drained from my face.

"Why, I want to ask if you'd be willing to accompany me to the movies this Friday night, Francie. And by the way, in case you're wondering — it's me, Harold Horvath!"

⊘⊘⊘

Friday after school, while I was whipping up an easy batch of applesauce muffins to calm my rangy nerves, Nana filled me in on a little family history.

"I remember your mother's first date," she said, feeding a sultana raisin to Rory. "Hair spiked to high heaven, safety pins through his nose. The first thing I said to him when I opened the front door was that if he touched one single hair on my daughter's head, I'd take those safety pins and stick them where the sun don't shine!"

"You did not," I said, licking a dollop of batter off the back of my hand.

Nana chuckled. "No, but I wanted to. Tell me, does your beau have safety pins?"

"Nobody has safety pins anymore, Nana, and nobody says 'beau,' either," I said with a squirmy feeling in my belly. "And even if they did, Harold wouldn't be mine. I'm only going to the movies with him because he wouldn't take no for an answer."

Nana looked scandalized. "He wouldn't take no for an answer, so you gave in?" she gasped.

"Nana, listen —"

"No, *you* listen," she interrupted. "I want you to promise me that if Mr. Smooth Operator tries any funny business, you'll kick him in the crotch as hard as you can and ask questions later. Understand?"

I pictured Harold Horvath writhing on the floor of the movie theater because he had the misfortune of startling me with the offer of a Junior Mint. "Nana —"

"Promise me!" she demanded, giving her cane a

tremendous thump. "Promise me, or I'll march right downstairs and tell your mother and father that your new beau is a filthy lech."

I knew it was wrong to agree to kick Harold in the nuts for no good reason, but all this talk about beaus and leches was making me feel light-headed and queasy and besides, this was my Nana, after all.

"All right," I agreed, grabbing the counter to steady myself. "I promise."

✑✑✑

When the doorbell rang at seven o'clock that evening, I was standing ankle-deep in a pile of clothes trying to decide what to wear. I needed something nice, but not too nice; sexy, but not too sexy. I wanted Harold to think I looked hot, but I didn't want him to think I wanted him to think I looked hot, and I also didn't want him to think that I was trying to look hot for *him*.

It was a great deal to ask from a shirt and a pair of pants.

Now that Harold was actually here, however, there was no time to lose. Every second spent in my bedroom was another second during which Nana could ask him some mortifying question about his intentions in the Funny Business department, and during which he could respond with some equally mortifying answer about how or what he wanted me to feel in the movie theater.

So, throwing on my favorite pair of jeans and a shirt that made me feel at least sixteen years old, I grabbed my lip gloss and the movie gift certificates Ricky and Vivian had given me for my birthday, then hesitated for only a moment before kicking aside my purple high-tops and sliding my feet into my furry platform shoes. Hurriedly flinging open my bedroom door and clattering into the front room, I was shocked to discover Harold juggling applesauce muffins with Rory perched on top of his head squawking "Love Me Tender" and trying to eat Harold's hair and ears in between verses.

"Bravo, bravo!" cried Nana, clapping her hands and laughing so hard that tears coursed down her powdery cheeks.

I rolled my eyes, wondering what had happened to the woman who wanted me to kick Harold in the crotch at the first sign of strange behavior.

As soon as he noticed me standing there, Harold abruptly set the muffins down on the coffee table. As Rory descended upon them like a feathered plague, Harold crossed the living room in three long strides and stood mere inches before me.

"You're even more beautiful than I remember," he murmured.

"I ... uh ... thanks," I replied, feeling flustered.

On the other side of the room, Nana thumped her cane and tried to give us a disapproving look, but she was still laughing too hard to do it right.

"Ready to go?" asked Harold.

I took a deep breath. "As ready as I'll ever be."

During the twenty-minute walk to the movie theater, Harold talked nonstop. This was a huge relief to me because frankly, I couldn't think of a thing to say. I was completely unnerved by the idea that I was on an actual date alone with a member of the opposite sex who clearly thought of me in *that* way and who would probably try to stick his tongue into my mouth at the first opportunity.

How could my own tongue possibly be expected to function properly under such circumstances?

By the time we arrived at the theater, I was freezing cold and my feet and back were killing me from walking so far on the icy sidewalks in my wretched platform shoes, so Harold suggested that I take a seat in the lobby while he stood in line for tickets and popcorn. Sinking gratefully onto a nearby bench, I tried to give him the movie gift certificates to pay for my share, but he immediately launched into a loud speech about how chivalry wasn't completely dead and how there were some men in the world who still knew how to treat a woman, so I hastily stuffed my gift certificates back into my pocket and mumbled that I was sorry I'd offered.

"You've got nothing to be sorry for, Francie," he called warmly as he swaggered away from me. "I'm just sorry you have such a low opinion of my sex that you would think I would expect you to pay your own way."

Several people turned and looked at me when they heard Harold say "my sex." Blushing furiously, I tried to appear as though I, too, was looking around for the intended recipient of his comment, but since there was no one to my right, and only a large, baby-blue-colored garbage pail to my left, I don't think I fooled anyone. Still, I stared intently at the garbage pail for another moment, just in case somebody watching actually believed that Harold had been talking to a pail of garbage about his sex.

"What are you looking at?" came a voice from my right side.

No, excuse me. Not "a" voice. *The* voice.

His voice.

Looking up, I saw Tate Jarvis standing before me in all his broad-shouldered, flat-bellied, slim-hipped glory. Staring up at him, I focused on trying to keep my mouth from hanging open as I tried desperately to think of something clever to say.

"Heh, heh," I finally said. "What movie are you here to see?"

"Hands in the Darkness," he grunted.

My eyes involuntarily darted to his hands — large and probably callused and yet, at the same time, capable of great tenderness and ...

"But isn't that restricted?" I squeaked.

"So?"

"Oh, right. Totally," I breathed, trying not to pant. Then, before I could stop myself, I pointed my index finger at him and made a bizarre clucking noise. I think that on some level

I was trying to appear as though I was cool with the idea of sneaking into a restricted movie, but Tate just stared at me like I'd sprouted a second head. Then he got a sudden, weird look in his eye and asked,

"Who are you here with?"

Aha! Lowering my head, I stared up at him through my long, goopy eyelashes. "Well, *actually,* Tate," I said, with a little catch in my voice, "I'm on a date."

"Yeah?" said Tate, looking around. "With who?"

Just then, I saw Harold strutting toward me. He had a box of Junior Mints and a bag of licorice tucked into the waistband of his slacks, and he was desperately trying to balance a gigantic tub of popcorn between the two large drinks he held in his hands.

Tate laughed as the tub of popcorn began to slip. Harold made a valiant attempt to save it and, in doing so, spilled soda all down the front of his white turtleneck. The popcorn hit the floor in a cascade of trans-fat-saturated glory, and in that moment, I was forcibly struck by the realization that being seen on a date with someone like Harold was going to do exactly nothing to send Tate into the jealous rage I'd been envisioning.

"Listen, Tate," I blurted, jumping to my feet. "It's been real, but I've got to go find my date now. See you around."

And with a self-conscious flip of my carefully crafted curls, I hurried off in the direction of the bathroom without a second glance at Harold *or* Tate.

৶৶৶

When I finally emerged from the bathroom, Tate was gone and Harold was waiting for me at the bench by the concession stand with a full tub of popcorn and fresh drinks. I didn't say anything about his soda-stained turtleneck, and neither did he. We headed into the theater and got settled just as the lights dimmed and the movie began. During the opening credits, Harold leaned over and politely offered me some candy, but I declined without telling him the reason — namely, that I wasn't about to eat anything that had spent time down the front of some guy's pants. The very idea was so distracting that I accidentally let my arm stray to the armrest between us. Harold promptly picked up my hand and clasped it tight in his own. Stunned, I tried to pull my hand away, but Harold just stared up at the big screen, pretending he hadn't noticed my escape attempt, so I didn't know what else to do but sit there letting my hand get hot and sweaty in his.

By the time the movie ended, my hand felt like a prune and I'd decided that holding hands was the most overrated activity on the planet. Following Harold out of the theater, I was so relieved not to be holding his hand anymore that I actually joined in when he began critiquing the movie's various kissing scenes. He seemed very pleased by this unprecedented display of enthusiasm on my part until, just before we turned down my street, he suddenly grew quiet and stopped walking. Puzzled, I stopped walking, too. As soon as I did, Harold seized me in his arms and murmured that all this talk about necking had really put him in the mood. I was so startled by the feel of his hot breath on my skin that after I squirmed out of his clutches, I blurted out what my Nana had said about him, and the promise she'd extracted from me.

"She called me Mr. Smooth Operator, did she?" He chuckled with obvious relish.

"She also told me to kick you in the crotch as hard as I could and ask questions later!" I hollered, lifting one foot in what I hoped was a threatening manner.

Harold laughed so hard when I did this that I started laughing, too, and pretty soon we both had the hiccups. Harold had the loudest hiccups I'd ever heard in my life, and hearing them made me laugh even harder. Then Harold did the most amazing thing: he took a deep breath and sprang into a handstand right there on the snowy boulevard. It was the most perfect handstand I'd ever seen — his toes were pointed and he wasn't wobbling or anything! — and the sight of him in his perfect handstand with his cheeks bulging and his serious face slowly turning blue from the effort of holding his breath to try to rid himself of his hiccups was too much for me. With a shriek, I collapsed onto the boulevard beside him and laughed until I cried.

When I finally stopped laughing, I asked Harold where he'd learned to do that.

"I take tumbling classes," he explained.

"Oh, you want to be a gymnast?" I asked.

"No, a circus performer!" he said, throwing his arms wide. "I also take juggling classes and have been pushing my mother to sign me up for a fire-eating seminar."

"They have fire-eating seminars?" I asked.

"Yes," he said. "Have I mentioned that I'm an accomplished mime?"

"No, you haven't," I grinned.

"Well, I am. I call this one 'Mime in a Box'," he said, opening his eyes very wide, sucking in his cheeks and pressing the palms of his hands against the invisible walls that contained him.

It was so good that I gave him a standing ovation. When I was finished clapping — and he was finished silently battling his way out of his invisible box — we continued on back to my place. We walked more slowly and talked more quickly than we had before. I learned that Harold had won second place in the National Junior Circus Performers' Rodeo three years in a row and that he was, in fact, my age; he learned that I loved to bake and that I wasn't really fond of the style of my platform shoes, either. It was almost as comfortable as talking to Holly, and for a minute there, I actually forgot that I was walking next to a guy who still had Junior Mints and licorice tucked into the waistband of his slacks.

It all came back in an unpleasant rush, however, when

Harold walked me up to the front of the café and then stood staring at my mouth with an expectant sort of smile on his lips.

"Can I tell you something?" he asked softly.

"I suppose," I huffed, the alarm bells in my head clanging so loud that I could barely hear him.

Harold's eyes did a lazy sweep of me from lips to toes and back again. "I'm going to be honest with you, Francie," he whispered, leaning closer. "When I first saw you, I thought you were just another pretty face — you know, a warm body to cling to on the dance floor, a willing hand to clutch in the darkness."

I wondered if I was going to throw up.

"But this evening, in the movie theater, when I saw you hurry off to the bathroom in an attempt to spare me the humiliation of thinking you'd seen me make that unfortunate mess with the popcorn and soda, I knew you were more than all those things. I knew you were that most elusive of creatures — *a decent person.*"

I stared at Harold, whose face seemed to be glowing with earnestness. Then I thought about why I'd really hurried off to the bathroom, and I felt like such a schmuck I hardly knew what to say.

"Now, give us a good-night kiss," Harold demanded huskily, raising himself up onto his tiptoes and closing his eyes.

"No!" I cried in alarm as I turned and clattered through the café door, which banged shut behind me. "No," I said more calmly, once I'd made sure the lock was securely fastened. "I'm sorry, but the answer is no, Harold. Thank you for a lovely evening. Good night."

Feeling enormously pleased with myself, I smiled at him through the window. For *once,* I hadn't let him rope me into something I didn't want to do. I'd been forthright and honest with him about my true feelings, and I'd conveyed my message politely and succinctly.

I'd been goddamn mature, that's what I'd been.

The question now was whether Harold could handle it. Would he take it like a man, or would he fling himself at the door, frothing at the mouth and moaning about his aching loins?

Clearly, I expected the latter, so it came as somewhat of a shock when he simply nodded politely and turned away. Walking to the curb, he crossed the street and sauntered off down the sidewalk without so much as a backward glance, and while I was obviously relieved by how the whole situation had played out, I don't mind admitting that I was just a teensy bit taken aback when it later occurred to me that Harold hadn't even *tried* to ask me out again.

12. The Mane Event

There once was a young girl named Francie
Whose shoes were incredibly fancy
She thought love was blind
'Til a mime changed her mind
And she wept, "I'm so glad I can see!"

From the private poetry collection of Harold Horvath

The next morning I lay in bed for almost forty-five minutes, staring at the cover of my latest True Romance novel and thinking about my date with Harold — the hungry look in his eyes when he'd seen me clomp into the living room in my platform shoes, the startling strength of his arms around me before I'd managed to squirm away from him. His breath had smelled pleasantly like Junior Mints, and with a small, involuntary spasm, I fleetingly wondered if his mouth would have tasted like Junior Mints if I'd allowed him to kiss me.

I also wondered why he hadn't tried to ask me out again.

I mean, I was obviously glad he hadn't, because I almost certainly would have had to turn him down. Harold was interesting in a weird sort of way, and the fact that he yearned for me was a definite bonus, but he was also short and skinny and generally not my idea of a heartthrob. Besides, after seeing Tate Jarvis at the movie theater and having had an almost normal human conversation with him, I was more in love with him than ever before.

Still, I thought. *Skinny or not, Harold gave me something very important last night.*

Inspiration.

There was no question that his desire to become a circus performer was a bizarre one, but to win second place in the National Junior Circus Performers' Rodeo three years in a row — well, that made my finalist finish in Lorenzo's contest feel like both more and less than it had before. More, because Harold seemed so proud of having come in second that it made making the finals seem like a genuine accomplishment. Less, because I had only ever put myself on the line once — and Harold had done it *three times*! Three times he'd entered that crazy rodeo hoping to win and three times he'd come close and failed. You had to hand it to the guy — he was a fighter.

And so was I.

Leaping out of bed, I hurried to the bathroom, eager to get a start on the day. After receiving the disappointing letter from Lorenzo, I'd half decided to skip my baking altogether this week. I'd had fun loafing around with Darlene last Saturday, and I'd already earned enough to pay for the trip to Portage la Prairie, so I hadn't seen the point of slaving away in the kitchen when my crummy recipes hadn't even been good enough to get me on some lousy baking show.

Now, however, I realized that if a person is truly dedicated to her craft, she can't give up that easily — and if she does give up that easily, she never deserved to succeed in the first place. *Besides,* I thought as I brushed my teeth with such vigor that minty foam spilled from my lips like soapsuds, *the story of how I rose above adversity is going to make a terrifically inspiring chapter in my autobiography someday!*

Dazzled by the thoughts of midnight crowds clamoring for a chance to be the first to read my life story, I spit, rinsed and spent a dreamy moment trying to calm my hysterical fans while at the same time writing a poetic dedication in the first-edition copy belonging to my dear devoted boyfriend, Tate Jarvis.

The sharp rap of knuckles against the door startled me out of my reverie.

"Francie?" called Nana sleepily. "What are you doing in there?"

Feeling suddenly, unaccountably giddy, I hollered, "MIME IN A BATHROOM!" Then I flung open the bathroom door so hard it banged against the doorstop and I stood there silently pressing my hands against the sides of an invisible portable toilet.

"Good Lord!" cried Nana, stumbling backward so fast she nearly tripped on the hem of her old blue-and-white-striped bathrobe. "What on *earth* has gotten into you, child?"

Swooping down on her like a great, benevolent bird with nearly perfect hair, I lifted her up into a fierce hug.

"Inspiration's gotten into me, Nana," I hooted as I planted an exuberant kiss on her cheek. "Inspiration!"

❧❧❧

I got dressed and ran almost the entire way to the grocery store, where I zoomed through the aisles, averting shopping cart–pedestrian collisions by such narrow margins that I left several early morning shoppers gasping in my wake. I didn't care who saw me, or what they thought of me. I was in hot pursuit of my destiny. The small opinions of small minds meant *nothing* to me.

Pausing briefly at the floral department to imagine how terrible it must have been for Darlene to have been abandoned by her mother amid such beauty, I hustled to the checkout and was in flight again the instant the cashier dropped the last brick of butter into my shopping bag. I made it home in record time, though I was sweating like a pig and gasping for breath when I burst into the café.

"Honey, what's wrong?" cried my mother as I lurched past her, dragging my heavy bags behind me.

"Nothing," I panted. "Inspiration!"

Up in the apartment, the first thing I did was to fetch the envelope containing my rejection letter from Lorenzo. Trying not to get choked up, I reread the letter once, then ripped it into a million tiny shreds, which I tossed to one side before commencing to rifle through the other contents of the envelope. The desktop photo calendar was stunning — picture after picture of my darling oozing raw sensuality and animal magnetism. With a pounding heart, I closed my eyes and pressed my lips against his. Then I opened my eyes again and propped the February picture of his face on the kitchen counter against the bags of chopped walnuts and milk-chocolate chips.

"Oh, Rory," I sighed. "Isn't he perfect?"

"OH, RORY! OH, RORY! ISN'T HE PERFECT?" sang my nana's demented bird while he proudly stared at his own reflection in the kitchen window.

After taking a moment to explain to Rory just how hideously imperfect he really was, I pored over the pamphlet containing the details of Lorenzo's current cross-country tour. When I'd initially read through my rejection letter, I'd been too busy wallowing in self-pity to give serious thought to other opportunities to showcase my talents. Now I realized that there was nothing stopping me from entering contests in other cities — maybe even in bigger cities, populated by vastly more influential baking critics!

As I ran my finger down the list of stops on the tour, one city name so grabbed my attention that it seemed to leap off the page.

Portage la Prairie!

Hardly daring to breathe, I looked to see what dates Lorenzo would be there.

They were the same dates the Performance Band would be there! I was so excited that I started to see black spots in front of my eyes. This was more than destiny. This was fate!

Elated, I checked the deadline for entering the Portage la Prairie contest. I read the date once, then twice. Then I rubbed my eyes, thinking the black spots must somehow have damaged my vision.

The pamphlet said the deadline was yesterday.

Yesterday.

I felt the inspiration drain out of me as surely as if someone had pulled a cork out of the bottom of my foot. If only I hadn't been so busy feeling sorry for myself! If only

I'd acted while there was still time! Slowly, I sank down into a chair so that I could more comfortably bury my face in my hands and weep with despair.

Then I stopped.

And I asked myself what someone like Harold Horvath would do in a situation like this.

"He wouldn't give up, that's for sure," I told Rory, who was too busy admiring his reflection to respond.

Filled to the brim with a fresh dose of inspiration, I hurried to my computer, wrote a heartfelt e-mail explaining why I'd missed the deadline (my parents had locked me in a closet to prevent me from spending even more money on delicious "Sinfully Yours" products) and asked Lorenzo's people to consider my submission anyway — or at least to give me the opportunity to be a member of the studio audience. As soon as I hit SEND I sat back, flushed with pleasure. I didn't know if I'd win, and I didn't know how I'd manage to ditch the Performance Band and get to the television studio if I did win, but nobody could say I hadn't tried.

Whizzing back to the kitchen, I unloaded the rest of my ingredients, put on my fluffy white hat and lugged out my pots and pans, all the while singing, "ME, ME, ME, ME, ME, ME, ME!" at the top of my lungs, as though I were a famous opera singer warming up before a concert. Then, without pausing for a breath, I bowed deeply to Rory and snatched up Glossy Two-Dimensional Lorenzo. After giving him a kiss that took even *my* breath away, I did a high-velocity pirouette and hit the music.

"DA, DA, DA, DUM!" I bellowed as the beat reached in and touched my very *soul*. "DA, DA, DA, DUM!"

I plunged into my baking with reckless abandon. I was messier than I'd ever been — but also more inspired. I baked without respite: rolling, stirring, mixing, sifting and beating as though my life depended on it. My rhythm was nearly thrown when I accidentally knocked over my last carton of eggs while attempting to cartwheel from the oven back to the counter, but a quick call downstairs confirmed we had plenty in the café cooler, and a grumbling Marguerite reluctantly agreed to bring them up when I explained that I was at a crucial point in my double-fudge chocolate-chunk nut bars and couldn't leave the kitchen.

After hanging up the phone, I paused to imagine that I was a genuine celebrity baker and that Marguerite was just one of the many minions who scurried around, eager to fetch ingredients at the snap of my fingers.

"Snap, SNAP!" I cried, dancing around and snapping my fingers at Rory while pretending that he was a minion who'd been incarcerated for disrespecting me on set.

Unfortunately, the thrill of pretending that Marguerite was my minion began to wane when she failed to appear with my eggs in a timely manner — so much so that by the time the doorbell finally rang I'd come very close to imagining her incarcerated as well.

"Marguerite, I called you almost twenty minutes ago!" I admonished as I wrenched the door open. "Where have you been?"

Darlene stared at me, a carton of eggs tucked neatly under one arm.

"Hello, Francie," she said. "Here are your eggs. You look like a lunatic."

I opened my mouth to disagree with her, then caught sight of myself in the mirrored lenses of her designer sunglasses. I *did* look like a lunatic. My crumpled baker's hat was perched askew atop my mop of disheveled hair, my sweaty face was dusted with flour and my eyes glittered feverishly.

Inspiration.

"Well? Aren't you going to invite me in?" asked Darlene, slipping off her sunglasses.

"Would you like to come in, Darlene?"

"I guess," she said, striding past me. "What's that smell?"

"Double-fudge chocolate-chunk nut bars," I said, trying to keep the note of pride out of my voice. "They're my own original recipe."

"They smell like they're burning."

"They're not. That's the toasted almond slivers you're smelling."

"Almonds give me hives. Do you want to come shopping with me today?"

"Oh!" I said, marveling at how out of place she looked in our messy little living room. "Uh ... I can't."

"Why not?" she asked. Then she glanced up at my puffy hat. "Is it because of your baking?"

When I hesitated, she smiled encouragingly, so I gave a sheepish little nod.

"I see," she murmured. Then, in a kindly voice, she said, "Francie, you *do* realize that this obsession of yours isn't normal, don't you?"

"It isn't an obsession," I said. "And it is so normal."

"It isn't, and you know it isn't. And do you know how I know you know it isn't?"

"How?" I asked in spite of myself.

"Because I've never once heard you mention it to anyone at school."

"That's not true. I've mentioned it to Holly. Millions of times."

"She doesn't count," said Darlene, with feeling.

"Why not?"

"Because she's your friend — she'd never tell you if she thought you were making a fool of yourself."

"I'm not making a fool of myself."

"I never said you were. Stop being so defensive."

"I'm not being defensive," I said, folding my arms across my chest. "I ... I think maybe you'd better go now, Darlene."

"Fine," she shrugged, slipping her fancy sunglasses back on. "But just remember this, Francie: I'm trying to be your friend."

"By telling me I'm abnormal?"

"By telling you the truth."

"I thought you said a friend wouldn't tell me the truth."

"I said Holly wouldn't tell you the truth. Something you should know about me, Francie, is that I'm a different kind of friend. The kind that isn't afraid to tell it like it is. So get angry with me if you will, but don't ever accuse me of not being a true friend."

I was very tempted to point out that I hadn't accused her of anything — and maybe to tell *her* not to be so defensive — but it seemed childish compared to her cool, sophisticated insights into the nature of friendship. So instead I thanked her for bringing up the eggs, apologized for not being available to go shopping and showed her to the door.

After she was gone, I wandered back into the kitchen.

"You don't think I'm making a fool of myself, do you?" I asked Glossy Two-Dimensional Lorenzo. He didn't respond, but I had a sudden vision of Harold Horvath standing in the middle of the street, miming his way out of an invisible box, and a single word sprang, unbidden, to my lips.

Inspiration.

❦

Sunday morning, the café was hopping with customers marveling over my latest creations and also congratulating me on having bounced back so well from my grotesquely disfiguring life-threatening illness. Later that afternoon, Holly — who also took Life Skills but was in the morning class — came over so we could work on our projects together. Presentations were scheduled to start the week after the Performance Band festival in Portage la Prairie, and neither one of us had made any significant headway. Mr. Simmons had categorically refused to accept Holly's outline stating that she wanted to be the first flutist in history to sell out a sixty-thousand-seat arena in under eight minutes, and although I'd tried to do research on becoming a lawyer, I found the whole prospect so uninspiring that I was having a hard time staying focused.

"This is a stupid project," announced Holly after she'd spent fifteen minutes diligently drawing red heart clusters on her bare arm. Flinging down her pen in frustration, she put her juicy wad of half-chewed bubble gum down on my mother's coffee table, reached into her knapsack and pulled out her flute case. "Want to hear my solo?"

"You know I do," I said quickly, relieved to have a reason to set down my own pen.

The piece that she and Mrs. C had selected was a slow, melancholy one, and Holly played it so beautifully that it brought a lump to my throat. As the last note died away, I quietly asked her if she would tell me if she thought I was making a fool of myself.

"Why, do you think I'm making a fool of myself?" she asked, with a shocked look on her face.

I leaped up off my perch at the edge of the coffee table. "No, of *course* not. That was so beautiful I nearly *cried*. I just mean — would you tell me if you thought I had an obsession that was ... unhealthy?"

"You mean like Tate Jarvis? Yes, I would tell you. In fact, I have told you. Many times. He's definitely an unhealthy obsession and what's more, I think his lack of dental hygiene is starting to catch up with him."

"What are you talking about?" I cried. "Tate has a beautiful smile."

"That may be, but I'm almost positive he doesn't floss, and I think the bits of food caught between his teeth must be starting to decay, because in case you haven't noticed, he's beginning to develop intolerably bad breath."

"He is not. And P.S. — that is disgusting."

"It certainly is," agreed Holly, peeling her bubble gum off the corner of the coffee table in order to give it a few chews before putting it back for safekeeping. "Now, will you listen to me play again? Rick says I should make the most of any opportunity I have to play in front of a live audience."

My heart did a funny kind of lurch when she said this, because I knew it meant she'd been sharing with Ricky a passion that up until now she'd only shared with me. And I knew she'd probably had more fun sharing it with him because he was a dedicated musician just like she was, and also because they'd probably rolled around on the floor French-kissing after their sharing session was over. It made me feel left out, left behind and inadequate, and I remembered what Darlene had said about there being different kinds of friends, and I wondered what kind of friends Holly and I would become now that Ricky had become more her friend than mine.

"Francie?" asked Holly. "Will you listen to me play again?"

I took a very deep breath and smiled.

"Of *course* I will," I said as I accidentally plopped down on her slobbery wad of gum. "I can't believe you thought you'd have to ask."

☙❧

The next day, Mr. Simmons called an impromptu meeting of the Social Committee to discuss the proposed Performance Band pep rally. Apparently, Mrs. C had bumped into the music teacher from the nearby private school at a recent professional-development seminar, and the two of them had decided it might be fun to bring the two schools together and have a "Battle of the Bands"-themed pep rally, since both schools were sending bands to the Portage la Prairie festival.

"It's going to mean a lot more work, pigeons," declared Mr. Simmons sourly as he sucked at a piece of food lodged between his grungy front teeth. "More posters. More introductions. More coordination if we expect not only to pack another five hundred goobers into the gymnasium, but also to keep you lot from sneaking off to suck face with the private-school nitwits who have the cutest rear ends."

I huffed so explosively when he said this that my lungs practically *collapsed.*

"Mr. Simmons," I said, rising to my feet with great dignity. "I believe I speak on behalf of every student in this room when I say that is the most disrespectful thing I've ever heard in my life."

"Couldn't agree with you more, Freewater!" bellowed Mr. Simmons as the lodged piece of food suddenly popped free, sailed through the air and landed next to my tuna-salad sandwich. "That's why we're going to plan this one down to the last nitwit, people. I won't have a bunch of hormonally challenged morons ruining the good name of this fine school."

෴

I was so steamed at Mr. Simmons that I didn't raise my hand once during Life Skills class, even though, as a result of my baking business, I knew perfectly well how to design a personal budget, and even though class participation was worth twenty percent of our overall grade. Afterward, Holly and I hurried off to Performance Band rehearsal. With less than two weeks to go before the festival, Mrs. C had started scheduling rehearsals on a daily basis.

"I want us to head into that festival knowing we couldn't possibly have done anything more to perfect our pieces," she explained passionately as she handed out a note containing important details regarding transportation and accommodation. "The competition is going to be fierce, but if we stay focused and use the time remaining to put the final polish on our performance, I truly believe we'll have a shot at bringing home top honors!"

Everyone cheered at this, even me, despite the fact that I was a lot more excited about finding out our hotel room assignments than I was about bringing home top honors.

"We're in the same room together!" I bubbled as I bounded over to Holly after we'd been dismissed.

"With us!" chorused Sharon and Jody, flopping up behind me.

"And I'm right down the hall," added Ricky, reaching for Holly's hand.

"With me!" blurted Randy Newton, staring at Ricky's and Holly's entwined fingers with a stricken expression on his face.

I felt so sorry for Randy that I immediately sidled up to him and asked if he'd consider heading up the sub-committee in charge of pep-rally posters.

"After all," I murmured as we wandered out into the hallway, "we're on a very tight schedule, Randy, and everyone knows you're the best visual artist in our grade, and — oh my god."

I stopped so abruptly that Ricky stumbled right into the back of me.

For across the hallway, nonchalantly chewing on a coffee stir stick and leaning up against a locker like the brooding hero in some old black-and-white movie, was Harold Horvath. He was wearing gray wool slacks and a maroon blazer with a golden crest on it. The minute he laid eyes on me, he threw down the stir stick, stood up and inhaled deeply.

"Well, well, well. Francie Freewater. We meet again," he said, striding toward me with an air of great purpose.

I didn't know what to say. I didn't want to be unkind, but showing up at my school? Without first asking my permission? It was too much, even for Harold.

Still, I didn't see any reason to humiliate him in front of all my friends, so I took him by the elbow and steered him back to the other side of the hallway.

"Listen, Harold ..."

"Yes?" he murmured, looking deep into my eyes.

The intensity of his gaze threw me for a moment, but I quickly rallied. "Uh ... well, the thing is, Harold, that night we went out? I had fun with you and everything, and I'm *totally* flattered that you'd come here in the hope of seeing me again, but ... the truth is I ... I just don't have *those* kinds of feelings for you."

I cringed when I said this last part, certain that I'd hurt him terribly, but Harold, if anything, looked more in love with me than ever.

"Oh, Francie," he said exultantly. "I had fun with you, too, and I wholeheartedly agree we shouldn't rush into any kind of emotional commitment — though I'm not at all opposed to exploring the physical side of our relationship at your earliest possible convenience. However, in the spirit of honesty, which I hope will continue to prevail between us, I must tell you that I didn't actually come here to see you."

"You didn't?" I blurted.

"No, I came to meet up with my cousin."

"Your cousin?"

"Randy."

"Randy?"

"Your fellow percussionist. It was he who invited me to the dance where we first met," explained Harold as he gently brushed a lock of hair out of my eyes.

"Oh," I said, too stunned to slap his hand away.

"But perhaps someday I *will* come here in the hope of seeing you again, dear Francie," he murmured with a little bow of his head. "Until then, fair lady, I bid you adieu."

❧❧❧

Following my encounter with Harold, I felt inexplicably let down, but I didn't get a chance to talk to Holly about my feelings because Ricky had invited her over for dinner and he said if they were late getting home his mom would feed the tofu casserole to the cats. Out of the corner of my eye, I watched as the two of them happily set off down the hallway, smiling and bumping up against each other every second step. Then I watched as Randy and Harold left together, and then as Sharon and Jody did. At that point, I realized that the only other person in the hallway besides me was the janitor. So I nodded once at him, slung my knapsack over my shoulder and slowly headed for home.

⁄ᗜᗜ

That night, after a quiet evening spent mostly alone, I booted up my computer and saw that there was an e-mail from Lorenzo LaRue Productions. I stared at it without opening it for a very long time, trying to convince myself it might be good news. When I finally double-clicked on it, however, it was a "Dear Cherished Viewer" note thanking me for my submission but pointing out that it had been received after the deadline for the Portage la Prairie contest and was therefore ineligible for consideration. After a few seconds, a video clip of Lorenzo blowing kisses popped up, along with an animated advertisement for his "Sinfully Yours" product line.

I closed the advertising pop-up, watched the video clip to the very last kiss, then shut off the computer, got into bed and waited for sleep to come.

⁄ᗜᗜ

The next day in chemistry class, Mr. Flatburn announced that he was finally going to let us conduct an experiment using the Bunsen burners. We were all pretty excited, and there was a lot of chattering and jostling as we headed back to the supply cabinet to get our Bunsen burners, rubber gas hoses, test tubes and metal clamps. At first, I felt a little awkward around Darlene because of the way we'd left things on Saturday, but she didn't seem at all uncomfortable and in no time, she, Tate and I were busy setting up for our experiment.

We'd just put a little of the first mystery solid into a clamped test tube so we could try to measure its melting point when I noticed that Tate was giving me a strange, sideways glance. Giving my lower lip what I hoped was a sultry little nibble, I gave him a very tiny smile. He immediately leaned over, closed his hand around mine and moved it three inches to the left while whispering in my ear, "I think you actually have to hold the test tube over the flame if you want that crap to melt, Francie."

It was the first time Tate had ever said my name — let alone whispered it in my ear! — and I was so excited that for one awful minute I didn't think I'd be able to start breathing again. Then respiration kicked in and, with a sexy smile and a toss of my hair, I thanked Tate for his advice.

His return smile turned into a look of such horror that I wondered if I'd just blown a booger onto him without realizing it. Suddenly, quick as a cat, he reached into his bag, grabbed his stinky old gym shorts and began smacking me in the side of the head with them. I was so stunned by this gross boy behavior that I didn't even *try* to defend myself, and the next thing I knew, Mr. Flatburn was standing next to me with a panicked look on his face.

"Is she okay?" he asked.

"I think so," said Tate importantly as he shoved his shorts back into his bag. Leaning close to me, he asked, "Are you okay?"

Recoiling slightly at the smell of his breath — which *was* kind of putrid — I ignored his question in favor of indignantly asking Mr. Flatburn why on earth he'd asked Tate if I was all right when Tate was the one who'd been hitting me!

"Because he was standing right beside you when your hair went up in flames," snapped Mr. Flatburn. Then he turned to the class, pointed to my head and said, "You see, people, what happens when you don't take proper precautions around the Bunsen burners?"

Wide-eyed, everyone nodded. I felt like a seven-eyed mutant being used to illustrate why people shouldn't go swimming in toxic waste dumps.

"Good," said Mr. Flatburn. Then he turned to me and

said, "I'm not going to punish you for your carelessness, Francie — clearly, what has happened to your hair is punishment enough. Just go clean up and when you get back to class, see if you can finish the experiment without lighting any other part of your body on fire."

✎∞

Darlene came with me to the bathroom, though I was in such a panic after Mr. Flatburn's comments about my hair that she could barely keep up with me as I sprinted through the empty halls. Banging open the bathroom door, I flew across the grubby tile floor and came to a screeching halt in front of the mirror.

"My hair!" I wailed in horror. "My nearly perfect hair!"

It looked awful — no, worse than awful. Frizzy and singed and uneven, it made my poor head look like a big fat coconut that had been dropped in a campfire. Desperately, I twisted my head this way and that, wondering if there was anything at all that could be done to salvage all those long, painful months of growing it out.

"Ruined," I concluded miserably. "Utterly ruined."

"Oh, so what," said Darlene as she carefully reapplied her lip gloss. "I'm sure you're going to look just fine with short hair. Besides, I have some news that is so exciting you're going to forget all about your hair."

"Really?" I asked as I stared mournfully at my ruined mane.

"Yes," said Darlene. "Do you remember the suggestion I made when you came over to my place a few Saturdays ago? About getting you and Tate together?"

How could I forget? Her suggestion was that I meet up with Tate in a secret location at a prearranged time for the sole purpose of necking with him. The way she figured it, if I was good enough, it might finally give Tate a real reason to like me.

"I remember telling you I'd think about it," I muttered.

Darlene laughed. "Well, I know you said that, Francie, but after careful consideration I decided that as your friend, I just couldn't leave the decision up to you."

"Excuse me?" I said slowly, looking away from the devastation in the mirror for the first time.

"I could see the idea made you nervous," explained Darlene as she touched up her mascara. "And as the days wore on without you ever mentioning it again, I just knew you were going to come up with some stupid excuse not to go through with it. So last night while Tate and I were studying, I went ahead and asked him if he'd be willing to meet you for a private make-out session next Friday during the Performance Band pep rally and he said yes."

I opened my mouth and moved my tongue, but no words came out.

"Not bad," smirked Darlene. "But when you're French-kissing Tate, try to lose the stunned look on your face, okay? After everything I've told him about you, Francie, he's going to be expecting big things."

13. An Unexpected Tragedy

Scientists have proven that in many ways parrots are more intelligent, sensitive and loyal than human beings like my ex-husband.

From The Big Book of Parrots *by Olive Byrds*

I spent the rest of the day in a fog, trying to figure out what to do. I couldn't believe Darlene had set this up without my permission — permission I never would have granted her in a million, billion years. I wasn't some cheap tongue-for-hire, and as much as I liked Tate, if he couldn't find a reason to like me that didn't involve us exchanging saliva, then I was more than willing to give up on him.

The problem was that if I tried to call it off now, I was going to look like a big stupid baby who was all uptight about doing something everybody else probably did as casually as brushing teeth. Plus, as much as I hated to admit it, there was a very tiny part of me that *wanted* to go through with it. I knew it was wrong to feel this way, but I was tired of being the only fourteen-year-old girl on the planet who'd never kissed a boy. And to share my first kiss with Tate? I got dizzy every time I thought about it. In fact, I nearly fell out of my desk during Life Skills class when it suddenly occurred to me that Tate might even sweep me into his big strong arms before kissing me.

"Problem, Freewater?" barked Mr. Simmons, flinging a piece of chalk in my direction.

"No, sir," I blurted, still feeling the heat of Tate's phantom embrace.

After school, Mrs. C gave me permission to skip Performance Band rehearsal in order to go get my hair fixed, so I ran all the way home and showed my parents what had happened. The minute I pulled off my black fisherman's cap, my mom gasped, flew to my side and anxiously examined every inch of my scalp. When she was satisfied that my head wasn't a giant, oozing heat blister, she cupped my face in her hands and said, "How on earth did you light your hair on fire?"

"It was Mr. Flatburn's fault," I explained as I nicked a French fry straight from the deep fryer basket. "He's the one who insisted on putting Darlene at my desk even though I warned him that three was a crowd and that a crowd wasn't the best thing to have around a Bunsen burner."

"Uh-huh," said my mom, folding her arms in front of her. "And how is it that you managed not to get severely burned?"

"Tate Jarvis — he's just this, uh, guy who sits next to me in chemistry class — well, anyway, uh, he noticed my hair catch fire and quickly put out the flames."

"I remember Tate Jarvis," said my dad, smiling broadly as he handed me a paper plate heaped with piping hot, freshly salted fries. "He was that young hunk who clogged the toilet with paper towel at your birthday party, wasn't he?"

"Young hunk?" I squeaked as I felt my face go very red. "Oh, please, Dad. Don't make me *barf!*"

My mom and dad both started laughing at this, then my mom told me to go down to the beauty parlor after I finished my fries and see if Mrs. Watson could fit me in. Luckily, she had an opening, and after several minutes spent fussing over my poor hair, she snatched up her scissors and began happily prattling on about my genius in the kitchen. Many, many snips of the scissors later, she triumphantly spun the swivel chair toward the mirror and made a big production out of telling me how wonderful it was to finally be able to see my beautiful ears again.

Shell-shocked, I thanked her in a hollow voice, then slid out of the chair, pulled my cap as low on my head as it would go and headed for home. As soon as I got there, I locked myself in the bathroom, wet down my hair and began furiously restyling it in an attempt to see if there was any possible way to recapture the sexy perfection I'd come so close to achieving.

I'd just tried a side comb-over that made me look about as sexy as an old bald man when I heard the phone ring. Bursting out of the bathroom, I nearly trampled Nana to death in my haste to get to the phone first.

"Hello?" I asked breathlessly, snatching up the receiver with such gusto that I sent the rest of the phone clattering to the floor.

"Hi," said Holly. "It's me."

"Oh. Hey."

"You sound disappointed," she chuckled. "Were you hoping it might be someone else?"

"No," I lied, wondering how in the world Harold Horvath could claim to be madly in love with me when he couldn't even be bothered to call me once in a while. "I'm super-glad you called. There's something I need to talk to you about."

"The make-out session you and Tate Jarvis have scheduled for next Friday afternoon?" guessed Holly, sounding suddenly very serious. "I know. I heard all about it. It's the reason I called."

I was stunned. I'd just assumed the whole thing was a secret between Darlene, Tate and me. It had never *occurred* to me that anyone else would find out about it — or that it would sound so ugly coming from someone who obviously didn't approve.

"I overheard Greg Podwinski laughing about it in gym today," continued Holly. "After beaning him with a bladder ball so hard I nearly knocked his retainer right out of his head, I told him he was full of it because you would never stoop to doing something so degrading with a rot mouth like Tate Jarvis. I was right, wasn't I?" she asked.

"Don't call him that," I said, as a hot flush rose to my cheeks. "You don't hear me calling your boyfriend names, do you?"

"Tate isn't your boyfriend," said Holly.

"Well, maybe he will be after next Friday," I huffed, hurt by how thoughtlessly she'd pointed out the fact that Tate couldn't care less about me.

"What's that supposed to mean?" she asked.

"That you heard right," I said, making a sudden decision. "Tate and I *are* planning to hook up."

"Oh, Francie, come on!" groaned Holly in dismay. "Don't be a chump. The guy has never treated you with the slightest bit of respect!"

"He saved my life."

"He slapped you in the face with his gym shorts."

"It wasn't like that, and anyway, I don't care what you or anyone else says," I retorted stubbornly. "You're not the only one who can get romantic with the boy of your dreams, okay? I like Tate and he likes me enough to agree to make out with me, so next Friday I'm going to sneak out of that stupid pep rally, meet up with him at a secret location and French-kiss his freaking socks off!"

For a long moment, Holly didn't say anything.

"Well," she said at last, "it sounds like your mind is made up, so I guess the only thing left for me to say is good luck. Oh, and Francie?" she added in a gently teasing voice that I knew was meant to ease the tension between us. "If you do manage to French-kiss Tate's socks off, I suggest you plug your nose because between you and me, he's never struck me as the kind of guy who washes his feet on a regular basis."

❧❧❧

The next morning, Darlene and *Gary* showed up at the café and offered me a drive to school. The minute Darlene saw my new haircut she burst out laughing and asked if she should shove over to make room for Tweedle Dee, or if I was the only one going to school today. I guess I looked hurt, because she immediately told me to lighten up, then whispered that I shouldn't worry about what Tate was going to think of my brutal new haircut because we were going to be making out in the dark, anyway.

"What?" I whispered anxiously. "In the dark? But why?"

"It's more romantic that way, dummy," murmured Darlene in a voice too low for her father to hear. "Plus, Mr. Simmons said there are going to be teachers monitoring the halls, remember? Don't you think they're going to notice if all the lights in the band room are on?"

"The band room?" I whispered even more quietly. "Is that the secret location you've decided on?"

Darlene nodded.

I hesitated, then asked, "Are you sure it's a *secret* location?"

"What do you mean?" asked Darlene, wrinkling her freckly little nose at me.

"Well, I was talking to Holly last night and she knew about our plans even before I told her. She ... she made it sound like everyone was laughing about it behind my back," I said, flushing with embarrassment.

Darlene gave a derisive snort. "She is *hardly* one to be spreading rumors about you. Do you know what I heard about her? I heard she let that friend of yours take her bra off and stick his hand up her shirt."

"*What?*" I gasped as my arms instinctively flew up to protect my chest.

"Uh-huh, and there's also a rumor going around that she's agreed to have —"

"Stop," I said, so loudly that *Gary* glanced back at me. I lowered my voice before continuing. "I don't want to hear any more, Darlene. Holly would never spread rumors about anyone — least of all me — and if she's let Ricky feel her up, well, that's her business. She may not understand about me and Tate, but she's still my best friend and I just don't feel right talking about her this way."

For an instant, Darlene looked almost as hurt as she had

the night of the winter carnival when Ricky had walked away from her without a backward glance. Then she smiled broadly.

"Fine, Tweedle Dum. Whatever," she shrugged as the car pulled up in front of the school. "It's just as well, anyway. I've put a lot of effort into setting things up for next Friday and I don't want you screwing them up because you can't stop thinking about someone else's love life."

✍❦✍

Saturday morning I got up early, but instead of getting straight to my baking, I dragged my comforter into the darkened living room, curled up on my dad's old recliner and watched the taped episodes of *Getting Baked with Lorenzo* that I'd missed on account of Performance Band rehearsals. As I watched my darling knead a lump of biscuit dough with such passion that his whole body started undulating, I wistfully thought about how close I'd come to baking at his bare, tanned, muscular, sweat-soaked side.

"I know I should get to my baking," I sighed as Nana quietly thumped into the room and sat down on the couch. "But ever since I found out that I missed my shot at baking with Lorenzo in Portage la Prairie, I've been having a hard time feeling inspired. How am I supposed to keep fighting to succeed if I don't feel inspired?"

"Do your baking or don't do your baking," shrugged Nana without taking her eyes off the extreme close-up of Lorenzo's extremely kissable lips. "Just don't make excuses."

"I'm not making excuses," I spluttered indignantly. "I'm talking about my *feelings*."

Nana harrumphed.

"The world is full of talented people who gave up when the going got tough and who spend the rest of their lives moaning about what might have been," she said, still staring at the TV screen. "But the truth is that a life goal is a marathon, not a sprint. You can trip and fall many times along the way and still make it to the finish line — but only if you keep plodding along, inspired or not."

Shifting my gaze to the living room window, I stared in silence at the cold winter sky, and at the faint pink streaks on the horizon that hinted at the coming dawn. Then, abruptly, I huffed as loudly as I possibly could.

"Well, jeez, I know *that*," I said, flinging the comforter to one side, scooting off the recliner and hurrying to get dressed. "It's not like I *wasn't* going to get to my baking, okay?" I hollered from my bedroom. "I mean, *sheesh*, Nana, can't a person watch their favorite television show around here without getting a big, fat lecture?"

"You watch your tone, young lady!" warned Nana, hammering her cane against the floor. "And another thing —"

"Yes?" I asked, popping my head out the bedroom door.

"When you make it to the finish line, try not to forget those of us who stood on the sidelines and cheered ourselves hoarse as you plodded past," she said with a small smile.

"I'll do my best, Nana," I grinned, blowing her a juicy kiss. "But I'm not making any promises, so enjoy me while you can."

❧❧❧

The next day, I was down to my last few items for sale when the café door flew open with a bang and Sharon and Jody tumbled inside. They were so covered with snow that it looked like they'd been rolling in it, and their cheeks and noses were red with cold. Spying me behind the counter, they each gave me an exuberant wave, then began to clomp across the café toward me, leaving big puddles of melting snow in their wake.

"Cool hat," announced Sharon, before I'd recovered my senses enough to snatch my poufy white hat off my head.

I felt my face grow warm.

"Can I try it on?" asked Jody.

Not knowing what else to do, I handed it over to her.

Enthusiastically, she jammed it down on her head. "Wow. I look totally awesome," she breathed, after leaning over to examine her reflection in the glass countertop. Straightening up, she looked past me to my baking trays. "Aw, you've hardly got anything left!" She turned to give Sharon a slug in the arm. "I told you this would happen if we didn't get here early," she said. Turning back to me, she cheerfully explained, "A while back, Darlene was showing around this poster advertising your baking business and ever since then we've been meaning to come by and check it out. Unfortunately, *some people*" — she bugged her eyes out at Sharon — "can't seem to get up before noon unless some other people drag them out of bed by their ears."

"Oh," I said. "Uh, okay. Well, um, do you want a muffin or something?"

"Uh-huh, sure, that sounds great," said Jody, bobbing her head at me.

In unison, she and Sharon reached down and started laboriously digging through their big bulky boots.

"What are you doing?" I asked, leaning across the counter to watch them.

"Getting our money," grunted Sharon, nearly losing her balance.

"Don't worry about it," I said hastily. "It's on the house."

"No, that's okay," panted Jody, standing up suddenly and flinging some very sweaty change across the counter at me. "We can pay."

I looked down at the money and then across at my disheveled fellow percussionists — who didn't seem to think I was making a fool of myself at all — and then I smiled.

"Come on," I said. "I'll show you to my favorite table."

☙☙☙

We ended up spending the afternoon together teaching Rory swear words, playing KerPlunk! and asking the Ouija board to predict the future. I was dying to ask if there was any chance Tate Jarvis was going to like me after I French-kissed with him on Friday, but I was too embarrassed to ask in front of Sharon and Jody. Every time I thought about what I'd gotten myself into, I wanted to crawl into the nearest hole and never come out.

This feeling only got worse over the next five days. Whenever I passed Tate in the halls he gave me a knowing smile, and once he even waited for me by my locker in order to ask if he could borrow my notes from chemistry class. Too flustered to tell him he should have taken better notes himself, I hurriedly thrust them at him and fled.

Suddenly, it was the day before the pep rally.

"Oh, relax," said Darlene as we loafed in the northeast stairwell during our free period. "It's not like you've never necked with anyone before, is it?"

"No, of course not," I panted, pressing a wad of dampened paper towels more firmly against my forehead.

"All right, then," she said. "So here's the plan: tomorrow afternoon, just before the Performance Band marches into the gymnasium, you tell Mrs. C you think you're going to throw up."

"No problem," I said as I clutched at my stomach, which was already churning.

"She'll have no choice but to allow you to go to the bathroom," continued Darlene. "Wait there until you hear the other band geeks being cheered as they march into the gymnasium, then count to a hundred and sneak back into the band room."

"Okay," I said, nodding convulsively.

"It'll be dark," Darlene reminded me. "And also quiet, because I've told Tate not to say a word until you're in his arms."

I clutched my stomach harder. "Why?" I breathed. "Why can't he say a word?"

"Why do you have to ask so many questions?" complained Darlene, throwing her spindly arms into the air. "I'm your friend. Don't you trust me?"

"It's not that —"

"I should hope not," said Darlene primly. "Now, promise me you're not going to be a big baby and chicken out, no matter what."

"Okay. I promise," I babbled. "Only — one more thing."

"Yes?" asked Darlene impatiently.

"Do you think Tate is going to floss and brush beforehand?"

"*What?*"

"Never mind."

⌇⌇⌇

The next morning, my hands were shaking so badly that I poked myself in the eyeball with my eyeliner pencil four times before I finally finished putting on my makeup. Hurrying into my bedroom, I put on a bra, a tank top, a T-shirt *and* a sweatshirt to make sure I had as many barriers as possible between my breasts and Tate's potentially meandering hands. Pulling on my favorite jeans and slipping into my purple high-tops, I dashed to the kitchen and poured myself a glass of pineapple juice. Just as I was about to gulp it down, however, I heard a loud screech and turned to see Rory flying straight at my head! With a cry, I flung up my hands to protect my face and, in the process, poured pineapple juice all over myself.

"You idiot!" I hollered, slamming down my cup and chasing him into the living room. "How did you get out of your cage?"

"YOU IDIOT," he squawked excitedly as he settled down on top of my school things. "GET OUT!"

"Rory, stay," I commanded, creeping toward him.

"STAY," he sang, taking a poop on my knapsack before sailing into the air again.

"Rory, what do think Nana is going to say if I don't get you safely back into your cage before I go to school?" I cried, making a grab at his tail feathers.

"YOU IDIOT," he suggested as he landed on the remains of the toasted raisin bagel that was sitting on a plate next to my dad's recliner.

"Yes!" I said. "But she'll be talking to you, not me."

"YOU, NOT ME," he agreed in a garbled voice, not bothering to distinguish between the bagel and the greasy paper napkin beside it in his haste to gobble up his prize.

He was so distracted by his feeding frenzy that I was able to grab him. Dumping him back in his cage, I carefully locked the door, grabbed a fresh roll of paper towel and cleaned up the pineapple juice mess as best I could.

"I'll get you for this, Rory," I promised as I set the paper towel roll down on the counter next to his cage and hurriedly began to peel off my many layers of soaking breast protection. "Mark my words."

⌖

The morning was a blur, and then suddenly I was milling around the band room with my fellow Performance Band members, trying not to puke my guts out. I was so nervous I could hardly breathe.

"I don't know if I can go through with this," I confessed to Holly.

"Then don't go through with it," she urged, gripping my hands so tight it hurt. "Please! I have a really bad feeling about this, Francie. *Really* bad."

I started to ask her what in the world she was talking about, but just then Mrs. C rapped her little conductor's baton against the side of a music stand and called for attention.

"Okay, they're almost ready for us in the gym, so look sharp, everybody," she said as she nervously ran one hand through her *achingly* beautiful hair. "Before we go, however,

I want to share some exciting news with you. This morning I was advised that the Portage la Prairie finals in both the band and solo competitions will be televised in front of a live studio audience and broadcast on public television!"

I was so flabbergasted I couldn't even join in the cheering. I knew for a fact that there was only one TV studio in Portage la Prairie. This meant that if our band made it into the finals, there was a good possibility we'd end up in a studio right down the hall from where Lorenzo was taping his show. If that happened, how hard could it possibly be for me to figure out a way to get in to see him? And if *that* happened, how could he possibly ignore the passion with which I spoke about my baking?

He couldn't. It was just that simple.

Nana was right: it didn't matter how many times I stumbled, it only mattered that I got back up and kept trying. As long as I did that, the dream could never die.

My head was spinning, but the sight of my fellow band members beginning to file into the gym stopped it cold because this was my cue — my chance to keep another dream alive.

The dream of Tate.

Feeling more confident than I had all week, I ran up to Mrs. C and blurted that I thought I was going to throw up. She looked exasperated — especially since Randy had just gone to throw up a minute earlier — but as Darlene had predicted, she just ordered me to the bathroom as quickly as possible. Once there, I crouched down, put my head between my knees and counted to one hundred like Darlene had told me to do. When I was done, I stood up, freshened my lip gloss and, like a girl in a fog, crept out of the bathroom. Mr. Simmons was at the other end of the hall, walking in the opposite direction, so I tiptoed as fast as I could to the darkened band room and slipped inside.

For a moment, I just stood there letting my eyes adjust to the dimness. Then, unsure of exactly where Tate might be waiting and mindful of the fact that he had orders not to say a word until he had me in his arms, I began to silently pick my way around open instrument cases, music stands and stray pieces of sheet music. I'd made it through the woodwind and brass sections with no sign of Tate and was just beginning to wonder if it had all been a cruel joke, after all, when a small figure popped up from behind the tympani drums, not two feet from where I was standing. With a shout of surprise, I stumbled backward and fell, hitting my head squarely on the gong.

"I couldn't let you do it, Francie!" shrieked Harold Horvath. "I couldn't let you go through with it!"

Faintly, I heard Mr. Simmons bellow and begin trundling toward the band room as fast as his nicotine-ravaged body could carry him.

"What are you talking about?" I hissed as I scrambled to my feet. "Oh, Harold, you *idiot*. You've ruined everything!"

"No, no," he protested. "I've *saved* you. I know you were told you were going to be sharing an intimate moment with some fellow named Tape — "

"Tate."

"Yes, exactly. But it was a lie! When I arrived with my fellow band members to participate in the pep rally, Randy took me aside and told me this Tape character had told him that someone had arranged for a lecherous senior to be waiting for you instead," explained Harold urgently. "When I heard that, I realized you could be in mortal danger."

"Mortal danger?" I said skeptically.

"Yes!" he cried, clutching his head as though boggled by my attitude. "Alone, in a dark room, with a stranger who is bigger and stronger than you? There would have been no way for you to stop him if he'd decided he wanted to do more than kissing, Francie. No way at all! That's why I ordered Randy to detain the lech while I hurried past the leviathan with the ashtray breath to wait here and explain the situation to you."

The leviathan with the ashtray breath was mere seconds away from discovering us.

"I know this has been a terrible shock for you," continued Harold frantically, his voice getting higher pitched with every word. "But I want you to know that if you feel the need to show your gratitude toward me in the form of a warm embrace and possibly some light necking, I'm on board that ship and ready to set sail!"

With that, Harold puckered up his lips, reached out his arms and started lurching toward me like a lovesick zombie.

"AHA!" cried Mr. Simmons, bursting into the room and turning on the light with a triumphant flourish. "Freewater!" He staggered backward and clutched his chest in shock. "I don't believe it. Well, I guess it just goes to show that you knuckleheads are all the same, after all. Come along, pigeons."

"Mr. Simmons, let me explain ..." I began desperately.

"Save it, Freewater," he sneered. "We're going to the office and I'm calling your parents. You can explain to them why I caught you sucking face with this pint-sized Romeo when you should have been making beautiful music with the rest of the band."

∽∾∾

It was ages before my dad finally showed up, and when he did, he looked as upset as I'd ever seen him look.

"I can explain," I blurted. "It's really complicated, though. The main thing you need to know is that I wasn't doing anything inappropriate with Harold, I promise! He's just a friend and besides, I didn't even know he was going to be there." I clasped my hands under my chin. "Oh, Dad, you've got to believe me!"

"I believe you," he said distractedly. "Just get your coat, Francie. We have to leave."

Something about the way he said that made my blood run cold.

"Why?" I asked, not moving an inch. "Why do we have to leave?"

My father pressed his palms together and held his hands to his mouth. He looked like he was praying to find the right words to tell me something *awful*.

"What is it?" I asked in alarm, rising to my feet. "Is it Mom?"

My father shook his head.

"Is it Nana?" I asked. "Did something happen to Nana?"

My father took my hand. "No, honey," he said gently. "It's not Nana."

"Then who is it?" I cried.

"It's Rory," he said softly. "Rory is dead."

14. The Confession

All any lady needs to know about nutrition is that the four major food groups are chocolate, strawberries, champagne and me.

From Morsels to Live By *by Lorenzo LaRue*

"He choked to death on a mouthful of paper towel," my father explained when we got into the car. "Nana came home and found him lying on the bottom of his cage. She tried to clear his airway and resuscitate him, but it was too late."

The blood drained from my face as I remembered tossing the paper towel roll onto the counter next to Rory's cage that morning. I pictured Nana trying desperately to revive her beloved pet — alternately weeping and thumping her cane on the floor as though she might somehow be able to command him to live.

"How is she doing?" I asked in a very small voice.

"She's pretty upset, honey," said my dad, patting me on the knee. "Remember, she got Rory right after Poppy died, and she always said he helped her feel less alone in those first difficult days." My dad paused before adding, "She's decided to have a small memorial service for him on Sunday and she asked me to ask you if you'd bake a batch of bran muffins to serve to the guests."

"Of course — they were Rory's favorite," I said. And then, suddenly, I was crying. "That bird was an *idiot!*" I blubbered as I leaned over to sob on my dad's shoulder.

"I know he was, honey," he agreed softly, putting his arms around me and kissing the top of my head. "I know he was."

☙☙☙

Sunday afternoon, my parents closed the café for an hour so that Nana could hold Rory's memorial service there. Along with Rory's empty cage and food dish, Nana brought down some of the things Rory had most enjoyed chewing on — including my mother's favorite shirt, Malibu Barbie, the plastic ivy from on top of the dish cupboard and my old toothbrush — and arranged them around a large, glossy picture of Rory as though hoping they would accompany him on his journey across the River Styx to the Underworld.

Besides my parents and me, the only other guests were Nana's gentleman friend, Mr. Darnell, and Marguerite.

"I am terribly sorry for your loss, Mrs. McNamara," whispered Marguerite respectfully as we waited for the service to begin. Rummaging around in her big straw purse, she pulled out a couple of photos. "I took these at Francie's birthday party," she explained, handing them to Nana. "I thought you might like to have them."

The pictures were all of Rory — Rory with my parents, Rory with Nana, Rory using his scratchy left foot to try to drag the edge of a plastic tablecloth into his cage.

"Can I see those?" I asked in a low voice.

Wordlessly, Nana handed them to me. For a moment, I stood transfixed by the frozen image of Tate and me standing in front of Rory's cage. I was smiling and Tate had just reached out to brush the hair off my forehead. If I didn't know better, I would have said it looked as though he actually kind of liked me.

"I'd like to begin the service now," murmured Nana, thumping softly to the front of the room.

Hastily, I wiped my watery eyes and shoved the pictures into the back pocket of my second-best pair of black dress pants. As Nana began to quietly eulogize Rory, I heard someone tiptoe up behind me.

It was Holly and behind her, Ricky.

"Sorry we're late," whispered Holly. "Your mom said she'd leave the back door unlocked for us."

"Oh," I replied, feeling slightly confused. "Uh ... what are you doing here?"

"I heard what happened," she murmured, giving my hand a sympathetic squeeze.

I didn't know if she meant that she'd heard about Rory dying or that she'd heard about what happened to me in the band room with Harold, but I didn't care. I was just glad to have her there — so glad I didn't even mind the fact that I was sharing her with Ricky.

"... and so, in conclusion," Nana was saying, "the best thing about Rory was that he was my friend. He wasn't perfect, goodness knows, but he made me laugh and he kept me company and he listened to me and occasionally even sang with me, and no matter what else happened, I always knew I could count on him to sail alongside me through life's stormy seas."

Holly and I smiled at each other and squeezed hands again.

"And now," said Nana, reaching for a knife, "I'd ask you to all butter your muffins and gulp them down as fast as you possibly can in loving memory of my dear departed Rory."

❧❧❧

After the memorial service was over and Nana had gone upstairs, my dad asked Ricky to help him bring some boxes up from the basement and my mom brought out ice-cream sodas for Holly and me.

"I just can't believe she double-crossed you like that," said Holly, after I'd told her how Darlene had arranged for some perverted senior to take Tate's place in the band room. "It makes me wish I'd never tried to include her in anything — and it makes me feel like a fool for ever having felt sorry for her on account of what happened to her mother."

"What do you mean?" I asked, taking a big slurp of my soda. "What happened to her mother?"

Holly looked from side to side and then leaned forward. "This is just between you and me," she warned in a low voice.

I nodded eagerly. It had been a long time since it had

been just Holly and me sharing secrets together, and it felt *wonderful*.

"Okay, remember how you once told me that you thought Darlene might be motherless?" breathed Holly. "Well, she is. Seven years ago, her mother went into the hospital for a routine tonsillectomy, only this mentally unstable operating room attendant purposely pulled a switcheroo between her file and this old diabetic patient's file, so instead of taking out her tonsils, the surgeons ended up amputating both of her legs. Three days later gas gangrene set in, and Darlene had to spend her seventh birthday in the intensive care unit watching her mother die."

"That's impossible," I said flatly. "Darlene told *me* that her mother abandoned her in the floral department of a grocery store exactly two weeks before her eighth birthday."

"Why would her mother abandon her in the floral department?" asked Holly.

"Why would surgeons amputate two perfect healthy-looking legs?" I asked.

For a moment, Holly and I just stared at each other. Then we both burst out laughing.

"What are you laughing about?" asked Ricky as he walked up to the table.

"None of your business," said Holly affectionately, patting the seat beside her.

Just then, the door of the café slammed open and Harold Horvath staggered inside clutching a beautiful white rose in one hand and lugging an absolutely enormous instrument case behind him. The moment he saw me, his eyes widened but he didn't smile. If anything, he frowned more deeply. Pivoting on one heel, he turned toward me and stumped his way over to the table.

"Oh, brother," I muttered, sinking into my seat.

"Francie," panted Harold, setting his instrument case heavily at my feet and handing me the white rose. "I would have been here sooner if I'd known."

"Known?" I asked, staring at the rose in embarrassment.

Harold swooped into the seat beside me and scooped up my hand. "On Friday, after your father picked you up from school, Randy was sent to the office for holding the lecherous senior hostage in the boys' washroom on the third floor while I attempted to extricate you from the band room with your body and dignity intact."

Pulling my hand away, I gave a quick, embarrassed glance at Ricky and sank farther into my seat.

"Randy heard the secretaries talking about Rory's passing," continued Harold mournfully. "Unfortunately, he didn't think to mention it to me until this morning when he and Auntie were dropping me off at Performance Band rehearsal. I waited until they'd driven away, then snatched up my bass bassoon and hurried here as fast as I could to offer my condolences to you and your family at this difficult time."

"Oh," I said, feeling a little nonplussed. "Well, thanks."

"So, how did he ... go?" inquired Harold in a deeply sympathetic voice

"Rory? Well, he choked to death on a wad of paper towel," I explained, my face flushing uncomfortably.

Harold looked startled, but quickly smoothed it over. "It's okay, it's okay," he soothed, rubbing my arm. "How old was he?"

"I'm not sure." I shrugged, taking a deep sniff of my rose.

Harold stared at me with his large, thickly lashed eyes. "Well, was he older than you or younger than you?" he prompted.

I shrugged again. "I really don't know, Harold. You'd have to ask my nana."

"What about your parents?"

"Oh, they didn't have much to do with him," I said. "To be honest, Nana was the only one who really liked him." I chuckled ruefully. "Between you and me, the rest of us thought he was kind of a pain in the neck."

At this, Harold sprang to his feet. "How ... how can you speak about Rory that way?" he demanded, his whole body quivering with outrage. "Where is your decency? Where is your humanity? For pity's sake, that poor child was your *brother!*"

After a moment of stunned silence, I burst out laughing. So did Holly and Ricky. Harold looked ready to hit somebody.

"Harold," I said as my giggles subsided, "Rory wasn't my brother. He was my nana's pet bird."

"Oh," said Harold.

I was about to tell him not to feel foolish on account of the misunderstanding when he threw back his head and let out a great, deep, booming laugh that sounded so out of place coming from his skinny little body that the rest of us started laughing all over again. This made Harold laugh harder — which made us laugh harder. Somewhere in between all that laughing, my mom brought out a plate of fries and two more ice-cream sodas.

"Well!" said Harold, plopping back down and digging into the plate of fries with gusto. "I'm certainly glad to learn that you're not prostrate with grief, Francie, because I wouldn't have wanted our first weekend away together to be marred by tragedy."

"Our first weekend away together?" I spluttered, choking on a French fry.

"In Portage la Prairie!" said Harold exultantly. "Randy tells me we'll all be staying at the same hotel. By the way, Auntie says that a very popular television baker will be in Portage la Prairie taping his show at the same time we'll be there. His name is Lorenzo LaRue and she says that his book *Don't Let Him Knead You* changed her life forever. Have you heard of him?"

It was on the tip of my tongue to say I hadn't, or to say I had but to act as though Lorenzo was no big deal to me one way or another. But sitting next to a guy who, on our very first date, had admitted to his dream of becoming a circus performer, I couldn't bring myself to lie.

"Heard of him?" I said boldly. "I'm practically his number-one fan!"

"It's true, she is," concurred Holly quickly. "She watches his show every week, she's a member of his Birthday Club *and* she was recently selected as a finalist in a contest where the winner got to bake with him on TV!"

"Really?" said Harold, looking impressed. "You never told me that."

"It never came up." I shrugged. "Plus, I was pretty disappointed that I hadn't won. I guess I just wanted to forget about it."

"I know what you mean," said Ricky. "Last year, my band placed second in the Morden Corn and Apple Festival Talent Competition behind a troupe of ten-year-old highland dancers. For weeks afterward, I couldn't stand the sight of corn *or* apples."

He looked so glum at the memory that I reached across the table and gave his arm a friendly squeeze. Holly smiled at me, then leaned her head on his shoulder.

"Anyway," I continued. "I'm not disappointed anymore because I've decided to figure out a way to get in to see Lorenzo in Portage la Prairie. Meeting him is the first step in my dream of becoming a famous baker." I didn't bother to mention that it was also the first step in my dream of someday becoming the ravishingly beautiful young Mrs. LaRue. "I mean, I know it won't be easy — first our Performance Band has to make the finals, then I have to figure out a way to give Mrs. C and Mr. Ashtray Breath the slip, then I have to find Lorenzo and get him to listen to me and take me seriously — but I'm going give it my very best shot."

"Good for you, Francie," breathed Harold, his eyes glowing like live coals. "Why, if I had a chance to meet Claude Depardieu, I wouldn't hesitate for an instant, either."

"Who is Claude Depardieu?" I asked.

Harold rolled his eyes. "Only the finest mime this country has produced in the last fifty years!" he clucked.

Holly, Ricky and I started laughing again. When we were finished, the four of us brainstormed possible solutions to my Lorenzo roadblocks until Ricky said he had to go jam with his band. Holly immediately let out a sigh and asked if she could tag along and watch him. Ricky flushed with pleasure at the thought of having his very first groupie, then accidentally knocked his ice-cream soda mug off the table. When we were done cleaning up the mess, Ricky and Holly hurriedly left, and I walked Harold to the front door of the café.

"You know, Harold, I never did get a chance to thank you for trying to preserve my dignity and ... everything ... on Friday," I said, blushing furiously.

"You're welcome," he murmured. "And may I take this opportunity to say how very lovely you look when you blush?" He brushed the backs of his cool fingers against my burning cheeks. "Just when I think you can't get any more beautiful, you make a fool out of me."

Jerking my head away, I tried to think of something to say.

"Shhh! Don't say anything," whispered Harold, placing his finger against my lips. "Only know that the austere white rose I brought you out of respect for the passing of what I thought was your beloved brother was always, in my heart, blood red with passion. So if at any time you feel that a little sexual healing might help you recover from the death of your grandmother's bird, never forget that I am only a phone call away."

And with that, Harold picked up his bass bassoon and stumped out of the café leaving me, stunned and speechless, in his formidable wake.

୭୭

That afternoon, I picked out five of my all-time favorite original recipes and baked a batch of each to absolute perfection. Then I selected the finest samples from each batch, wrapped them in wax paper and packed them carefully in a large Tupperware container so that when I finally met Lorenzo and confessed to being an inspired baker, he wouldn't just have to take my word for it.

Just as I set the last chocolate toffee cheese square into the container, Nana thumped into the kitchen.

"What's all this?" she asked, peering at the cooling racks crammed with goodies.

"I don't know," I said, shoving the Tupperware container to one side so she wouldn't guess what I was up to. "I, uh, just felt like doing a little baking, I guess. Would you like anything?"

Nana shook her head, then sat down at the kitchen table, placed her chin in her folded hands and gazed at the spot near the counter where I used to drag Rory's cage when I was pretending he was my studio audience. Turning away from her, I puttered about, rinsing pots and scrubbing burned bits of batter off cookie sheets until I couldn't stand the silence a minute longer.

"I've got to go finish my Life Skills project now, okay, Nana?" I said loudly as I pulled off my apron.

"Okay," she nodded.

"Then I've got to pack for my band trip. The bus leaves tomorrow morning at eight o'clock sharp," I informed her.

"All right," she said.

She seemed so distant that for one awful moment I wondered if she knew about the part I'd played in Rory's death.

"Nana?" I began timidly.

"Yes, Francie?" she said, looking up at me.

"Nothing," I said hastily, turning away.

⁄◦◦◦

My Life Skills project took me most of the afternoon to finish. I wasn't entirely displeased with the final result — the research was solid and even included a personal interview with a lawyer who just happened to be one of my Sunday morning baking customers. Over an extra-large cup of black coffee and a free maple walnut muffin, he'd told me all about how he'd nearly killed himself in law school, how the older lawyers at his firm treated him like a personal slave and how he was going to have to work eighty hours a week, fifty-two weeks a year, for the next ten years if he wanted a shot at making partner.

"But it's not all bad news," he'd explained with a hollow smile. "If I can make it to forty without getting divorced, having a heart attack or suffering a nervous breakdown, there's a good chance I'll be able to afford the kind of lifestyle most people only dream about."

It sounded like exactly the kind of thing Mr. Simmons was looking for — real world, no nonsense, tell it like it is. Of course, it also sounded like hell on earth. Who in his right mind would want to wait until he was forty for a *chance* at the kind of lifestyle most people only dream about? Even if he succeeded, what would be the point? He'd be *forty* — so old he might as well be dead!

But that was neither here nor there for me — I'd completed a project that was worth at least an A minus and that was all that mattered. Setting my homework to one side, I pulled out my duffle bag and began to pack for the band trip. Sneaking into the kitchen, I grabbed my cookbook, my baker's hat and the Tupperware container full of samples. Running back to my room, I carefully arranged these things at the bottom of the bag, then piled on top of them several different dark-bottom-white-top combinations to wear during performances, several changes of casual clothing, my pajamas and slippers, my stuffed frog, my makeup bag, my toiletry bag, two pairs of shoes (including my platform shoes), my three favorite romance novels (with the smutty parts marked by dog-eared pages), my sexy one-piece bathing suit (just in case the hotel had a hot tub), my camera (so I could get my own, personal photos of Lorenzo shirtless), my tape recorder (so I could record Holly's winning flute solo performance and give it to her for her next birthday), a giant bag of Skittles (even though we weren't supposed to bring snacks), three extra bras (just in case the straps of two bras broke simultaneously) and all the feminine protection I could find under the sink in the bathroom (I wasn't due to get my period, but it couldn't hurt to be prepared).

It was getting late by the time I breathlessly managed to get the bulging bag closed, so after giving my teeth a good brush, I crawled into bed and turned off my light.

Minutes later, the door creaked open.

"Francie?" whispered Nana.

"Yes?" I asked, staring at the wedge of yellow light that streamed across my darkened floor.

Quietly, Nana thumped over and sat down at the edge of my bed.

"I just wanted to say good-night, and also to wish you good luck at your band festival," she said.

"If we make it to the finals, it's going to be televised," I told her.

"Is that so?" she said in surprise. "Did you know that Lorenzo is going to be taping his show in Portage la Prairie at the exact same time?"

"What?" I exclaimed loudly, sitting up on one elbow. "Really? Wow. That's quite a coincidence, isn't it?"

"It certainly is," agreed Nana.

Giving me a powdery kiss on the cheek, she gently pushed me back down onto the pillow, pulled the covers up to my chin and started back out of the room. She was almost gone when I burrowed completely under the covers and called her back.

"Nana, I'm sorry about Rory," I mumbled, my voice sounding muffled even to my own ears.

"I know," she said.

"No," I blurted. "I mean ... I'm the one who accidentally

left the paper towel by his cage. I also yelled at him the last time I saw him. I ... I called him an idiot."

For a moment I didn't hear anything. Then I heard Nana softly chuckling. Flinging off the covers, I sat bolt upright in bed.

"What's so funny?" I demanded.

"Rory is!" said Nana, slapping her thigh. "Honestly, what kind of bird chokes to death on a wad of paper towel?"

"So ... you're not mad at me?" I asked.

"Of course not," said Nana. "Whatever made you think such a thing?"

I shrugged helplessly. "Today ... in the kitchen ... you seemed so distant."

"I was a little distant, I guess. But not because of you or anything you did, Francie," she informed me with a little thump of her cane. "I was sad, that's all. I loved Rory with all my heart, but he got what he had coming to him, make no mistake about that. In this life, we take our chances and in the end, the best we can hope for is that the thrill of the moment was worth the price we paid."

With that, Nana kissed me again, thumped out of the room and closed the door behind her. With a shiver, I lay back down in my now badly rumpled bed and stared into the darkness, thinking about the days ahead and wondering what price I was going to have to pay if I was lucky enough to have the thrill of meeting Lorenzo LaRue.

15. Hope and Other Forms of Torture (Part II)

Randall, I have decided that you are like maple sugar candy — undeniably irresistible in your way, but likely to cause stomach upset, diabetes and tooth decay in large doses. So get up off your knees and get the hell out of my way. I've got places to go.

From The Cad Who Loved Me by Ima Dormatt

The next morning, my mom drove me to school so that I wouldn't have to lug all my stuff on the bus.

"Now, are you sure you have everything?" she asked, after we'd loaded my bag onto the luggage compartment of the big touring bus the band was taking to Portage la Prairie.

"I'm sure," I said distractedly, patting her arm as I scanned the noisy crowd for Holly. "Don't worry. Everything will be fine."

My mother nodded. "Do you have your toothbrush?" she asked. "Your retainer? A change of underwear?" She leaned close and whispered. "Some Imodium in case of diarrhea?"

I exhaled very loudly. "Mom," I ordered, *"relax.* I'm going to be just fine."

"I know you are," she laughed, throwing her arms around me.

Just then, Holly's car came to a screeching halt at the curb in front of the school. In the backseat, I could see Holly using her flute case to parry blows from Tabitha, who appeared to be trying to bash her brains in with an alto recorder. In the front seat, I could see Mrs. Carleson scrunched down behind the steering wheel looking about 185 million years old.

"Holly is here," I said happily, wriggling out of my mother's arms. "You can go now, if you like."

"I don't mind staying until the bus leaves," she said.

"It's okay," I replied, trying hard not to sound impatient.

My mother rolled her eyes. "All right, *fine*. Here you go," she said, pulling a bag out of her knapsack. "A little gift from Dad and me for the bus ride there."

Peering inside the bag, I saw a large bag of chips, a chocolate bar, a box of Sourpuss candies and a jumbo bottle of soda — more junk food than I was normally allowed to eat in a year. "Oh, wow!" I cried. "Thank you! Thank you so much! This is so awesome. You guys are the best!"

"Yeah, yeah," she chuckled. Pulling out her car keys, she gave me one last kiss and then said, "Oh, I almost forgot."

"I packed some pads," I whispered with a grimace.

My mother shook her head. "That's good to know, but that's not it," she said. "This morning, after you'd gone down to the car, Nana asked me to give you a message. She said, 'Tell her to say hello to Lorenzo for me.' Does that mean anything to you?"

Even though I was totally shocked, I *instantly* managed to turn my face into a mask devoid of all emotion.

"I have no idea," I said in a slightly robotic voice.

My mother gave me a strange look.

"None at all," I insisted.

"Okay," she said, jangling her keys at me. "Good luck at the festival and we'll see you when you get home."

⁊⁊⁊

It was another twenty-five minutes before we got everyone's stuff loaded onto the bus. By that point, Mrs. C was having a conniption fit over the possibility that we might be late for our first set, and Mr. Simmons looked as though he might start bleeding from the ears at any moment. Holly and I didn't care — we were too excited. The Performance Band Festival was finally here!

"This is so great," I enthused, kneeling up in my seat to bounce and gawk at the people seated behind me.

One of the French-horn jokers lifted up a straw and caught me with a spit ball right between the eyes before cranking up the volume on his MP3 player. I stuck my tongue out at him, then slid back into my seat and took a big swig of my soda. At the front of the bus, Mr. Simmons was bellowing for everyone to be quiet and Mrs. C was desperately trying to take one final head count. The next instant, the bus was pulling away from the curb.

"HURRAY! HURRAY!" we cheered as we pounded on the windows and made faces at all the sad sacks who were going to be stuck in regular classes for the next two days.

Suddenly, I noticed Darlene and Tate standing with a group of popular seniors who were disdainfully watching our display. Darlene pointed toward the bus and laughed. Then she said something, and Tate and the others started laughing, too.

Feeling slightly subdued, I sat back in my seat and took another swig of soda. "This is going to be great, isn't it?" I said to Holly — and also to Ricky and Randy, who were sitting right across the aisle from us.

"Absolutely," said the boys, looking up from their video games.

"The greatest," said Holly.

"Well, now, that depends on you, don't it?" drawled Jody, popping up to dangle over the seatback in front of me. The kerchief she usually wore to keep her long, blond hair out of her face was tied over her nose and she was pointing one of her drumsticks at me. "I seen what's in that there bag your mama handed you, ma'am, and the fact is I'm powerful fond of Sourpuss candies. So just hand 'em over and no one'll get hurt."

Holly, Randy and Ricky started to laugh. I took another sip of soda.

"I don't want to use force," said Jody, dropping her voice

even lower and performing such an explosive drum solo on the top of Sharon's baseball cap that her iPod earbuds popped out. "But as you can plainly see, I will if I have to."

⚯⚯⚯

An hour and twenty minutes later, the bus pulled into the half-circle driveway in front of the concert hall in Portage la Prairie.

"Okay, listen up, people," called Mrs. C anxiously. "There's no time to lose — we're expected on stage in less than ten minutes. Leave everything but your instruments and your sheet music and come with me." She turned to hurry off the bus, then abruptly turned back. "And just a reminder — according to the festival charter, once we enter that hall, you are expected to conduct yourselves as musicians of the highest caliber."

"Yeah!" snarled Mr. Simmons, who was clearly in the grip of nicotine withdrawal. "That means no running around like pigeons with your heads cut off!"

"It also means immediate point deductions for any student who fails to take the stage prepared," added Mrs. C, with a sideways glance at Mr. Simmons, who had begun to sweat badly. "So be sure you have a spare reed, keep a tight grip on your music and follow me."

All around me, kids bounded up and excitedly filed into the aisle. I sat hunched over in my seat, worried that the slightest movement might cause my overfilled bladder to spontaneously release.

"Come on," urged Holly, as the last few people straggled off the bus. "Get up."

"I can't," I croaked, hunching over farther as I silently cursed my parents for giving me that jumbo bottle of soda.

"You have to," said Holly firmly. "You can't sit here all day — you'll wet yourself *and* get into trouble. Think of it this way: the faster you get off this bus and find a bathroom, the faster you'll be able to go. Won't that feel good?" Closing her

217

eyes and smiling blissfully, she sighed, "Ahhhhh."

"Stop it!" I cried. Gingerly, I got to my feet, followed her off the bus and hobbled up to Mrs. C, who was busy rifling through a stack of sheet music.

"I have to go to the bathroom," I whispered.

"Not now, Francie," she said distractedly.

"But Mrs. C ..."

"Not now," she repeated, more firmly this time. "The last time I let you go to the bathroom before a major event you ended up sneaking off to meet some boy in the band room, remember? Just take your place in line. You can use the facilities after we've finished our first set."

I nodded mutely, and then, as she wheeled around to snatch the spit-ball straw out of the mouth of the French-horn joker, I slipped off to find a bathroom. I didn't want to disobey Mrs. C — I really didn't — but I had no choice. There was no way I was going to be able to hold it through the first set. It was either find a bathroom now, or pee my pants during the second movement of Mozart's favorite symphony, and I just didn't see how I was going to be able to get away with that without the judges docking us points.

I only meant to be gone for a minute, but the first-floor bathroom was closed for cleaning and I had to search for one on the second floor. When I found it, I was so excited to finally see a toilet that I popped the button of my best pair of black pants in my haste to yank them down. Several exquisite minutes later, I pulled my pants back up, zipped up and washed my hands for as long as it took to hum half the alphabet. Then I took off down the long, deserted second-floor hallway at a dead run, flew down the stairs and bolted into the foyer in search of Mrs. C and the band. Worrisomely, I didn't see them anywhere, but from the big hall to my left, I *did* hear the sound of Mrs. C's unique interpretation of Mozart's favorite symphony — being played without any maracas!

The sound filled me with such dread that I think I might actually have fainted if I hadn't at that very moment seen Mr. Simmons just outside the foyer mashing his cigarette out in a barrel full of sand. I knew if he came in and saw me standing there, I was dead pigeon meat. So, turning on one heel, I ran lightly to the door of the big hall, yanked it open and slipped inside. Tiptoeing along the side wall, I reached the stage in seconds, slunk up the stairs, picked up my maracas and began to play. I avoided looking Mrs. C in the eye, but I couldn't avoid the glare of one of the judges — a thin-lipped woman whose lipstick had bled into the cracks around her mouth. Sucking her already sunken cheeks in, she leaned over and made a precise notation on the score card in front of her.

When the set was over and we'd filed off the stage and out of the big hall like musicians of the highest caliber, Mrs. C stormed over and chewed me out in front of everybody. I tried to explain myself, but this only made her angrier, especially when the head judge marched outside and posted our results on the big bulletin board.

"We got docked twenty points for that little stunt of yours, Francie," fumed Mrs. C, her hair bouncing like something out of a shampoo commercial. "Do you realize how close to perfect our next two sets are going to have to be if we're to have any hope of making the finals tomorrow?"

I was horror-stricken at the thought that we might not make the finals. Not only would my more dedicated fellow band members almost certainly kill me, but my entire plan to meet Lorenzo — and fulfill my *destiny* — hinged on making them.

"Don't worry, Mrs. C," I said fervently. "I'll talk to everyone. We'll make sure our next sets are not just close to perfect, but better than perfect!"

She gave me a moody toss of her glorious hair, then turned and walked over to calm Mr. Simmons, who'd caught a tenth grader using his trombone to lift up the back of an older girl's skirt. I ran over to where Holly and Ricky were standing with my fellow percussionists.

"Mrs. C says I might have screwed up our chances of making the finals," I blurted. "I'm so sorry, you guys. I'm such a jerk!"

"It's not your fault you had to go to the bathroom," said Holly firmly. "Mrs. Cavanaugh really ought to have tried to delay the first set a few minutes."

"Yeah!" said Jody.

"I suppose you're right," I said, relieved that no one seemed to be mad at me. "Only, what am I going to do? My chances of meeting Lorenzo are next to zilch if I'm not at that television studio tomorrow!"

"Who is Lorenzo?" asked Sharon eagerly.

I quickly explained to her, Jody and Randy who he was, and why it was so important that I meet him. All three of them nodded as though they understood completely, then listened carefully to the sketchy details of my plan.

"You're going to need to figure out a way to give the warden the slip, you know," said Sharon, jerking her thumb toward Mrs. C.

"I know."

"And a way to get past studio security," added Jody. "And a way to get past Lorenzo's handlers, and a way to get him to believe you're as good as you say, and a way to —"

"I know! I know! I know!" I shrieked, flapping my hands in her face.

"Don't worry, Francie," murmured Randy, patting my shoulder with surprising tenderness for such a beefy guy. "Harold told me he was working on a plan that would solve all those problems, and I just know he's going to come through for you."

"Yeah," said Jody, who was staring at this new, tender Randy with such a lustful look in her eye that he broke into a visible sweat.

"I hope you're right," I said grimly. "Because the way

things are looking right now, I'm going to need all the help I can get."

❧❧❧

That afternoon, Holly did such an amazing job on her flute solo that she made it into the finals with flying colors. The band got perfect marks for our second set, but then, right near the end of our third set, disaster struck when Jody looked up from her snare drum and licked her lips at Randy, who immediately suffered a spasm so violent that his left tympani mallet flew out of his hand. In horrified disbelief, I watched as it flew slowly through the air. For a minute it looked like the rogue mallet might actually overshoot the thin-lipped judge — who was hunched over scribbling notes at the time — but just as it was about to sail safely over her head, she suddenly sat up and was caught right between the eyes with it.

And just like that, it was all over.

Later, as I stood in front of the results board staring at the crumpled piece of paper that said we'd missed making the finals by just five points, I tried to tell myself it wasn't the end of the world. Sure, I wasn't going to be at the TV studio tomorrow, but that didn't mean my chances of meeting Lorenzo were zilch, right? They were only *next* to zilch. After all, Lorenzo was still in Portage la Prairie, and so was I. All I needed to do was to think up a completely new plan — one that included, among other things, an expensive cab ride across town. Paid for by money I didn't have.

Afraid that I might start to cry if I stood there a minute longer, I turned abruptly and nearly tripped over Randy, who looked even worse than I felt.

"I'm sorry," he mumbled, his shaggy head drooping miserably. "We would have made it to the finals if it wasn't for me."

"We would have made it to the finals if it wasn't for *me*,

Randy. I was the one who showed up late for the first set, remember?" I reminded him.

Looking somewhat cheered, Randy nodded. Then his face clouded over again. "Harold is going to kill me for wrecking your plans," he said morosely.

In spite of everything, I started to laugh. "You're a wrestler who outweighs him by at least a hundred pounds of solid muscle, Randy," I said. "What's he going to do — talk you to death?" Impulsively, I threw my arm across his meaty shoulders. "Come on, let's go find the others and get back to the bus before it leaves for the hotel without us."

⚬⚬⚬

On the bus ride to the hotel, a rather despondent Mrs. C explained that all the bands that hadn't made it into the finals would be going back to the concert hall the next day in order to watch a live satellite feed of the televised performances of the finalists. Several disappointed musicians from the woodwind section hollered catcalls at this news, and one of the oboe players even spat gross bits of chewed reed at Randy and me. On that pleasant note, Mrs. C began handing out room keys and listing the many exciting hotel-based activities that could result in a midnight telephone call to our parents and permanent expulsion from the Performance Band.

"I don't care what she says," confided Jody as we stepped onto the elevator. "I'm going to sneak out tonight."

"Me too," said Sharon.

"Not me," said Holly. "I'm heading into the solo finals in first place and I don't want to do anything to mess up my chances of bringing home gold."

"What about you, Francie?" called Jody as she bounded like a gazelle down the narrow, hideously carpeted hallway.

I started to answer her, but faltered when I saw a single rose lying in front of our door. It looked exactly like the one Harold had given me the previous weekend, only instead of being white, it was red.

Blood red with *passion*.

"Well, looky here!" cried Sharon, snatching it up and giving it a deep sniff. "I wonder who this is from?"

"Search me," I squeaked, hoping no one would notice how red my face had suddenly gotten.

But no one was paying any attention to me. After several impatient attempts to use the magnetic room key, Sharon shoved the key at Holly, who got us in on the first try. Whooping like a pair of overexcited five-year-olds, Sharon and Jody raced into the room, chucked their bags to one side and leaped onto the beds.

"This is our bed!" shrieked Jody, bouncing up and down as hard as she could.

"No — this is!" cried Sharon from the other bed.

"Forget it!" hollered Jody, leaning over to wallop Sharon with a pillow.

Sharon immediately snatched up her own pillow, launched herself across the chasm between the beds and began pounding Jody on the head with it. When they'd worked themselves into a dripping sweat, they flung the pillows to one side and announced that they were off to find the ice machine. Flopping past Holly and me, they threw open the hotel room door and screamed like a pair of banshees when they discovered Harold Horvath standing before them.

"I knocked several times," he explained in a dignified voice. "But I gather you were unable to hear me."

"I gather you're right," agreed Sharon, giving him a hearty smack on the back. "So, Harry, what's up?"

Harold winced at being referred to as Harry, then said, "Ladies, I've come to tell you that following dinner this evening, I will be hosting a clandestine gathering in my hotel room."

"Awesome," said Jody. Sharon nodded eagerly.

"And that's not all," he said. Looking past the others, he caught me with his eyes. Once again, I felt as though I was under the spell of an evil hypnotist.

"What else, Harold?" I asked in a faraway voice.

"Once everyone has arrived and the lights have been dimmed," he murmured, "we are going to quietly gather together in a circle ..."

"Yeah, yeah?" breathed Sharon and Jody.

"... and take turns randomly selecting members of the opposite sex with whom to share a brief but deeply fulfilling embrace."

There was a brief, confused silence. And then: "OH!" hollered Jody excitedly. "YOU MEAN WE'RE GOING TO PLAY SPIN THE BOTTLE?"

"Exactly," said Harold.

And with a smile that made me tingle all over, he turned on his heel and sauntered away.

☙☙☙

After he was gone, Sharon and Jody bounced out of the room in search of the ice machine, leaving Holly and me to ourselves.

"I'm really happy you made the finals," I said.

"I'm really sorry you didn't make the finals," she said at the very same instant.

We laughed a little, then I cried a little. Then we racked our brains for a way to get me over to the TV studio the next day. When we came up empty, I cried some more, then dug the Tupperware container full of samples out of my bag and stretched out on the bed next to Holly.

"I really believed it was going to happen, you know?" I sniffled as I gulped down a perfect little lemon custard puff pastry.

"I know. Me too," Holly mumbled through a mouthful of blueberry crumble squares. "Now, um, not to change the subject or anything, but are you going to kiss Harold tonight at the Spin the Bottle party?"

"I don't know," I huffed, stuffing half a raspberry white chocolate scone into my mouth.

"I think you should," said Holly, spraying me with bits of crumble. "I've never seen a boy with nicer lips, and I've noticed that his breath always smells like Junior Mints. I bet he's a great kisser."

At the mention of Harold's lips, I started to choke so hard on my giant mouthful of scone that I almost didn't manage to get Holly pinned in a position that would allow me to tickle her bare feet until she begged for mercy.

Almost.

That evening we went to dinner at the Pizza Pizzazz restaurant across the street. Mrs. C forbade us to get the Parmesan noodles on the grounds that they smelled like vomit, so I had a Hawaiian pizza and an order of cheesy breadsticks. After dinner, Sharon, Jody, Holly and I went back to our room and used the tape recorder I'd brought to record the sound of us laughing and talking together. Since Holly wasn't going to be sneaking out to attend Harold's party, she'd agreed to play the recording any time she heard Mrs. C or Mr. Simmons lurking in the hallway trying to make sure we were all in our rooms.

Shortly after nine o'clock, after checking to make sure the coast was clear, Sharon, Jody and I snuck out of our room and headed down to Harold's room on the second floor. Harold — who was dressed in a maroon velvet housecoat — wordlessly ushered us in. After taking me aside to tell me how very sorry he was that my band hadn't made it to the finals and to urge me not to give up hope, he led Sharon, Jody and me over to the corner of the room, where Randy Newton was already sitting in a circle with some kids we didn't know.

"Hello, everybody," said Jody, plopping down cross-legged

and reaching for the half-empty ketchup bottle somebody had swiped from Pizza Pizzazz. "Can I go first?"

Nervously, everyone laughed and said that she could. Clamping her tongue firmly between her teeth, she gave the bottle a vigorous spin, then stuck out her foot so that it came to a dead stop pointing straight at Randy. Grinning broadly, she clambered across the circle on her hands and knees, wrapped her gangly arms around Randy's neck and gave him a long, wet kiss. When she was done, she sat back on her heels with a satisfied expression on her face.

Randy looked like he'd been petrified.

"Your turn, Randy," said Jody, leaning over to give him an encouraging punch in the shoulder.

His mouth dropped open a little, but otherwise, he didn't move.

"I'm his cousin. I'll take his turn for him," said Harold, giving me another slow smile.

My mouth went dry as I watched him reach for the bottle. Everything seemed to be happening in slow motion — the spin, the stop and the realization that the bottle was pointing directly at me.

"Harold ..." I croaked, my heart hammering so hard I could hardly hear the sound of my own voice.

But before he could answer, "Stairway to Heaven" began bleeping from the pocket of his velvet housecoat. Sitting back on his heels, he reached in and pulled out a cell phone. After listening intently for a few seconds, he announced, "You'll have to excuse me. I need to take this call."

And without seeming to notice the shocked expression on my face, he got up, strode across the room and locked himself in the bathroom.

16. The Great Cheesecake of Life

There was an experienced dater
Locking lips was just part of his nature.
But he heard duty call
And sacrificed all
In the hope that she'd give it up later.

From the private poetry collection of Harold Horvath

The party broke up before Harold finished his phone call. One of the monitors from his school heard Sharon shout, "Holy moly!" when an oboe player from another band tried to slip her the tongue, and the gig was up. Bursting into the room, the monitor caught us red-handed. Luckily, Sharon, Jody and I managed to get away with nothing more than a lame speech about what people thought of girls like us. Racing back to our own room, we flung on all the lights and piled on top of Holly, pinching her awake and giggling about the night's adventures before settling down to demolish what was left of the treats in my Tupperware container.

The next morning, the band met in the lobby at nine o'clock sharp. The rest of us didn't have to be back at the concert hall until mid-morning, but Holly had to leave for the television studio right away and Mrs. C wanted us to give her a proper send-off.

"Where is she?" asked Holly anxiously, bouncing from foot to foot so hard that her flute case knocked against her thighs.

"She'll be here. Don't worry," soothed Ricky.

"Yeah," said Jody as she clamped her arm firmly around Randy. "In fact, there she is now."

We all turned in time to see Mrs. C catapult out of the elevator and bolt over to where we were standing.

"Mrs. C," I asked in alarm. "What is it?"

"Go ... go get dressed in your performance outfits. All of

you!" she panted breathlessly. "Everyone in the ... the brass section of the second-place band came down with food poisoning. They ... they think it was the Parmesan noodles." She leaned over with her hands on her knees, much the same way I did whenever I was trying not to pass out from excitement.

"Well ... don't just stand there," she gasped at last, flapping her hands at us. "Hurry and change! Then onto the bus! We're going to the finals!"

∽∾∾

I didn't bother to take the elevator back to my room — it would only have slowed me down. Flying up the stairs, I got there well ahead of Sharon and Jody. Cursing, I tossed aside my best pair of black pants because of the missing button and pulled on my second-best pair, along with a fresh white shirt and my platform shoes. Then, grabbing my knapsack, I hastily dumped the contents onto the bed and stuffed in my makeup bag, hairbrush, camera, tape recorder, cookbook and baker's hat. I cursed one more time as I accidentally stumbled over the empty Tupperware container, then I was out the door and on my way to meet Lorenzo LaRue — and, quite possibly, my destiny.

∽∾∾

Our bus pulled up outside the TV station at the same time as the bus transporting Harold, whose band had also made it to the finals. The minute I stepped into the lobby of the TV station, Harold pounced on me.

"You made it!" he cried exultantly, snatching up both of my hands and showering the palms of them with kisses.

"The second-place band got sick," I explained, pulling my hands away from his lips, which were distractingly soft.

"I know," he said.

Something about the way he said it made me stare. "Harold," I asked suddenly, "you didn't ..."

"Didn't what?" he asked in a guarded voice. "Poison them?" He leaned close — so close I could feel his breath on my cheek. "Are you *really* sure you want to know the answer to that question, Francie?" He let me gawk at him for several seconds before starting to laugh — the same great, booming laugh that had set the rest of us off on the afternoon of Rory's funeral service. "Of course I didn't poison them, Francie — though I might have, if it had occurred to me."

Just then, the monitor from the night before started shouting to Harold's band that it was time to head into the studio. Harold reached for my hands again. "The bands will go on first," he murmured urgently. "Then, after a short break, the soloists will perform. Meet me by the first-floor vending machines during the break and don't be late."

"But why —"

"Don't ask questions," he interrupted. "Just trust me, okay?"

My heart thumping like a jackrabbit, I stared into his thickly lashed gray eyes for a very long moment. Then, abruptly, I gave his hands a little squeeze and said, "Okay."

Grinning broadly, Harold darted off into the crowd. I started toward the bathroom to make sure my makeup and hair looked perfect for my rendezvous with Lorenzo, but Mrs. C put the block on me so fast I nearly got whiplash. Not wanting to give her any reason to watch me more closely that she already was, I hastily told her I could wait to pee, then hurried over to where Holly was standing.

"You know what?" I whispered to her as I touched the spot on my cheek that had felt the touch of Harold's breath. "You were right. His breath does always smell like Junior Mints.

∽≈≈

Our band didn't do very well at all. Right before we took the stage, Jody dragged Randy behind a curtain and planted another sloppy kiss squarely on his lips, effectively eliminating his ability to function like a normal human being, and although I tried hard to concentrate, the knowledge that I might actually be breathing in air molecules that had previously passed through Lorenzo LaRue's warm, wet mouth kept sending me into rhythm-annihilating full-body spasms.

Luckily, I couldn't have cared less about our brutal performance.

The instant the director yelled "Cut!" and Mrs. C told us to take five, I bolted for the nearest bathroom with Holly, Sharon and Jody hot on my heels. I nearly had a heart attack when I looked in the mirror and saw what the hot stage lights had done to me.

"I look like a corpse!" I exclaimed in horror as I fingered the melted mascara that had dribbled halfway down to my chin. "Oh, Holly, what am I going to do?"

"You're going to calm down," she ordered briskly, shoving her flute and sheet music at me and plucking the makeup case out of my hand, all in a single, fluid movement. "And while we fix you up, you're going to try not to think about the fact that you're about to meet a dreamy heartthrob with a totally weird absence of body hair and the power to make all your dreams come true."

And with a laugh, she went to work as though there was nothing more important to her in the world at that moment than making sure my bubble gum lip gloss was on so thick I couldn't lick it off if I tried. Not to be outdone, Jody tackled my poor hair with an enthusiasm that would have terrified me if I hadn't been able to see with my own two eyes that she was magic with a brush and hairspray, and Sharon fetched two large handfuls of cheap toilet tissue, which she tried to get me to stuff into my bra.

"How are you going to look eighteen if you don't have boobs?" she grunted, trying to pry my hands off my chest.

"I have boobs," I grunted back, trying to elbow her away without moving my head and wrecking the finishing touches Holly was putting on my face.

Just then, over the public address system, someone with a mouthful of saliva announced that the soloists would perform in ten minutes.

"Okay, I better go," I said, giving each of them a hurried hug. "Thanks for everything. Wish me luck!"

"Good luck!" they all cried

And then I was gone.

∽⊘⊘⊘

Harold was waiting for me beside the vending machines, just like he'd promised. There was no one else in sight.

"My god, you look incredible," Harold said in a wondering voice. "If I didn't know better, I'd say you were at *least* eighteen."

"Really?" I cried, throwing my arms around him. "Oh, Harold, that's the nicest thing you've ever said to me."

"Did I say eighteen?" he murmured, burying his face in my bare neck. "I meant twenty. Or even thirty."

"Okay, that's enough," I said, wriggling out of his grasp. "So, what's the plan?"

"Do you see the door at the end of this hall?" he asked.

The lights at the far end of the hall were off, so I had to strain my eyes to see. "You mean the one on the right?"

Harold nodded. "On the other side of that door is your celebrity baker. There's a notice on the door that says an alarm will go off if you open it, but it won't because the crew from the other sound stage disabled the alarm years ago."

"Why?" I whispered.

"Because of these," said Harold, nodding at the vending machines. "If the people working on the other sound stage go through that door, it takes them a minute to grab a soda and chips. If they have to go around the other way, it takes them ten."

"Oh," I said. "How do you know this?"

"The Amazing Arnold told me," replied Harold.

I smiled. "Who is the Amazing Arnold?"

"Do you remember when I told you I'd won second place in the National Junior Circus Performers' Rodeo three years in a row? Well, the Amazing Arnold won first place. He's performed at the Portage la Prairie Public Television Telethon for the last two years and I'd been trying to get hold of him ever since I first learned of your burning desire to meet this Lorenzo fellow. Last night, he finally returned my call."

"While we were playing Spin the Bottle," I guessed.

"Correct," said Harold.

"So ... you gave up a chance to kiss me because you had a chance to help me?" I said in a small voice.

"Correct."

I felt my face flush. "Thank you, Harold," I said.

"You're welcome," he replied. "Now, get going. I hear someone coming."

At that moment, Mr. Simmons rounded the corner. I stepped back behind the vending machines just in the nick of time. With the grace of a dancer, Harold leaped away from me.

"I recognize you!" barked Mr. Simmons. "You're that punk from the band room. Why are you out here? All students are supposed to be in the sound stage waiting to watch the soloists perform."

The only response was silence.

"What the hell are you doing?"

More silence.

"Answer me!"

More silence.

"Oh, you think you're a funny guy, do you?" snarled Mr. Simmons. "Well, I'll show you funny, mister. You're coming with me, and when I find your teacher, I'm going to make sure he comes down on you like a ton of bricks. Now, cut it out!"

I could tell that Mr. Simmons had turned around and was going back the way he'd come, so I risked a quick peek to see what Harold was doing that was making Mr. Simmons so furious. And when I saw what it was, I nearly laughed aloud.

Mime in a Box.

✎✎✎

With the coast clear, all I had to do was make it to the far door and pray that Harold was right about the alarm being disabled. The clunk of my platform heels against the floor in the empty hallway sounded loud to my ears, but not nearly as loud as the beating of my own heart. I'd dreamed about this moment for so long it was hard to believe it was actually here.

And then the door was there in front of me, along with the sign saying that an alarm would go off if it was opened. A vision of a hulking security guard dragging me off by my hair bloomed before me, but faded again almost as quickly.

I'd come this far — nothing was going to stop me now. *Nothing.*

Suddenly, another announcement blared out over the public address system, so loud I nearly jumped out of my skin. The soloists were going on in three minutes; the doors to the sound stage would be locked in two.

As soon as the announcement was over, I took a deep breath and slowly pushed my shoulder against the door.

The door opened a crack, but no alarm went off.

No alarm went off, but *I could hear Lorenzo LaRue talking as clearly as if he was standing in my very own kitchen!* He was in the hallway just beyond sight, and it sounded as though he was complaining to someone about how his hair looked. I took a brief moment to compose the world's most flattering hair comment and was about to shove the door open all the way when I looked down and noticed something so awful my heart nearly stopped.

Holly's flute and sheet music.

I was still holding them in my hand.

I stood for what seemed to be an eternity, paralyzed by indecision. Without her instrument and music, Holly would be disqualified. But Lorenzo was *right there* — all I had to do was push the door open another few inches and pour out my feelings of passion for him and baking. If I could do that before his handlers pounced on me, I just knew I could make him see that I was the real deal. And if I could do that, I believed with all my heart that anything was possible. *Anything.*

Pushing the door open another inch, I thought about how hard I'd worked and how much I'd sacrificed for this chance to meet Lorenzo. Then I stopped. And I looked again at Holly's flute and sheet music. And I thought about how Holly had worked on my makeup even though she probably should have been warming up, and I thought about how she must be feeling at this moment, knowing how close she'd come to winning it all only to watch it slip through her fingers.

And I suddenly knew it was a price I wasn't willing to pay, not even for the thrill that awaited me beyond this door.

And so, letting the door slam shut so fast the noise echoed down the empty hallway, I kicked off my platform shoes, stuffed them into my bag and ran toward the sound stage as though my life depended on it.

Holly gave the performance of a lifetime, even though she was badly shaken by the fact that I'd shown up just seconds before she was called to the stage. I was so proud of her I couldn't stop clapping, and when the festival coordinator announced that she'd won first place, Jody, Sharon and I went so crazy that the stage manager had to ask us to tone it down because our cheering was causing feedback in the sound system.

"Oh, Francie," cried Holly, flying off the stage and hurling herself at me so hard I body-slammed backward into Ricky, who was standing right behind me waiting for *his* hug. "I'll never forget how you came back for me. Never! This is the best day of my entire life and you're the best friend a girl ever had," she said, hugging me tight enough to cut off the oxygen supply to my brain.

I hugged her back just as tightly. In that moment, everything felt so good and right that missing my chance to meet Lorenzo didn't even feel like a sacrifice. The tears I was blinking back were tears of happiness, I was almost sure of it. Nana had said that in this life, we take our chances and in the end, the best we can hope for is that the thrill of the moment is worth the price we have to pay. The moment *had* been worth the price I'd had to pay, even though the thrill had been Holly's, not mine.

Wiping away my tears with the back of my hand, I happened to glance over Holly's shoulder to the back of the studio.

And what I saw made me gasp aloud.

No, it wasn't Lorenzo.

But it was the next best thing.

"I don't believe it," I said, my arms falling limply to my sides.

"Don't believe what?" said Sharon.

Wordlessly, I lifted my hand and pointed to the back of the room.

"Hey, isn't that the bimbo from your baking show?" said Holly.

I nodded without taking my eyes off the Lovely Lydia.

"How come you brought her here?" she asked.

"I didn't," I said in a bewildered voice. "I didn't meet her. I ... I almost met Lorenzo, but there was no time ... I had your flute ... and if I didn't get back ..."

My voice dribbled off. Holly's eyes widened with understanding but before she could say anything warm and tender, Sharon gave each of us a jab in the ribs and pointed out that Lydia was heading for the nearest exit.

"Out of my way!" bellowed Holly suddenly, using her flute to cut a path through the crowd for us. "Come on, move it! Shove over! I'm not kidding, buster. Let's go!"

Holly got to the Lovely Lydia just as she was pushing open the door to leave. Not knowing what else to do, she leaned over and gave the Lovely Lydia a poke in the rear end with her flute case, startling her so badly that she gave a little yelp and whirled about to face us.

"Can I help you?" she demanded.

Ricky, who was standing right beside Holly, immediately started to blush. He looked so guilty that I think the Lovely Lydia might have started to rip into him if Jody hadn't at that moment planted her elbow between my shoulder blades.

Jerking forward with a cry, I blurted, "My name is Francie Freewater! I watch your show every week and I was a finalist in the Winnipeg contest to take over your job and I'd do *almost* anything to meet Lorenzo and there's nothing in the world I want more than to become a famous baker just like him and ... why are you wearing a business suit, Lovely Lydia?"

She blinked for a moment, as though trying to recover from my outburst. Then she laughed. "Call me Lydia," she said. "I'm wearing a business suit because I'm the president of Lorenzo LaRue Incorporated and the executive producer of *Getting Baked with Lorenzo*. That means I have to meet with a lot of important people who expect me to dress like a professional."

I gaped at her. "*You're* L. Barnes — the one who sent me my "Dear Loser" letter?" I cried. "But that's impossible! L. Barnes had a bunch of important-looking credentials behind his name. No offense or anything, but all you do is let Lorenzo lick chocolate sauce off your finger every week!"

Lydia laughed again. "Playing the part of the Lovely Lydia is like playing dress-up. It's not my real job, Francie, it's just something I do because it's fun. Plus, it allows me to monitor Barney more closely."

"Who is Barney?" I asked, mystified.

"Oh, I'm sorry. You know him as Lorenzo."

"His real name is *Barney?*"

"That's right," said Lydia. Then she cocked her head at me. "Oh, wait a minute. I remember you now. Francie Freewater. You're that eighteen-year-old who said she'd missed our Portage la Prairie deadline because her parents had locked her in a closet." She gave me a wry smile. "I'm pleased to see that you managed to escape, but may I ask what a grown woman like yourself is doing at a high school Performance Band Festival?"

"The same thing you are, of course," I bluffed.

"I just came to relive the old days," mused Lydia. "I was in my high school Performance Band, you know. I played percussion."

"I play percussion!" I shouted.

Lydia started to reply, but before she could, Harold burst out of the crowd, hurried over to me and snatched up my hand.

"Well?" he asked hopefully, staring so deeply into my eyes that he didn't even seem to notice Lydia, who looked stunning in spite of her boring business clothes.

"The fire door didn't work out," I muttered under my breath. "Something came up but" — I wiggled my eyebrows in Lydia's direction and whispered — "his assistant is here."

Turning sharply on one heel, Harold regarded Lydia intently. Then he lowered his chin slightly and fixed her with his hypnotic gray eyes.

"Ah, yes," he murmured, taking a step toward her. "I recognize you now. And may I say that while some men may prefer the slinky white evening gowns you so unwisely choose to wear while baking on television, I find the power, intelligence and animal heat you radiate in this simple suit of raw silk intoxicating almost beyond endurance." Harold took another step toward Lydia. He was so close now that I was sure she could feel his warm Junior Mint breath on her collarbone. "Lydia. May I call you Lydia?" Without bothering to wait for an answer, he gestured toward me. "Lydia, you have no idea how dedicated this stunning young woman is to her craft, and how much it means to her. Up at the crack of dawn every weekend, struggling past the disappointment of collapsed cakes and singed strudels, never resting in her pursuit of the perfect pastry. Do you realize that she earned every penny required to come on this trip by selling raspberry white chocolate scones so good they are practically a religious experience?"

"Is that true?" murmured Lydia vaguely.

I nodded.

"My dearest Lydia," breathed Harold in a quivery voice, "you, and you alone, have the power to grant this paragon of loveliness her fondest desire, which is to have a short, closely chaperoned meeting with your Lorenzo for the purposes of using him as a lowly stepping stone in her quest for baking greatness." I tried to protest that I didn't want to *use* Lorenzo, or have my visit with him chaperoned, but Harold ignored me. "The only questions you have to ask yourself, Lydia," he continued, "are what it would have meant to you to have *your* fondest desire granted to you when you were her age, and whether you'll be able to look at yourself in the mirror tomorrow morning if you turn your back on her and walk out that door today."

For a long moment, Lydia just stood there, staring deeply into Harold's eyes. Then, with an abrupt shake of her head, she said, "We finished taping the show a while ago, but if we hurry, we might be able to catch Barney before he heads back to the hotel. Do you need to ask your teachers for permission to slip away for a few minutes?"

Holly, Ricky, Randy, Sharon, Jody, Harold and I looked at each other.

"No, ma'am," said Jody and Sharon in voices so sweet that I hardly recognized them.

"Of course not," added Ricky and Randy.

Holly and I grabbed hands and squeezed. Harold beamed.

"Fine," said Lydia. "Then follow me."

⚬⚬⚬

As I clattered along behind Lydia, I marveled at how it had all worked out in the end. I'd given up a chance to come face-to-face with Lorenzo so that Holly could pursue her dream, and now here I was, jogging along behind the executive producer of my favorite baking show, on my way to receiving a proper introduction to the man of my dreams. Of course, he was slightly *less* the man of my dreams now that I knew his real name was Barney, but still.

I wondered what Nana was going to say when she found out I'd met him.

When we got to the soundstage, someone told Lydia that Lorenzo was already on his way to the VIP parking lot, so she hurried after him while we followed along behind her like a brood of ducklings. Faster and faster we went, turning this way and that, until all at once, Lydia hung a sharp left and shoved open a set of double glass doors. Eagerly, I looked around for Lorenzo's limousine. As if sensing what I was thinking, Lydia shook her head and pointed to a little blue rust bucket that backfired loudly, then jerked out of the parking lot and puttered off down the road.

"The blue one — that was his car," she said, reaching down to massage a stitch in her side. "I'm sorry, Francie. He's gone."

⚬⚬⚬

Nobody said much of anything as we followed Lydia back to Lorenzo's dressing room so that she could give us each a signed photograph and a couple of coupons for the "Sinfully Yours" product line. There was really nothing to say.

Nothing to say, that is, until I crossed the threshold of Lorenzo's dressing room and discovered one of things I cherished most about him lying on the counter.

"WHAT IS THAT?" I shrieked, pointing at it.

Lydia chuckled. "Barney's hair."

"His *hair?*"

Lydia chuckled again. "Francie, you didn't honestly believe that gorgeous mane was his real hair, did you?" she said. "Between you and me, old Barney is as bald as a cue ball. I think the only place he still has hair is on his back."

I made a small gagging noise. "But I've never seen a picture of him with hair on his back!" I exclaimed, feeling a nameless sort of outrage.

"Oh," shrugged Lydia. "Well, that's because our makeup department makes him wax."

"Told you so," piped Holly.

"That being said, I'm going to ask you kids to keep this information to yourselves," continued Lydia, looking at her watch. "Barney is prone to throwing such temper tantrums that I have quite enough trouble keeping staff as it is. I wouldn't want to think how much worse it would get if word got out he wasn't quite the man his fans think he is."

Stunned by these revelations, I staggered over to the nearest chair and collapsed in a heap. It felt like the foundation stone of my dream had crumbled. I'd spent all these years being inspired by Lorenzo when he was really nothing more than a bald man named Barney with a hairy back and a tendency toward hissy fits.

"Does he even like baking?" I asked dispiritedly as I pulled my baker's hat out of my knapsack. "When he said all those inspiring things about feeling the recipe and having the courage to listen to our inner baker, was he ever speaking from the heart?"

"The shows are scripted, Francie," said Lydia with a small smile. "Barney reads off the teleprompter."

"So in other words, no," I said glumly, staring down at my crumpled baker's hat.

Lydia shrugged.

Then Harold walked up and stood behind me. Placing his hands on my shoulders, he said, "You know, Francie, Claude Depardieu is my hero, but if I ever found out he mumbled under his breath the whole time he was miming, it really wouldn't change anything for me. I would still love being a mime. I would just have to find myself a new hero."

I thought about this for a long moment. Then, ever so slowly, a feeling of calm descended upon me as I realized that Harold was right. Lorenzo wasn't who I thought he was, but that was his problem, not mine. He'd been part of my fantasy, but he wasn't part of my dream.

My dream belonged to no one but me.

Straightening my back and lifting my chin, I picked up my baker's hat and plunked it on top of my head.

Harold fluffed up the pouf for me and then smiled at my reflection in the fancy lightbulb-ringed makeup mirror.

Reaching up to give his hand a squeeze, I grinned back at him.

Suddenly, Lydia walked over and stood beside me. "You know what, Francie?" she said as she picked up a blush brush and absently swept it across my cheek. "You've just given me a wonderful idea."

17. Unfinished Business

After you've combined the basic ingredients, it may not look like much, but don't worry. This is just the beginning.

From the yet-to-be published recipe book by the Great Francie Freewater, Baker Extraordinaire

I stood behind the granite countertop, willing my legs to stop shaking, trying to focus on the stainless steel mixing bowls that were laid out in front of me. The studio lights were so hot I could feel trickles of sweat rolling down my back, and my skin itched beneath the pancake makeup that had been slathered onto my face, neck and hands.

"Two minutes, Ms. Freewater," said a man with a headset as he dashed past, calling instructions to his stagehands.

I blinked and shielded my eyes against the glare of the lights, trying to penetrate the darkness beyond in the hope that I could catch a glimpse of my studio audience. Almost immediately, a woman scurried on stage, pushed my hand away from my face and dusted my forehead with powder.

"I think I have to go to the bathroom," I croaked, but nobody seemed to hear me.

"Thirty seconds, Ms. Freewater."

I gripped the countertop, wondering if I was going to be able to do this.

"Milk-chocolate chips, two cups, right, Ms. Freewater?" asked an anxious-looking man.

When I nodded wordlessly, he carefully set the cupful of chips next to the mixing bowls and hurried off stage.

"Five ... four ... three ... two ... and ... Action!" cried the man with the headset, pointing at me.

In the dead silence that followed, I tried to think of what to do first, but my mind had gone completely blank. As I desperately shifted my weight from foot to foot, trying to think of how to begin, I felt something move in my pocket. Reaching back, I pulled out the photos of Rory that

Marguerite had given Nana at the memorial service. I'd put them in my pocket right before Nana had started speaking and forgotten to take them out afterward. The photo on top showed Rory tearing into a piece of birthday cake, while Nana looked on in dismay. With a sudden smile, I turned the picture toward the camera.

"I'm dedicating this show to Rory the parrot, who was not only a good friend to those who loved him, but also the most enthusiastic studio audience any baker ever had." I waited for a moment so that the cameras could zoom in on the picture of Rory and Nana. Then, setting it to one side, I bowed my head, lifted my hand and said, "Cue the music."

And just like that, the familiar throb of the world's most perfect rock bass line filled the air. Looking up, I flashed a dazzling grin and reached for the mixing bowls. I combined pre-measured dry ingredients, then threw a silver fork into the air, did a wobbly sort of spin on my platform heels and caught the fork on the way down. The six members of my studio audience went wild.

My television debut had officially begun.

Nineteen exhilarating minutes later, the man with the headset raised five fingers in the air, counted backward to zero and then hollered, "Cut!" Someone else killed the stage lights; still another person hurried over and began clearing away my dirty dishes. Holly and the others scrambled up on stage and crowded around me, laughing, asking me how it felt to be a superstar and telling me they'd never seen anything like it before in their lives.

"It was pretty good," agreed Lydia with a chuckle as she stepped out from behind the black velvet curtains at the back of the set. "How did it feel?"

"It was a lot harder than I thought it would be," I admitted, wiping my itchy, dripping brow with the hem of my apron. "And a lot more tiring. Plus, I dropped an egg on the floor and accidentally added the chocolate chips before pouring the liquid ingredients into the well I'd formed in the dry ingredients. They were rookie mistakes. I've never made them before."

Lydia smiled. "There's a big difference between baking in the comfort of your own kitchen and working under the hot lights of a professional studio. There's pressure. Chaos. Expectations. But if it's really what you love to do, you get used to it," she said. Then she handed me a DVD, which I hadn't even noticed she was holding.

"What's this?" I asked.

"Your demo recording," she said. "You're going to need one when you're finally *truly* old enough to take a serious stab at breaking into this business."

I stared at the DVD as though it were made of solid gold. "Thanks," I breathed.

Lydia smiled, then walked over and picked up one of the quick-bake hazelnut mocha drops I'd just finished making.

"Mmmm," she said, closing her eyes as it melted in her mouth. "These are delicious."

"It's an original recipe," I said eagerly, scrambling to show her my cookbook.

"I know," she replied. "We're including it in Lorenzo's next cookbook."

"You ARE?" I cried. "Well ... well, that's so *great*." I spun around and faced my friends. "Did you hear that? Did you? My recipe is going to be in a cookbook!"

Harold mimed extreme joy. Everyone else stood up and cheered.

"Actually," said Lydia over the noise, "it's not your recipe anymore."

We all stopped cheering and looked at her. Harold mimed extreme surprise.

"What are you talking about?" I asked.

"When you sent the recipe in, you acknowledged the fact that by submitting it, you were irrevocably conferring all rights of ownership to Lorenzo LaRue Incorporated," explained Lydia in a matter-of-fact tone of voice.

"But ... but ..." I stammered.

Lydia looked at her watch. "I've got to go now. Fabio will escort you and your friends out of the building," she said, pointing to a short, lumpy security guard with body odor so bad it made my eyes water. "Good luck with everything, Francie, and in the future, don't forget to read the fine print. It's a dog-eat-dog world out there and if you don't watch your back, no one else will."

"I don't know if I agree with you, Lydia," I said, smiling at my friends, who had backed me every step of the way. "But I do know I'll never forget what you did for me here today. Never."

☞☞☞

"And so, in conclusion," I said, pointing the remote at the DVD player and clicking it off, "when I grow up, I want to be a celebrity baker with a half-hour television show in the coveted four-to-six time slot. I want to publish a cookbook every two years, make regular contributions to national magazines and someday maybe even launch my own line of packaged baked goods. As a result, I could end up wildly rich and living the kind of lifestyle that most people only dream about, but I could also end up dead poor and busting my hump just to pay rent. Or I could end up with a totally different job that lets me make the money I need to survive so I can pursue my baking in my spare time. But whatever happens at least I'll be able to live my life knowing I'm doing everything I can to make my dream come true."

For a long moment, no one in my Life Skills class said a word. In her seat near the back, I saw Darlene grin and whisper something to the girl sitting next to her. The girl giggled and made the cuckoo sign at her temple. I felt like an idiot. That morning, I'd stuffed my demo recording into my knapsack on an impulse and at the last minute, instead of reading from the essay I'd written about becoming a lawyer, I'd decided to play the recording for the class. They'd laughed when they'd first seen me in my baker's hat, again when they'd watched me dedicate the show to Rory, and yet again when I'd dropped the egg. After that, they hadn't said a word.

I was just about to tell Mr. Simmons I'd made a terrible mistake when, without even bothering to raise his hand, Greg Podwinski announced, "You know what? I don't really want to be to a chartered accountant when I grow up. I want to be a professional hockey player."

Mr. Simmons glared at me and then, in a strangled voice, explained to Greg that his chances of making the NHL were worse than a pigeon's chances of becoming president of the United States.

Greg shrugged. "I know, but there's still a chance, right?"

"That's right," I said quickly, before Mr. Simmons could make any more pigeon-related comparisons. "I mean, it's a very small chance, but that's no reason not to *try*, right?"

"Right," said Greg with a broad grin.

Sharon leaned forward and gave him a slug on the arm. "Hey, Greggy, when you negotiate your NHL contract, make sure they give you time off so you can play at the Olympics, okay?" she said. "I'm going to be there, because I'm going to be captain of the women's national basketball team."

"Co-captain," interjected Jody. "I'm going to be captain, too, remember?"

Everyone started talking at once, babbling excitedly about fantasies no grown-ups in their right mind would consider a serious plan for the future. A couple of kids wanted to be rock stars; a couple of others wanted to cure cancer or figure out a way to rid the world of poverty. Randy wanted to move to Montreal, set up an easel in a crowded street and charge passersby twenty-five dollars a pop for portraits sketched in charcoal; a girl I'd never really noticed before said she wanted to work as a translator at the United Nations in New York City. To my surprise, Mr. Simmons didn't even bother to try to control us. Instead, he sat down at the edge of his desk and stared moodily out the window without saying a word until the bell rang, when he abruptly stood back up and ordered me to stay after class.

The United Nations girl gave me a sympathetic shrug, then scurried away. I turned my DVD over and over in my sweaty hands, hoping that by the time Mr. Simmons was through with me, I wouldn't regret having taken the chance I had.

When the last student was gone, he slowly walked over, shut the classroom door and turned to stare at me.

I blinked up at him nervously, wondering how fast I'd be able to duck if he suddenly lifted up a desk and threw it at me.

"Mr. Simmons —" I began.

"That was a fine piece of work, Freewater," he growled. "Damn fine."

I gaped at him.

"I asked that projects be presented in a format that would blow my mind and you delivered," he continued brusquely. "It was edgy. It was different. It got people talking. I like that."

I was so startled that the DVD slipped out of my hands and clattered to the floor. In an *unprecedented* display of respect for a person who was still young enough to dream about the day she'd grow into an underwire bra, Mr. Simmons silently leaned over and picked it up for me.

"Thank you," I spluttered, looking up at him as though seeing him for the first time.

"You're welcome," he grunted in reply.

You're welcome? Unprecedented!

Marveling at how quickly a relationship can change when two people are willing to treat each other with respect, I smiled warmly and said, "So, I guess this means I get an A on my project, huh, Mr. S?"

"The name is Simmons and you guess wrong," he barked. "What do you think, I rode in here on a load of turnips? You think I don't know you snuck off and recorded that claptrap in Portage la Prairie when you were supposed to be mingling with the rest of the Performance Band yahoos? You think I don't know that damn mime was in on it the whole time? I haven't yet figured out how you managed it all, but I will, Freewater, I will." He dug furiously at something caught between two of his molars. "In the meantime, you get an F and a chance to do a whole new project."

Stunned though I was by the swiftness with which Mr. Tobacco-Stained Fingers had turned on me, I nevertheless had the presence of mind to reach into my knapsack and pull out my essay on becoming a lawyer.

"Nice try!" brayed Mr. Simmons, swatting it to one side. "I said a *new* project, Freewater, not some recycled garbage you couldn't care less about. In the immortal words of the world's most famous baking teenybopper, show me how you're going to live your life doing everything you can to make your dream come true. And, Freewater?"

"Yes?"

"This time, try to do it without risking felony trespassing charges."

With that, Mr. Simmons grabbed his ugly tweed coat with the suede patches at the elbows and headed outside for a much-needed smoke break. I gathered up my knapsack and headed into the hall, feeling oddly elated by how things had turned out. True, I'd just gotten my first F ever, but I'd also been called edgy, and I'd gotten people talking. Even better, I'd laid it all on the line — who I really was, and what mattered to me — and nobody had treated it like a joke.

Well, almost nobody.

"I have to tell you, Francie, I never thought you'd take it that far," said a laughing voice as I headed down the hall toward my locker.

Turning, I saw Darlene leaning against a wall. On her lips was an elfin smile; at her side was Tate Jarvis. He looked at me once, then hastily looked away. I wondered how it was that I'd never before noticed how small and thinly lashed his eyes were.

Darlene prattled on. "When I told you I knew that you knew your obsession with baking wasn't normal because I'd never heard you mention it to anyone at school, it wasn't meant to be taken as some kind of challenge," she said, rolling her eyes. "I mean, *really*. A baking show dedicated to a parakeet? What were you thinking?"

I hadn't talked to Darlene since she'd pulled the band-room-boy-switcheroo. She was grinning at me now the same way she'd grinned at me in the pool changing room all those weeks ago. Like if I said what I was supposed to, she might continue to let me hang out with her — not as her true friend or anything like that, but as someone she could safely ignore or tease or humiliate or manipulate or stab in the back whenever she got bored or angry or hurt.

"Rory was a parrot," I said quietly.

"Rory was a parrot," she repeated in a mocking voice.

Tate laughed appreciatively, but shut up fast when I stepped right into his personal space and, in a *deadly* calm voice, asked, "Did you ever plan to meet me in the band room during the pep rally, Tate, or was it always your intention to send in an older, stronger stranger who could have hurt or even killed me if he'd wanted to?"

For a moment, Tate just stood there, staring like a deer caught in the headlights. Then he cast a furtive glance at Darlene and cleared his throat, sending a cloud of sour breath wafting in my direction.

Wrinkling my nose, I took a step backward.

"Oh, lighten up," said Darlene, with a little toss of her head. "It was a joke, okay?"

When I didn't say anything, her eyes narrowed almost imperceptibly. "I told you before, Francie, I don't think much of people who can't laugh at themselves," she reminded me.

I folded my arms across my chest. Slowly, Darlene walked

forward and stood so close to me that our noses would have been touching if she hadn't been such a shrimp boat.

"You're being a drag," she warned softly. "Such a drag, in fact, that I'm starting to think you're not the girl I thought you were."

We looked at each other for a long moment. Then, biting the inside of my cheek to keep from giggling, I solemnly rose up onto my tiptoes until I was practically looming over her.

"I'm not the girl you thought I was, Darlene," I said gravely as I looked down my nose at her. "And the truth is, I never was."

∽∂∂∽

That weekend, my parents grounded me for getting an F on my Life Skills term project, then hauled our TV and DVD player downstairs on Sunday morning and proudly played my demo recording over and over while I stood behind the counter and served my customers. My mother didn't go so far as to tell people she thought I was going to become a celebrity baker someday, but I didn't hear her bragging to anyone about what a great lawyer I'd make, either. It was a start.

I spent the rest of the day working on my new term project, ate a chicken pot pie for dinner, then took a long, hot bubble bath and got into bed. For a while, I lay in the dark with my hands behind my head, staring up at the glow-in-the-dark stars on the ceiling. Then I turned onto my side and closed my eyes. A few minutes later, my door creaked open.

"Francie?" whispered Nana.

I opened my eyes. Nana was silhouetted in the doorway.

"I just wanted to say good-night," she said, "and also that it was very sweet of you to dedicate your first show to Rory."

"You don't have to keep saying that, Nana," I said, snuggling deeper under my covers. "Believe me, it was enough to have seen you break down and sob like a baby the first time you saw the recording."

"I did not *sob*," she said haughtily

"Yes, you did, and now you're lying about it," I chuckled drowsily.

Gasping at my cheekiness, she lifted her cane high, but before she could thump it against the floor, I said, "Nana, are you still going to watch Lorenzo even though you now know he's a bald man named Barney who couldn't care less about baking?"

"I suppose I will," she said. Then she paused and added, "Until something better comes along, that is."

"Something better will come along, Nana," I promised, believing with all my heart that it was true.

"I know it will, Francie," she replied quietly. "Sleep well."

"You too, Nana."

⁕⁕⁕

The following Friday night, I had a party and invited all of my friends — Ricky and Randy, Sharon and Jody, Harold and Holly. Nana was out for the evening and my parents had agreed to stay downstairs except for bringing up plates of fries and trays full of frosty mugs brimming with black-cherry ice cream in orange soda.

We had the place to ourselves.

The girls arrived before the boys and then crowded into the front hall giggling and cooing when Ricky showed up and pulled from the front of his leather bomber jacket something that at first glance appeared to be the head of an old mop, dyed orange and dragged behind a bus for three miles.

"My mom asked me to bring him over," said Ricky, carefully handing me a mangy mongrel cat. "Your nana has decided to adopt him. To keep her company now that Rory is gone."

We all looked down at the cat. He squirmed onto his back, carefully arranged his scrawny back legs so that we all had an excellent view of his crotch, then closed his eyes and began to snore so loudly it sounded like a freight train was bearing down on us.

"What is that?" asked Harold, walking in the open door with Randy right behind him.

"My new cat," I said.

"He doesn't look very new to me," said Harold with a disapproving glance at the cat's crotch.

Everybody laughed. Then Holly took Ricky's hand and dragged him into the kitchen to share an ice-cream soda, and Jody clamped her long arm around Randy's meaty shoulder and marched him off to the living room in order to discuss their relationship. Sharon scooped the cat out of my arms and scampered after them, loudly threatening to drop the cat crotch-first on Randy's face if the two of them started necking and refused to play Twister with her.

Smiling at how nice it was to have not just one best friend, but a whole bunch of friends, I'd just started after Sharon when Harold pulled me back. Wordlessly, he pulled something out of the deep front pocket of his trench coat.

"What is that?" I asked, squinting in the dimness of the unlit hallway.

Harold lifted up the object and held it before my eyes.

Inhaling sharply, I recognized it as the half-empty ketchup bottle we'd used to play Spin the Bottle in his hotel room.

With a smile so slow and sexy that it practically made my hair stand on end, Harold leaned over, placed the bottle on the floor and gave it an expert spin. We both watched in silence as the bottle spun, then slowed, then finally came to a stop — pointing directly at me.

Reaching up to give my bangs a fluff, I swallowed hard.

Harold took a tentative step forward.

"This," he whispered, leaning so close I could feel his Junior Mint breath on my trembling lips, "is unfinished business ..."

THE END.

Maureen Fergus used to be a fourteen-year-old girl with uncooperative hair and a tendency to blush and trip over things in the presence of cute boys. Today, she is a writer and a business professional. Her first book, *Exploits of a Reluctant (But Extremely Goodlooking) Hero*, was the LOL diary of a thirteen-year-old boy. She regularly bakes up a storm for her husband and three kids in Winnipeg, Manitoba.